SPY GAME

A Cold War spy novel

John Fullerton

Burning Chair Limited, Trading as Burning Chair Publishing
61 Bridge Street, Kington HR5 3DJ
www.burningchairpublishing.com

By John Fullerton
Edited by Simon Finnie and Peter Oxley
Book cover design by Burning Chair Publishing

First published by Burning Chair Publishing, 2021

ISBN: 978-1-912946-16-7

By The Same Author

The Soviet Occupation of Afghanistan
The Monkey House
Clap (writing as JW Diaz)
A Hostile Place
This Green Land
White Boys Don't Cry
The Reticent Executioner

"Those who believe in their truth—the only ones whose imprint is retained by the memory of men—leave the earth behind them strewn with corpses."

E.M. Cioran, *A Short History of Decay*, translated from the French by Richard Howard, Penguin, 2006.

1

February, 1983

'Stop. Stop right here.' Brodick leaned forward and pointed, right arm extended between the front seats and inches from the driver's ear.

'That's it. Now, lights. Lights, dammit—switch them off. And turn off the engine.'

The two men were motionless. Brodick sat forward on the edge of the back seat. The only sound in the taxi was their breathing.

Brodick counted up to five.

So far, so good—though his hands were trembling as if he was running a high temperature, but this was no fever. This was his own doing; he was sure it marked the end of an all-consuming dream, his life's ambition—and Brodick was about to go against everything he believed in, or once thought he did.

'You wait, okay?'

There was just a smidgen of pale light low in the east, but Brodick was relieved that it was otherwise still very dark. No moon. Streetlights were few and far between, and in any case they were ineffectual in a city swathed in the smoke from countless wood fires.

No traffic, no footfall, no voices.

Brodick opened the back door a crack.

He expected the muzzle of a pistol pushed into his face, a round racked into the chamber, hands grabbing him before he could make a run for it. Anything was possible and none of it was good. Paranoia was his default state of mind.

The cold night air and distinctive stench of Pakistan's North West Frontier insinuated itself into the taxi: smoke, dust—always dust—and diesel, three constituents varying according to the time of day and season.

'Give me the keys.'

The driver half turned: surprised, worried.

Brodick's open right hand was over the driver's shoulder and close to his throat.

He hissed the words. 'Give. Me. The. Keys.'

'Okay mister, okay.'

Brodick stepped out and stood next to the taxi, holding the door ajar, holding his breath so he could hear better. Nothing but the first sounds of the dawn chorus and, in the general direction of the main road into the centre of Peshawar, the long, forlorn wail of a truck's horn. No doubt contraband of some sort on the move, thundering down from the Afghan frontier.

This was failure; its taste was bitter. He'd given up his marriage, a well-paid job, his dog, and his home for a career in intelligence. It had meant everything to him, and he'd been willing to pay almost any price. It was all for nothing, too, and it wasn't anyone's fault but his own. The dream had turned out to be a mirage. He was throwing his future away, a future he'd earned the hard way. He'd had his orders and he was disobeying them, wilfully. He wouldn't be able to say he didn't know, or that it had been an accident. His case officer was no fool, and sooner rather than later Century House would know too.

His chances of promotion to a fully qualified intelligence officer were finished, and so was he.

End of story—almost.

He padded quickly, silently, to the corner and, before he vanished down the suburban side street, he turned on his heel and looked back at the driver behind the windscreen. All he could see was the man's white skullcap. The driver was a stranger, picked at random; Brodick hadn't used his services before this morning. He would have preferred to use his usual taxi driver, Ahmad. Ahmad was reliable and understood English and he spoke a little, too. But it wouldn't have been safe, and security was paramount. Ahmad would have reported their journey to Pakistani Special Branch sooner or later, and that would not have been helpful.

Brodick jogged halfway along the first block of houses and stopped outside a bungalow; he looked over the top of the metal gate. Normally the guard would have been hard to spot, just a shadow leaning or squatting against the wall of the building, but the glowing tip of his cigarette, rising and falling as he drew on it, gave his position away. At least he was awake.

'*Salaam aleikum.*' Brodick kept his voice steady.

The pinpoint of light fell to the ground and went out. In its place appeared the gleam of a Kalashnikov, raised to waist height, cradled in the guard's arms as if he was holding an infant.

'*Waleikum salaam.*' The shadow detached itself from the wall and came forward, wary, sandals slapping the cement of the yard, the muzzle pointing at Brodick's chest.

'Wake him up.'

'Mr Richard, is you? Too early, Mr Richard.'

'The hell it is. Wake him up. They must come now. Both of them. Quickly.'

'You come in?'

'I'll wait here. Get them up. They must hurry. Now.'

'Okay, okay.'

Brodick saw a light come on in the interior.

He waited. Maybe a minute, maybe ten. To Brodick, at any

rate, it felt as if he'd aged in the interim.

The man with the gun, one of the professor's several nephews or cousins who shared the duty of protecting their uncle and his wife, carried out the bags.

'This is it?'

'Two. No more.'

Mungoo had actually taken his advice and they'd packed a single overnight bag each. Perhaps they'd imagined—wrongly— that they'd be returning at some point very soon.

'Put them down. Are they coming now?'

'One minute, please.'

'Tell them to hurry for Chrissakes.'

'They know, Mr Richard. Please, sir, be patient.'

Brodick had an urge to grab the man's weapon and wrap it around his neck.

It turned out they hadn't gone to bed but remained dressed, snoozing on and off as they waited for him. It seemed remarkable to Brodick that, despite his friendship with the professor stretching back over these many months, this was the first time he had actually seen the man's wife. They were family in a way; he'd enjoyed their hospitality, eaten her meals, drunk her tea, enjoyed her cakes and desserts, but had never shared them with her or exchanged a word with her. That was the way it was here, even in the case of a woman well-educated, from a prominent family and tribe and related to the exiled Afghan king. An aristocrat, no less. Even now, she wasn't really visible because she was veiled, and she seemed to be wearing so many clothes that her shape was indistinguishable. She could have been sixteen or sixty for all Brodick could tell. Maybe that was the point.

Brodick put their bags in the boot, settled Professor and Mrs Mungoo in the back, and took his place up front next to the driver.

The voice in the back was deep, rich, slightly muffled. 'Is this really necessary, Richard? Really?'

Brodick turned around in his seat to face them. 'We've talked about it. Haven't we? We've been through it. Let me spell it out for you again: there's a contract out on you, Professor. Every hour you stay here in Peshawar, every minute, you risk being shot or blown to pieces. They could come for you at any moment. Listen. Here are your tickets.' He handed them to Mungoo. 'And some hard currency. No, please, it's not much and you will need every penny you can get.' He handed over a sealed white envelope.

'You've got your passports?'

'Of course.'

The sky to the east was turning pink and gold.

'The flight to Islamabad takes fifty-five minutes, all right? It won't be a busy flight. Not everyone likes to get up so early. Our friend will meet you in person and take you to breakfast. There'll be someone in the domestic arrivals hall with a sign and a letter M for Mungoo. You follow him and he'll take you to your host's car.'

'Ahlberg? Ahlberg will be there?'

Brodick nodded, but then gestured at the driver and shook his head, indicating to the Mungoos that they shouldn't mention anyone's name out loud.

'You'll stay at the residence as his guests. You'll have your own bedroom, sitting room and bathroom. Your own guest apartment. You'll be comfortable and have plenty of privacy. I suggest you shouldn't go out if you can avoid doing so. Stay away from American, British and Pakistani officials if you can. Journalists too. It will be safer that way and your host is well aware of the danger. He'll arrange to have your shopping done for you. His cook will prepare whatever you prefer to eat. You'll have the run of the gardens when no one else is around.'

'How long?'

'He's already organising your visa, asylum papers and your flight. I would say no more than four or five days at the outside. Be patient. Try to see it as a free holiday, a chance to rest.'

Mungoo nodded, looked at his wife.

'Questions? I think we've covered everything.'

'I think so, too, Richard. Thank you.'

Mrs Mungoo did have one question. 'Mister Richard, is it very cold in Stockholm?'

'I shouldn't think the winters are any worse than they are in Kabul, Mrs Mungoo. You will be comfortable. They will look after you. Sweden's a very civilised country, as you no doubt know.'

The taxi was slowing down, moving through the Peshawar airport checkpoint. The policeman on duty wasn't interested in the foreigner in the front passenger seat. He waved them through. They drew up outside the terminal. As Brodick had anticipated, there was very little traffic in or out and no sign of Westerners. The driver opened the boot and Brodick hauled the bags out.

Brodick's heart was dancing a jig under his ribs; even now there was a very good chance of their being intercepted.

'I'm going to miss you, Richard.'

The men hugged, slapped each other's backs.

'Professor, you know you are my very best friend. I couldn't have stuck it out here in Peshawar without your friendship and kindness. And we did good work together. We'll do so again.'

Mrs Mungoo looked up at him. 'Mr Richard, we can't thank you enough. Really, we can't. You must come to see us in Stockholm. And soon.'

Mungoo nodded. 'Of course you must. We will be waiting for you.'

He watched them go. They turned and waved, and he waved back. Brodick wondered what they would say to him if they knew the truth: that he—their very good friend, collaborator and saviour Richard Brodick—was the British spy tasked with Professor Mungoo's assassination.

2

Two Years Previously

'Head agent sounds rather romantic, doesn't it? But the reality is rather mundane, I'm afraid.'

James Dryden put his pint glass down in the grass, careful not to spill his lager on the Black Watch tartan rug. 'You'll be our cutout between Tim here, and your cameramen.'

Brodick observed the ritual of beer and rug. 'Understood.'

Yes, he did understand, or thought he did, but it still seemed surreal. Spies sitting on a rug on a lawn, quaffing beer under a blazing sun. Surrey-in-Pakistan. It might be February and winter, but it was still hot, at least during the day. He appreciated that he, Brodick, was a little naive and perhaps Dryden was sensibly trying to dampen his enthusiasm and put matters into perspective. This was something he'd truly wanted so badly and for so long; to make a difference, to do his bit in the Cold War, to live up to his father's legendary reputation. And here he was at last, poised on the start line.

It was an exciting moment, but he knew better than to let his exuberance show.

There had been a price. Brodick had cast aside wife, dog, friends, job and home—his previous life, in effect—and this, here, at last, was the pay-off. Or so he hoped.

'And of course you'll be the cut-out for anyone else you might recruit as a sub-agent, witting or otherwise.'

Dryden was a former Royal Air Force squadron leader. He looked like one. Perhaps it was the combination of Ray-Ban shades, colourful Hawaiian shirt, cargo shorts and sandals; at any rate there was something raffish, even performative, about his manner, something not quite public school. Brodick couldn't picture him lunching at Boodle's or holding up the bar at White's. He had identified himself as head of station, the most senior Secret Intelligence Service officer working under diplomatic cover out of the Islamabad High Commission where he held the official rank of cultural first secretary—way below his real place in the embassy hierarchy. But it was Tim—Tim Hermitage—who interested Brodick most of the SIS intelligence officers present, the man who would be his case officer—his boss, in effect.

Interesting? Sure he was.

Hermitage had arrived late, apologising in that way the English have of not meaning sorry at all, adding in an offhand manner he'd come from the villa next door where he'd played six sets of tennis with the Reuters bureau chief, a New Zealander named Cowley. Prodded and teased by his colleagues as he helped himself to a Tennent's lager from the ice box, Hermitage admitted he'd won—only just, he said self-deprecatingly, because his opponent was suffering from one of his frequent hangovers. Brodick thought Hermitage hadn't needed to explain—he was carrying a racket and wearing tennis clothes soaked in sweat.

He was a tall, long-limbed man in his mid-forties with enormous ginger eyebrows that seemed to Brodick to writhe and wriggle like unkempt, furry caterpillars, lending him an air of piratical intensity. He looked older than his colleagues and appeared so lean as to have not an ounce of excess fat on him; his most notable feature aside from the eyebrows, Brodick decided, were the eyes. They were deep-set, flat and unblinking, a glittering hazel and they were now levelled at the newcomer. Meeting Hermitage's gaze was disconcerting. It was like staring down the muzzles of a double-barrelled shotgun. Not that it was an accusing or hostile stare; rather it was a frank visual inspection, the scrutiny of someone who sees everything, or tries to.

Hermitage was ex-Army. Brodick knew little more than that — other than Hermitage having served a dozen years with the Royal Irish Hussars, including three tours with the Special Air Service Regiment amid the dying embers of empire: Aden, Borneo, Oman. He'd achieved the rank of major but, as usual in such cases, was promoted lieutenant-colonel prior to resigning his commission, and was referred to simply as Colonel Hermitage.

Hermitage was a hard man and Brodick would have a tough job impressing him.

Dryden was still speaking. 'They'll be watching you, of course, you must expect that of them, but we don't anticipate any difficulty. You won't be armed. It won't be necessary. My advice would be to concentrate initially—the first couple of months or so—on establishing your cover. You need to work on that. Everyone's going to think you're a spy and you can only persuade them otherwise not by denying it but by being conscientious in producing plenty of material for your media outlets. They'll see your by-line—often, hopefully. I really do want the Pakistanis to relax, to accept you as just another member of the foreign press corps, albeit one who breaks the rules by living in Peshawar and not here, in Islamabad. We don't want them to regard you as any kind of threat. That's the essential thing. They'll ask the High Commission about you and our answer will be that we have no reason to think you're anything other than a freelance correspondent, suitably accredited. No hidden agenda we know of. Not up to any political mischief. No axes to grind. No ideology to worry about. Harmless. Our press attaché has been briefed.'

Quite a speech, then, an informal induction into the local SIS Station. Was this normal? No, not really, not if Brodick's limited experience was any guide. Previously he had only known his current case officer, and not the latter's colleagues by sight or by name. He had been passed from one handler to another over time, but now Brodick felt he was getting special treatment, that he was being told very clearly that he was one of them—almost one of them anyway, a probationer, that he was privileged in some sense yet still falling short of full membership. His birth in Beirut and schooling in Africa had ensured he had no automatic pass when it came to his positive vetting and, notwithstanding his late father's outstanding career as an intelligence officer, Brodick would have to work his way through what was known as an S-type engagement, earning his spurs the hard way in the ranks as a head agent on contract for a minimum of nine months but more likely two years.

Did they know about his father—about his extraordinary achievement in turning and then running an Abwehr officer as an agent in place in 1943? Of course they did, but were too circumspect to bring it up. Perhaps they resented Brodick, imagining that he'd somehow used his father's reputation to leverage a contract worker's job with the Service.

They were sizing him up: politely, without staring—except for Hermitage—and without making it too obvious. They'd know all about him already, surely, having had his personnel file and training report from Century House. They probably knew more about him than he did.

They sat on the front lawn of the rented home of James and Sarah Dryden, overlooking a bank of hydrangeas and one of the very quiet streets of Islamabad's diplomatic enclave. Designed on a grid as a garden city, Islamabad had at its centre a gigantic mosque, not unlike an English cathedral city. In fact, the rug and the beers seemed to him to be an attempt to replicate English suburbia, though it was far too hot, even in winter. They were all sweating. Brodick felt it trickle down his back, behind his ears. No, this wasn't Godalming or Guildford, no matter how hard they might pretend.

It surprised Brodick that his hosts didn't seem to mind being seen together and so openly. Anyone with a camera—or an automatic weapon, come to think of it—would have been able to capture, or kill in a single shot or burst, almost the entire SIS station. Or at least its senior intelligence officers, along with their latest contract recruit. But then Islamabad was the seat of government and hence well protected by the country's security forces.

Brodick saw his chance to raise an issue that mattered to him, one he hadn't mentioned in London but which had preoccupied him ever since leaving Heathrow. 'When it comes to my cover, Mr. Dryden, you do realise that I will have to go into Afghanistan. No journalist worth his salt would be willing to sit out the war in Peshawar. I have to go, at least for a couple of weeks, and soon.'

Dryden and Hermitage exchanged looks. 'I don't see why not. Do you, Tim?'

Hermitage's eyebrows wrestled each other to a draw. 'Perhaps we should clear it first with London. I don't see any reason why he shouldn't go if he wants to, particularly if it helps him establish his cover. That's the important thing.'

They were talking as if he wasn't present, and Brodick had a notion of what they were thinking and not saying. What if he were captured? How much could he divulge that would damage the Firm? Not much was the answer, and Brodick was counting on that being their view, too.

He'd never been to the drab SIS headquarters at Century House in south London; they'd made sure of that. He was still an outsider, not a career intelligence officer, though that was his aim, his lifelong ambition. All he had in the way of knowledge of the trade of espionage was his brief training at Fort Monckton at Gosport, and the names of the dozen case officers who had been his contacts with the Service over the years, along with the occasional insight and gobbet of gossip provided off-the-cuff by his otherwise taciturn and distant father, now deceased. Even so, his previous case officers had not used their real names, or so Brodick assumed. He had very little that would be useful to feed his captors even if they did succeed in making him talk, perhaps in return for an eventual pardon. But the Soviets would recognise the name: Brodick. They'd make the connection. Giving the son of a celebrated former SIS director, the star role in a Kabul show trial would at the very least be a propaganda coup for the KGB and its Afghan client service, the Khad or *Khidamate Aetilaate Daulati*. Brodick supposed it wouldn't really matter very much what he confessed to or if he confessed at all.

He was encouraged by what seemed to be a positive response. He would surely make the trip.

Mrs Dryden collected the bottles and plates with the help of the youngest SIS officer, an athletic young man with a strong jaw, five o'clock shadow and a placid expression. Around Brodick's age and named Harwood, he seemed anxious to please. 'Let me,' Harwood said, and repeated the phrase again and again as he loaded plates into arms bulging with muscles and ferried them up to the villa, then returning for more.

Brodick remembered to thank Sarah Dryden for the picnic.

He found himself standing next to Hermitage as they prepared to disperse. The ever-willing Harwood was folding up the rug.

'How's the hotel?'

'Seems okay, sir. No problems.'

The "sir" had slipped out inadvertently. Brodick felt the blood rush to his face. He was embarrassed by his embarrassment.

The three-star hotel was fine. The muzak sound system, though, was not. It blasted out in reception, the dining room and corridors, seeping into the guest rooms, playing over and over, twenty-four hours a day, a 1980 hit by the Australian group, Air Supply. Not that Brodick expected someone like Hermitage to understand, but the lyrics repeated themselves endlessly in his head, a cerebral indigestion, and he was sick of it.

'Tim. Call me Tim. We thought it better that you stay somewhere modest at the start; you'd attract too much of the wrong kind of attention at the Holiday Inn and to be honest we thought the rates would be a little steep for a young freelancer.

Sorry there's no pool.'

'Bit chilly for swimming anyhow.'

'I'm going up to Peshawar myself in a couple of days. Let me give you a lift.'

Perhaps this was an opportunity to bond with this rather forbidding boss.

'Thanks, but I think I should go as soon as possible. It might seem a little odd for a newly arrived journalist to get a lift with a senior British diplomat straight off.'

Brodick told himself he was explaining more than was strictly necessary. Shut up, you fool. He couldn't bring himself to use Hermitage's first name. He would use his military rank

'Fair enough.' Hermitage fiddled with a pipe, filling it from a leather tobacco pouch. 'Good luck, Richard. You'll do well, I'm sure.' Those glittery eyes said something else entirely. It seemed to Brodick they posed a question: Is he up to it?

Brodick was relieved no one had mentioned his father.

Two hours later, he was squeezed onto the grubby back seat of a small, battered taxi on his way northwest along the Grand Trunk Road. According to Brodick's travel guide, it was one of Asia's oldest and longest land routes, stretching all the way from Chittagong in Bangladesh, west to Howrah in India, through Delhi and Amritsar, Lahore and Peshawar and finally to Kabul. Brodick faced just a three hour long, potholed stretch of it during which he counted no fewer than nine road accidents of one kind or another, most of them involving buses, motorcycles and livestock and, in two cases, all three modes of transport. He saw casualties, too: goats and men sprawled on the verge, broken and bloody, but Brodick urged his driver not to stop, conscious that crowds of angry locals could all too easily pick on a foreigner as scapegoat.

At Attock Bridge, Brodick sensed he had at last left the Indian subcontinent behind for Central Asia. He didn't need a map to know it; it was something about the change in the light. The colours were more intense; the warm, late afternoon air smelled different. It was as if a burden had been lifted; Brodick realised he had crossed into North West Frontier Province.

Thus my real journey begins, he told himself. He was about to play his walk-on role in the final act of the Great Game. Brodick was elated; Attock marked the geographical start to his adventure, the dream he'd had as long as he could remember, of playing a secret warrior like his dad, only for real this time, and yes, he was going to make the old man proud, even if Brodick senior would never see his son fill his shoes. 'Just fucking watch me,' he said under his breath, but loud enough for the driver to glance at him in the rear-view mirror.

They arrived in the green oasis of Dean's Hotel as the sun was setting, Brodick stiff and dusty and greatly relieved; sweat dribbled down his back, legs and face. He wiped it from his chin to stop it dripping onto the pages of the registration book; he used the front of his shirt to dry his right hand so he wouldn't make a mess of signing in under the inscrutable gaze of modern Pakistan's founder, Muhammad Ali Jinnah. Then it took the combined strength of Brodick, two staff and his taxi driver to propel his trunk, bought in a Rawalpindi bazaar and secured with two padlocks, to his room. With much heaving and shoving and fierce imprecations in at least three languages, they managed to stow Brodick's humdrum paraphernalia of espionage under his bed.

He paid off the cab, tipped his helpers, took a shower, changed, and lay down. Peace at last. The vague and unfamiliar sounds of dusk—a bird's repetitive cry, distant footsteps and voices, the chuffing of a steam train—held his attention but momentarily.

Somehow the strangeness of it all seemed like a homecoming.

3

He was being watched.

Of course it might conceivably be no more sinister than curiosity aroused by his promenades through the city. Brodick was foreign, after all: conspicuously so, being fair-skinned, blue eyed and blond. And now that he'd been in place almost two weeks, most people interested in the 'English' would know about as much as it was possible to know, from his eating habits to his room number. Some might even know the true nature of his work, or think that they did. Every time he left the hotel on foot, innumerable pairs of eyes observed his passage and no doubt tongues wagged in Dari, Pashto, Urdu. Brodick felt the collective stare boring into his back; there was nothing he could do about any of that other than to vary routes and times. It was just the way things were in Peshawar. Brodick had to accept he was a novelty, an exotic creature. But this morning was different; the oddity's skin prickled with an uncertainty bordering on fear.

He was trapped between the solitariness of his hotel room and the sensation of paranoia on these streets. The loneliness of Dean's Hotel drove him out, but the city and unease of being followed forced him back to endure his own company.

He was careful to keep a leisurely pace, though his leg muscles twitched with a suppressed desire to break into a run. Despite the awareness of being tracked he kept his hands in his pockets as any visitor might: his right held his grubby rupees, his left his keys. What no one except Brodick knew was that the rupees he held were soaked in sweat from the furious fist that squeezed them, and that the keys cut into the palm of his left hand, also bunched tight as if he was about to step into the ring and fight for his life. The pain helped. He felt liquid ooze between the fingers of both fists; he hoped that in the case of his left it wasn't blood that would soil his pants, but he refrained from looking down to check. He was no threat, for it would surely be obvious to everyone watching that he carried no weapon. That in itself was a departure from the norm; in this corner of the planet, especially rural areas of the North West Frontier Province, no self-respecting male over the age of fourteen wanted to be seen without one. It was a matter not of style or fashion but honour.

Brodick made a point of gazing about without a particular aim in mind. No, he wouldn't show concern—nothing about his demeanour showed nervousness. That was the intention anyhow, in sharp contrast to how he felt. On the contrary, he hoped he appeared sure of himself, confident of his own safety, of his right as a Briton to venture wherever he fancied. *Savoir-faire* was his armour.

Although he knew it was useless trying to identify his follower or followers, he let his eyes slide across shop windows the way he had been taught to 'mirror' any tail. But the windows were too dusty, the pavements and street itself too chaotic: shrouded in toxic exhaust, teeming with pedestrians dodging scores of motorcycles. The motorcycles were a problem; they were perfect for surveillance and almost impossible to detect because they were agile and so numerous. And what purpose would be served by pinpointing whoever they were? Shaking off a tail, Brodick had been instructed, was only to be practiced in extremis, to protect oneself or the security of a contact. He reminded himself for the umpteenth time that being watched went with his new job.

Suck it up, chum.

He slowed then paused, turning to look at a shop entrance to his left as if deciding whether to go in or not and, having made up his mind, he strode through the doorway into the darkness and stillness of the tailor's.

Emerging a few minutes later, a brown paper parcel tied with string under his left arm, Brodick stood under the shop's tattered awning, feeling cold drops of sweat run down his back as he surveyed the street as if trying to decide which way to go. Left or right? Eenie meanie miney moe. Three small boys armed with sticks chased the metal rim of a bicycle wheel through the traffic, oblivious of danger. Another hawked newspapers with massive red headlines in Pashto splashed like blood on the front pages, holding them up to motorists who sounded their horns continuously, pointlessly. Across the street, a bald, thin man with a grey beard bent and slapped loaves on the red-hot sides of a clay oven.

'Rupee, Mister?' A male child perhaps five or six, barefoot in filthy *shalwar kameez*, tapped on the arm that held the parcel and stood waiting, snot or tears or both leaving streaks on his muddy cheeks. With each tap the same plaintive note. 'Mister? Mister? Mister?' Brodick pretended not to notice. Give one refugee starveling a coin and he would have a mob of juveniles to contend with.

'No, absolutely not. Fuck off, will you.' His lips moved; it made him feel better saying it aloud. A vengeful breeze whipped up dust from the road into Brodick's face and made the torn wall posters gyrate, distorting the features of Pakistani politicians, martyred Afghan 'freedom fighters' and Bollywood stars. They seemed to mock Brodick, punishing him for his arrogance. Peculiar then that this normal stuff was happening while just a few score miles away Afghans and Soviets were killing one another.

Brodick's attention was taken by a woman—no, two women—both covered head-to-toe, one in shiny pink, the other neon blue, walking side by side, heads close together, carrying shopping bags and deep in conversation, each face masked by cotton latticework that reminded Brodick of a medieval portcullis. One nudged the other; they glanced back at him with their blank grills and moved on. Brodick's eyes followed, noticing how their figures swayed under the tent-like burkas. Rewarded with a glimpse of pale ankle strapped into a high-heeled golden sandal, Brodick was aroused in an instant and almost laughed out loud notwithstanding his apprehension. He'd only been in the place less than a month and already he felt a grievous want. Even a burka could excite.

Which was presumably why his handlers had routinely asked if and when Marion would join him. At first, the question had been, 'Have you told her?' Then, a while later at a subsequent meeting, 'How did Marion take it?' Still later, 'Is your wife in favour of what you'll be doing? Has she said whether she'll go out there with you?' Brodick lied and lied again. He had told her, he said, untruthfully, and in fact had only done so at the last possible opportunity because he was afraid of what she would say, of what he knew she would say.

She had assumed all along, ever since he insisted they would be going abroad, that it would at least be somewhere agreeable: more than agreeable, somewhere exciting, romantic, artistic. Paris, perhaps, or Barcelona. Florence. Amsterdam. When he finally spelled it out, she had told him straight: she wasn't going. No way. She didn't know anything about the place, had never heard of it, but didn't like the sound of it one bit. It was another of his palm tree-and-shithole locations that her peculiar husband loved so much. She didn't like his new 'friends' either, or their line of work. She didn't understand why he would want to have anything to do with such people. Thugs in expensive suits with posh accents, she called them. Marion had her career to think of. She had her own friends—real friends—and family. The latter would be perplexed and worried, the former appalled if they knew; her contemporaries would drop her instantly, she would be a social outcast. Why couldn't he stick with the glossy current affairs magazine he worked for? Okay, it was right wing, very pro-Thatcher. So what? It paid well. Couldn't his editor find him a foreign posting?

Brodick listened to this in silence, and when she finished he said he understood completely. He was sympathetic. It was fine if she didn't want to go, really it was, but perhaps she might reconsider later. That bit about reconsidering later was also a lie. The truth of it was that he wished that his marriage would die, withering away with the corrosion of time, distance and the chosen location. Above all without fuss. In the meantime, would she mind joining him on the short training course, pretty please? Just to show willing. The handlers' questions became more insistent. 'We think it's important that Marion join you—for your sake.' For the female companionship, they'd meant, for the sex. Oh, the irony. If they'd known how infrequently their head agent and his wife had fucked, they wouldn't have been so concerned. Or would they? They must have reasoned that Brodick on his own would be frustrated, vulnerable. Burkas. Ankles. Heeled sandals in gold glitter. Now he got it.

There were no real signs that he was being followed, but he still believed it.

Back in his hotel room, the door locked, he tried on his purchases: two sets of *shalwar kameez* for his foray into Afghanistan—he was relieved to find that he hadn't bled into his trouser pocket, after all. He then dragged his tin trunk out from under his bed—a single iron affair with a horsehair mattress—and unlocked it. He counted his Super 8 cameras and cassettes. The former had the advantages of being small, rugged, light and simple to use. The disadvantage was that the latter lasted only three minutes and the zoom feature was very limited; so limited that, to be effective, action had to be filmed close up. Very close. The cameraman had to be in the firing line with the *mujahideen*.

To Brodick's dismay most of the stuff brought back so far had proved useless—either taken so far away from the action as to be totally unusable, or else consisted of what Brodick labelled Afghan holiday snaps—endless video of the guys walking around in the mountains, praying, striking poses with their AK-47s for the camera, eating, smoking, praying, scratching themselves, applying kohl to their eyes with the aid of hand mirrors and generally doing what *mujahideen* do when not fighting. Bugger all, in other words. Rarely, very rarely, there were a few seconds of brilliance—a close-up of a BTR-60 ablaze and under fire, dead Russians in a ditch or a Soviet gunship directly overhead, strafing a village.

Over the previous year, Soviet soldiers had died in their thousands and had been shipped home in sealed metal coffins and buried in secret. Even their mothers weren't allowed to see the bodies. This was all very well and good, but where, Lord Carrington asked, was the coverage of the fighting? The Foreign Secretary wanted Soviet blood spilled in every British living room. The conventional wisdom had it that Afghanistan was far too inaccessible, the combat itself too dangerous and communications almost entirely lacking—no wonder the war failed to attract the usual media circus, and media visas were never granted by the communist authorities in Kabul unless the recipients were sympathetic to the Soviet cause and deliberately blind or indifferent to what was really going on. So without video footage reaching millions of television screens in the West, it seemed unlikely that politicians would feel any public pressure to support the resistance in any meaningful way.

Hence Brodick's labours. The cassettes—he turned them over in his hands: small, grey, plastic, oddly fragile—were passed on covertly and free of charge by the Secret Intelligence Service to a confidential contact in a wholesale television agency, which edited out the crap—and there was rather a lot of that—and put together whatever gems there might be, distributing these to the main television outlets.

Brodick checked the fourteen cameramen listed as being in the field, volunteers he'd inherited from his anonymous predecessor, no doubt another contract labourer. This then was his primary mission: finding, recruiting, equipping, training and paying young men willing to take on the task.

Room 19 was Brodick's refuge and his prison cell. It was around the corner from reception, away from the hotel entrance and front lawn. It was quiet, too quiet. It had two steps up to a little, half-walled stoep, its floor painted red and polished, which led in turn to the stable door that opened to a whitewashed sitting area with two 1950s-style armchairs and a small sofa dressed in loose, off-white covers, a very worn brown rug, a stained coffee table and, beyond that, the sleeping alcove and bathroom. High ceiling fans stirred the air in both sitting room and alcove, a sullen wheezing and juddering that seemed to make little difference to the atmosphere.

Built in 1913, Dean's was a colonial relic of sprawling brick and stucco. White and single storey, complete with ballroom and chandeliers, spread out across generous lawns and flower beds, it had in its imperial heyday played host to the famous and infamous: Rudyard Kipling and King Nadir Shah had been among its guests. It lay close to the railway station and just outside the Peshawar cantonment: the city's leafy garrison area from which the Empire's troops had set out, drums beating and flags waving, to wage several campaigns on the margins of empire, the Frontier and in Afghanistan itself. The cantonment's old guardhouse still boasted a mirror which was set in the cement outside the entrance, whereby NCOs could check that soldiers of the Black Watch were 'regimental': in that they wore nothing under their kilts as per regulations. Brodick had inspected it, too—sticking his tongue out at himself—finding it badly tarnished but still functional.

He told himself he would love playing his walk-on part in this late colonial drama even more if he wasn't so bloody petrified and lonely most of the time.

If someone had suggested that he too was a colonial relic, he would not have been offended, but would have found it mildly amusing and perplexing, chuckling politely along with his accuser. And if someone had asked him—they never did—whether he thought the British Empire had been, at the height of its power, beneficial or oppressive in the eyes of its subjects, he would have thought a moment and muttered something to the effect that it had probably been both, depending on time and place. But it would be better to ask them *their* views for Brodick, at least unconsciously, associated himself with coloniser, not colonised—despite an ancestor's lucrative slave trading from the Bight of Biafra to the plantations of Virginia in the 18th century, or perhaps because of it. For he could not find it within himself to speak for Africans or Asians. Brodick's thinking and imagination did not stretch that far. He might lack empathy but he was sure, however, that what he was doing was romantic. It was an adventure. It was patriotic. It was the right thing to do. He was making history and he was following in his father's footsteps. He wasn't about to let mushy liberal scruple stand in the way of opposing the Soviets, who were, after all, just the latest iteration of his old man's Nazi enemies.

He was going to prove himself or die violently in the attempt, the latter a constant possibility which made it all the more exciting. In theory, at least.

*

Several days would pass without the appearance of a cameraman or new recruit, giving Brodick plenty of time to focus on what interested him: the Afghan resistance movement and the war on the far side of what passed for a frontier, the Durand Line. After another silent, solitary breakfast of toast, scrambled egg and tea in the gloomy hotel dining room—he seemed to be the only guest— he strode out into a cool morning of hazy sunshine to the lone taxi, always the same taxi, a brown Toyota Corolla, with the same man dozing in the driver's seat, waiting just outside reception. This morning it would be the turn of Jamiat-i-Islami, a mainly Tajik organisation with a strong following north and northeast of Kabul and regarded by Brodick as one of the best organised and best led organisations. While it sought to replace the communists in Kabul with an Islamic order, its leader, the renowned Islamic theologian named Rabbani, seemed of a mild and benign disposition. Brodick liked Jamiat. He liked Tajiks generally, though he wasn't sure why.

Brodick opened one of the rear doors and climbed in. The driver woke and looked at his customer in the rear-view mirror.

'*Salaam Aleikum*, Ahmad.'

'*Waleikum salaam*, Mr Richard. Where to?'

Ahmad was a brown man who wore a brown *shalwar kameez* that matched his brown taxi. Even the worn seats were brown.

'Jamiat-i-Islami, please, Ahmad.

By now Ahmad—a local Pashtun, middle-aged, sleepy-eyed, unshaven and obese—knew his customer's several possible destinations, and Brodick was happy for Ahmad to doze behind the wheel outside the Jamiat-i-Islami office and wait for him while he settled on a chair in the press office, drank green tea below a poster showing Afghans merrily burying two coffins—one wrapped in the Stars and Stripes and the other the Soviet Hammer and Sickle—and exchanged pleasantries with the Jamiat spokesman, hopefully gaining some new insight into the conflict.

There was no doubt in Brodick's mind that Ahmad kept Special Branch or at least one of several Pakistani intelligence and security agencies informed of his activities. Brodick didn't mind. It suited him—he wanted to be seen to behave openly just as any foreign journalist would. On those occasions when Brodick needed to protect his interlocutors' identity, he would slip away from the hotel on foot, then take a motorised rickshaw—Thais would have called it a *tuk-tuk*—changing it at least twice before reaching his destination. Or he would leave Ahmad outside as usual, stroll out by the back door and then reappear later by the front an hour or two later as if he'd been there all the time.

It was possible that Ahmad had tumbled to this subterfuge, but why should Ahmad bother telling anyone? Brodick reasoned that as long as the driver was paid for his informing, and permitted to keep his prime spot as the sole taxi service parked inside the hallowed gates of Dean's, as well as pocketing Brodick's fare along with a generous tip on an almost daily basis, it wouldn't matter to Ahmad what the "English" really got up to. After all, each of the seven major resistance organisations headquartered in Peshawar was watched closely, with Pakistani secret police always outside the gates, noting every arrival and departure—and perhaps inside as well—with the help of Afghan informers. Brodick could usually identify the secret policemen—it was something about the way they wore their *shalwar kameez,* complimented by their round woollen hats, their aviator shades and the inevitable toothbrush moustaches, their well-fed bellies and their habitual smoking along with their insolent stares.

There was something this morning, albeit minor. The press officer—a suave young man with a white turban and a livid scar that stretched right across his face, from jawline to the cheekbone on the opposite side, stopping just short of the eye—had translated it from the handwritten note in Dari, a torn and grubby page of lined paper that had taken two weeks at least to reach Peshawar. Jamiat fighters, or more likely another local group affiliated to Jamiat, had downed a Soviet helicopter gunship—not an Mi-8 this time, but the real thing, an Mi-24, codenamed *'HIND'* by NATO, a huge, ferocious, armoured predator equipped with rockets and most lethal of all, a fast-firing 'minigun' in the nose and designed to provide close air support for the Red Army's 'combined arms' tank divisions on the plains of northern Europe. It was the one weapon the Afghans feared and regarded as almost indestructible.

Apparently the helicopter had been brought down—or perhaps it had suffered engine failure and crashed—in remote Bamyan Province in the north-central Hazarajat, a rugged area populated mainly by Hazaras, a Shi'ite people traditionally treated as second-class citizens by Afghanistan's majority Sunni Muslims. According to popular mythology, the Hazaras' Asian features were evidence of the DNA they'd inherited from the Mongols' conquering army.

Brodick knew the Mi-24's mini-gun was high on the local SIS station's Requirements list: in other words, its intelligence targets to which all UK departments—especially the Foreign Office and Ministry of Defence—contributed. Probably the MI-24's avionics were on the list, too, but Brodick couldn't recall; it was such a long list, comprising at least 200 items.

'Do you know when this happened?'

'There's no date. We think maybe the first week of January.'

'So, around six weeks ago. And where, exactly? Is there a village or town nearby?'

'It doesn't say where. Bamyan is all we know.'

'What happened to the three aircrew? Do you know?'

'Killed. All.' The spokesman passed the edge of his hand across his throat.

'Afghans? Soviets?'

'Afghans are not allowed to fly this helicopter. They were Russians.'

'Do you have their IDs?'

'What?'

'Their identity discs.' Brodick gestured with his fingers at his own throat. 'Or their papers.'

The spokesman shook his head.

'How did they bring it down?'

'The note doesn't say.'

'And is the writer of this note named?'

'Mullah Shariati. He is leader of the fighters who shot it down.'

'Is that his real name?'

The spokesman shrugged both shoulders, raising his hands, palms outwards.

'It could be that he named himself after Ali Shariati of Iran.'

The spokesman nodded and smiled, perhaps pleased—or amused—that the distinguished Shariati was known to this Westerner. 'It's possible, yes.'

Brodick thought it quite likely that the spokesman knew more of the incident than he was willing to divulge.

'Any pictures? Photographs?'

'No.'

If it was true, it was a rare thing. As far as Brodick knew, the resistance had as yet received no supplies of shoulder-fired surface-to-air missiles, such as the Soviet SAM-7. And it seemed almost impossible for a gunship to be brought down by fire from the guerrillas' standard anti-aircraft weapon, the DShK 12.7mm heavy machine gun, unless the latter was fired from above: deployed on a ridge in mountainous Kunar, for example, as the enemy aircraft flew low along a valley floor, with the firer trying to hit the rotor blades or engine.

'Can you get any more information?'

'We can, but it will take time. You want?'

'Yes, please. If it can be done.'

The spokesman said he would do his best, but it could be months.

Brodick would mention it to his case officer the next time he saw him. On second thoughts, he'd write it up as a very brief intelligence report. Material from the deep interior was quite rare, especially featuring a downed Mi-24.

He wasn't looking forward to his next engagement: a news conference called by Hezb-i-Islami, the largest and best-equipped Afghan resistance organisation led by the sinister Islamist, Burhanuddin, a man funded by the Saudis, armed and supported by Islamabad's generals with CIA help and actively assisted by Pakistan's Inter Services Intelligence, or ISI: the military espionage outfit charged with implementing Pakistan's so-called forward policy in Afghanistan. No doubt Burhanuddin would use the occasion to attack the Western media, his favourite target.

Burhanuddin was a murderous creature; Brodick had good reason to fear him.

Then it would be time to ditch the taxi and ring the changes, walking a little, doubling back, waving down a rickshaw, switching to another, then walking again—time-consuming precautions Brodick felt were essential before dropping in on his most important contact and best friend, Professor Mungoo.

4

'Richard! Come in, dear boy, come in.'

They were just like old friends, though they'd only known one another for a couple of months. Mungoo appeared delighted to have the young Westerner drop by. Brodick visited the old man several times a week, in fact, but his host always made a point of making him feel special. Maybe he did that with everyone. Mungoo clambered to his feet and, with one hand on his worktable for support, hobbled around it and shook Brodick by the hand, then flapped his free hand at a chair, indicating Brodick should take it. Then he returned to his papers but, before sitting down, turned to Brodick again and, looking at him over the top of his half-moon spectacles, explained he had been sitting for too long and his legs were stiff.

'You will have some tea, yes? How was your interview with Burhanuddin? Did he put a price on your head? He does that with most foreign journalists. He's a delightful fellow, now isn't he?' Mungoo's brown eyes fell on the bag Brodick held on his knee. 'Ha! Is that for me? A present?' His eagerness, his obvious delight in anticipating a gift was childlike—quite unlike his polite interest in Brodick's activities. Mungoo couldn't have cared less about the latter—any kind of derring-do he seemed to find silly and boring—and his disarming delight in whatever it was Brodick had brought was also a deliberate way—so Brodick thought—of laying claim to both Brodick and what Mungoo evidently thought was Brodick's duty as supplicant. That is to say, if Brodick sincerely wanted the old man's friendship and to tap into his wisdom as a kind of father figure, it was right and proper that he should bring gifts as a reciprocal gesture and as a sign of respect.

It was how the game was to be played, apparently, and Brodick wasn't going to argue.

At the start, back in February, they'd been wary of each other and sometimes downright suspicious, but now they'd worked out a modus vivendi. They both had what the other wanted and had reached an unspoken agreement on the terms of the relationship.

Perhaps it was linked in some way to Mungoo having been a professor and dean of the faculty of letters at Kabul University as well as sometime governor of Kapisa Province. He might live in genteel poverty in Peshawar, but he wanted his social, academic and political significance recognised. He needed acknowledgement. Who didn't, after all?

As for Brodick, he had no friends, no one he could confide in, no one with whom he could relax, drink and speak his mind. There was an emotional aspect that Brodick didn't really understand as yet, but he sensed that Mungoo fulfilled the role of mentor, a kindly uncle who's always around, willing to listen and to advise.

Anyhow, Brodick believed he knew what would come next, as it always did. Mungoo had grand ideas. He had ambitions, and he thought—or rather hoped and all but insisted—that Brodick might facilitate some of them. That meant money of course but, unknown to Mungoo, Brodick was already ahead of him, and more than willing to throw SIS cash Mungoo's way; if only small, irregular amounts to ensnare Mungoo for Brodick's own purposes. Or did Mungoo already guess what Brodick was and what he represented? Had he shaped his proposals in such a way that he knew Brodick would take the bait?

Afghans might roundly curse foreigners for interfering in their affairs, but they didn't hesitate to seek their material support.

To Brodick it resembled an arcane courtship dance, the methods and rules of which were a little murky and the end result even more mysterious. For a just moment Brodick wondered who it was who was being seduced. Was he really recruiting Mungoo? Or was he, Brodick, being recruited by this old man? Or was it mutual seduction, based on their respective needs: personal as well as professional? This seemed the most plausible interpretation.

He couldn't help liking Mungoo and he looked up to him, it was true. Mungoo was turning into the father figure Brodick recognised he lacked. A man of ideas and a true friend.

*

As for Burhanuddin—the man mentioned by Mungoo—he was, as everyone in Peshawar knew, the Islamist heading the biggest Afghan resistance organisation and the leader most favoured by Pakistan, receiving the best of the CIA-supplied weapons and the biggest share of the Wahhabi dosh doled out by the ISI. He was also something of a rabble-rouser, drawing huge crowds at his party rallies. Any Afghan male of military age signing on as a refugee in Pakistan was pressed to sign up for Hezb-i-Islami in return for the usual inducements: better and more plentiful food rations, a bigger and better tent for the refugee's family and a regular cash allowance. And ISI never failed to ram home the message to the CIA, Chinese intelligence and no doubt SIS, too: Burhanuddin was the man to back. The fact that the Pashtun leader—unusually, a Pashtun from the north of the country—would sell himself a hundred times over and resort to murder to achieve his dream of ruling Afghanistan once the Soviets had left wouldn't matter to the ISI. He was their man.

Brodick knew Mungoo to be a refugee, one of three million or thereabouts, and poor—though not so poor that he had to take up residence in a tent supplied by the UNHCR among the masses of his fellow countrymen camped out on a desolate moonscape outside town. He rented a small, dilapidated bungalow in the tranquil suburb of University Town, which Brodick thought was the nearest Peshawar came to having its own Putney or Dulwich. It was populated by doctors and dentists, lawyers and accountants and even a sprinkling of Gulf Arab newcomers connected somehow or other with the Afghan resistance. Brodick noted that some of the properties were concrete palaces, pretentious and ugly, funded by remittances from abroad. Mungoo lived with his wife—whom Brodick had never seen—and perhaps with his son, Fawzi. The rusty blue gate was always open and anyone could just walk in and across the yard still littered with the previous autumn's fallen leaves to the front room—technically, it was an annexe, the traditional reception for male guests—where Mungoo had his worktable, a few cheap upright chairs along with his books and papers piled haphazardly on shelves and the floor itself.

He was tall, balding—what little hair he had was white and long and wisps of it stood up of its own accord, giving him the air of a distracted Einstein—bushy grey eyebrows, immense brown eyes that seemed perpetually amused and he carried quite a paunch under a plain, off-the-shelf *shalwar kameez*. He shuffled about barefoot. Brodick put him in his late sixties, perhaps older. His pale skin was spattered with liver spots. He would run his hand across his non-existent hair frequently. He was not someone who had the time or inclination for regular exercise, and he seemed frequently short of breath. He was given to much shrugging, tucking his elbows into his sides, rolling his eyes, puffing out his cheeks and expelling air sharply from his expressive mouth.

Their meetings marked the high point of Brodick's otherwise solitary days.

Brodick noticed that old age had already taken hold; it encased Mungoo like a plaster cast, slowly smothering the youth that was. He was like a healthy tree, a mighty baobab, steadily succumbing to a predatory vine. The flesh on his face was loose, puffy and corrugated by deep fissures as if someone had taken a knife to him. Maybe he suffered from a medical condition Brodick had read about somewhere: the *Touraine-Solente-Golé* syndrome, sometimes

30

called bulldog-scalp.

Tea wasn't mentioned again for a while, and so too Brodick's encounter with the sinister Burhanuddin was forgotten. Even the mystery present on Brodick's knee was ignored.

Mungoo slapped the tabletop. 'I've decided.'

'Yes?'

'What do you know about Xerox machines?'

'Nothing. Sorry.'

'Are they easy to use?'

'I imagine so. But I've no experience of them.'

'Are they slow or quick? How many pages can they copy a minute?'

'I don't know. I'm a technical dunce, I'm afraid.'

'Dunce?'

'Idiot.'

'Ah.' Mungoo frowned at Brodick's woeful ignorance. 'How much is one of the machines?'

Brodick shook his head.

'I need one.' Impatient as ever, Mungoo tapped his knuckles on the table and sighed.

Brodick waited.

'Will you get me one?'

Brodick didn't answer, but waited for more.

Mungoo took off his glasses, pulled himself up out of his chair, shuffling about and rubbing his eyes. 'I've decided, Richard. I'm going to start a news service. An Afghan news service. It will be independent. It will be published in Pashto with Dari and English editions. I will want your help with the English. My son will help us with the Pashto, also.'

Brodick gave no sign of his excitement at the announcement.

'About the war, Professor?'

'Yes, yes. Of course. About the war. About Afghanistan. The war, certainly, also the politics and diplomacy. As well as the refugees. And some poetry. We cannot do without at least some culture, and all Afghans, regardless of their station in life, love poetry. Even the illiterate who are in the majority. What should we call it, do you think? I like the sound of the *Afghan News Bulletin*, or ANB. We'll send out free copies to major newspapers and embassies.'

'Why free?'

'For the publicity, to establish ourselves.'

'Institutions should pay more than individuals, perhaps twice as much, because they'll copy and distribute whatever they find interesting. If the material is reliable and original, you won't have to worry about publicity. You'll get plenty of subscribers and they'll pay well for it.'

'Maybe just at the start they can have the *Bulletin* free.'

'How often do you plan to publish, Professor?'

Mungoo shrugged. He didn't seem to have thought that far ahead. 'What do you think, Richard? Depends on how much material we have, I suppose. Sometimes we might devote an entire edition to an interview, or an investigation. Just occasionally we might devote one issue to literature. Especially if we run short of news. We don't have to publish regularly—or do we?'

Punctuality was not an Afghan strength. At the dawn of capitalism it was the Spanish who'd ensured that every colonial town was equipped with a clock tower. Time was seen as a commodity like everything else, from sugar and forest timber to slaves, and it was exploited and marketed along with the colonial labour force. What was the value of labour without time? Thankfully, the Afghans had escaped that imposition.

'If you are selling subscriptions I think issues should appear at regular intervals, so people know what they're getting for their money. If readers have to wait weeks for the next issue, they'll lose interest and cancel. They'll think you've given up. I suggest it should be monthly or bimonthly, perhaps with the odd special edition thrown in.'

Mungoo frowned, shrugged, pouted, scratched his bulldog scalp.

'Of course your name will go on the front cover, Richard. You will be my partner, a co-editor or associate publisher. How does that sound? This has to work for you too, my friend and comrade. It's our joint creation. You have a reputation to build, too, you know.'

'Wonderful, and I appreciate your generosity, but you should keep this an Afghan affair, Professor. Surely you've had enough of the British by now?'

Mungoo stared out of the window, deep in thought.

'Well. Perhaps you're right.

'Do you have a budget?'

'That's where you come in, Richard.'

Here we go. Brodick thought he could almost hear the cash register ringing in Mungoo's mind. It was a little unfair of him; the old man needed money, and it was Brodick not Mungoo who had first mentioned the issue of finance.

'Please ask your diplomat friends to contribute. Maybe one might donate a Xerox machine. I think we'll need to pay our writers eventually. There are so many journalists from my country living here in great hardship. They need help, too.'

'Do you know the Swedish ambassador, Professor?'

Mungoo sat down again and put on his glasses and took them off and cleaned them with the long tail of his shirt. 'Do you?'

'I'm seeing him tomorrow. Ahlberg. I'll give him your address, if I may, and suggest he visit you and you can explain your proposal and ask Ahlberg yourself. Maybe the Swedes can subsidise the first year's production of twelve bulletins. Or get hold of a Xerox for you. The ambassador seems keen to make a contribution in some way that doesn't tarnish his government's official neutrality. They already do a lot for the refugees here and donate medicines and equipment to the Afghan Surgical Hospital.'

'Tell your friend the ambassador I like *Glasmastarsills*.' Mungoo gave Brodick an extravagant wink.

'And chocolate, Professor. Don't forget the chocolate. I'll happily write and edit the English edition.'

'I know you will, Richard. I am counting on you. Now, what is it you have there for me in that little bag? And don't worry, I'm keeping my requests for chocolate for the Belgians and holding back on *Sachertorte* for the Austrians. Beggars must always be choosy, contrary to what you English say.'

Brodick watched Mungoo as he opened the bag and examined the red and chrome Walkman, turning it over several times in his hands with poorly concealed delight.

'I remembered you saying you missed your music, and that one of the Western composers you liked was Mahler. You said you like Shostakovich, too, if I remember.'

'It must have been expensive, Richard. This is so generous of you. And you remembered Mahler. I am touched. Truly. You are Boswell to my Johnson. See? I know about you English. And I do love Shostakovich.'

Brodick had already charged it to expenses. The Firm would pay.

'Tell me about this defector. The senior PDPA official you mentioned.'

'You really do want to meet him?'

'Of course I do.'

'Even if he insists that it's off the record?'

'Yes, if he insists.'

'You won't use his real name. It's his life at stake, Richard, not just the little freedom he enjoys in exile. I'm not sure he'll trust you, and for sure he won't tell you everything. There are some matters that could only come from him and, if known, would incriminate him. His caution is only natural. He has a family. You will have to be very patient. He has to worry not just about the Khad, but the resistance too, and the Pakistanis and their ISI. We both do. Our enemies are numerous.'

'I understand.'

'Do you? I did say you wanted to meet him, and he asked who you worked for. I confess I didn't remember and in any case he said you were probably a British spy. Are you a spy, Richard? You're certainly not your average journalist or you wouldn't be here living in Peshawar in the first place. You're a rule breaker.'

Brodick smiled, shook his head. 'It's one of those situations in which a denial only makes matters worse. Would a real spy ever admit to being one? If I say "yes" then I'm either a fool or a fantasist. If I say "no", then the notion only gains traction. Your question is best left unanswered.'

'Traction?'

'Credibility. When can I meet him? Did he agree?'

'Well, if you are prepared to wait or come back this evening and let me listen to this marvellous Second Symphony in the meantime, then you can ask him yourself. Stay for supper, why don't you. I enjoy your company, Richard. But I can't promise to persuade him on your behalf, and I don't think I should. Whatever is decided will be between the two of you. Leave me out of it. By the way, he does have a tendency to talk too much. You have been warned.'

Brodick loved invitations to dinner; it wasn't just the wonderful Afghan food, but the company, the conviviality of the event fuelled by alcohol of one kind or another and lots of contentious craic.

Mungoo slipped the cassette out of its case and into the Walkman.

'Do you know why Mahler called it the Resurrection, Professor?'

'Presumably he was religious in some way, and believed in an afterlife.'

'Do you?'

Mungoo pouted, blew air out of his cheeks as he positioned the little earphones. 'It depends on my mood, Richard, and how fragile I'm feeling. Ageing isn't very nice, you know. It's horrible, to be honest. It happens so fast. One morning you wake up and discover you're old and not twenty-four anymore. Belief is a kind of crutch and when you get old you will know how it feels. It's always a temptation.'

'I can imagine.' Not really, but Brodick admired his host's honesty and lack of dogma. 'I could do with that tea you offered.'

'Forgive me.' Mungoo pulled himself out of his chair once again, almost dropping the Walkman. 'I quite forgot. I'm so sorry—I'm a really terrible host.'

'You are, yes.'

They had a good laugh about Mungoo's very un-Afghan sense of hospitality and eventually tea was made—by Mungoo's invisible wife—and drunk. Brodick didn't admit that, to his shame, he knew precious little of James Boswell or Samuel Johnson.

5

He was a friend of Mungoo's and his assumed name was Mirwais, but it wasn't until May that they finally met. Brodick was getting used to the fact that everything related to Afghanistan took a very long time to happen, regardless of promises and good intentions.

There was something about the man that suggested to Brodick that he was an important find, that he would be of great benefit to his intelligence effort. That first evening, it was little more than a feeling, a sense of great things to come.

Mirwais began at once what would turn out to be a lecture. 'I won't insult you, Mr Richard, by recounting your own country's colonial history, starting in 1838 with your Lord Auckland's manifesto of intent to restore the weak and unpopular Amir Shah Shuja-ul-Mulk to the Afghan throne. It would only depress you, I think. And us, of course. I'm sure you know it, in any case. Let me instead quote one of your European philosophers, a certain Hegel, who said: "People and governments never have learned anything from history, or acted on principles deduced from it." It was true of the Soviets when they came in force to help us on the path of socialism just over fourteen months ago. The aims of the British Raj and our Soviet comrades were essentially the same, and both were doomed to fail.'

Brodick was surprised. 'You see the Soviet occupation as a failure—already?'

'Of course. No doubt at all. To use force is to fail, don't you think?'

'But you are a Marxist-Leninist, aren't you?'

'I was.'

'You've renounced your faith?'

'Ha! That's a good word for it: faith. You know why, Mister Richard? I'll tell you. Bolsheviks sought the coming of the kingdom of freedom, just as Jews and Christians and Muslims have waited in vain for the arrival of the kingdom of god. The traditional Jews tried obedience, the Essenes cleanliness and Christian heretics blind faith. These are all millenarian sects, Mr Richard. Cults that became sects led by radical fundamentalists. Along with liberalism and capitalism. They're all based on the same myth, the same fairy story of human progress, material or spiritual or both, and all of them a futile attempt to escape mortality, to defeat death. In my humble opinion, reality for human beings exists only in embracing the necessity of dying, but admittedly it's very hard to do.'

Humble? There was nothing humble about Mirwais or his opinions.

'But you were a Communist.' Brodick was impatient when it came to metaphysics.

'Ah, but I was never tied to Soviet apron strings. I was a member of the Khalq faction of the PDPA, Mr Richard, if you know what that is. There are thousands of us still in Afghanistan's jails. We were radicals in a hurry, impatient for the coming of socialism and with little patience for Moscow's cautious realpolitik.'

Mungoo, almost invisible in the dark, interrupted. 'Mirwais was a founder member of the Khalq, Richard. He was there at the start.'

Brodick threw in his penny's worth. 'The Saur Revolution. April 27, 1978.'

'So the Englishman knows something, after all.' Mirwais grinned at Brodick.

Mungoo again. 'Earlier, much earlier. Tell Richard. You were at the founding congress of the PDPA in 1965. You were just a kid. Like me. You were one of the twenty-seven founders of the Party and you were friends with Nur Muhammad who was then a journalist until it all went to his head and he developed a personality cult, calling himself the "Great Leader" and "Teacher and Great Guide".' Mungoo snorted with contempt.

'You're talking about Taraki.'

Mirwais clapped his chubby hands. 'We can't teach you a thing, Mr Richard, sir.'

Brodick knew he was being teased and he laughed along with it. 'No, no. Not at all. How did you and Professor Mungoo get to know each other? Unlike you, Mirwais, Mungoo's no Communist or PDPA member. You seem very different, in fact.'

'We are very different, though perhaps not in the way you imagine.'

For one thing, they were so unalike in appearance. Mungoo was tall and pale, Mirwais was short and dark. The latter was round, chubby, with thick lips and stubby hands and wore one of those ridiculous, round woollen hats that looked like a pie, a *pakhoul*, on the back of his head, giving him a clownish, Falstaffian appearance. He laughed a good deal, but he remained watchful even when rocking back and forth with amusement. He had smoked an entire packet of Brodick's Lucky Strikes, and Brodick made a mental note to remember to give him a carton of them the next time they met.

'Will someone explain?'

Mungoo stood up, shaking his head. 'My dear Richard, please— don't ask him. Unless of course you are willing to be inflict upon yourself more of my friend's standard lectures. If so, I suggest we have more tea to prepare ourselves for the painful experience.'

'It's not that bad.' Mirwais shook his fist, glaring at his host in mock anger.

Brodick was fascinated. 'I don't mind, really. I'd like to know more.'

Mungoo sighed and rolled his eyes. 'Don't torture the man just because he's British!'

First, they had the tea.

*

Mirwais rubbed his hands together like a man preparing to wield a spade or hammer—in his case, perhaps a hammer and sickle. 'My friend Mungoo here is what you English call "posh". I'm a commoner. He's a Kabul intellectual, an insider with connections, whereas I'm a simple provincial, an ignorant peasant without any patrons.'

Mungoo was about to say something, but Mirwais wasn't having it.

'No, don't interrupt! I'm an outsider, you see. Mungoo's not only of Durrani origin, but his wife is Muhammadzai, hence related to both our exiled King, Zahir Shah, and to the King's cousin, the late President Muhammad Daoud. If our Professor had seen the light and been a Marxist-Leninist, he would have found a natural home in the pro-Soviet Parcham faction of the PDPA and by now he'd be a top dog and someone to be feared. I would have to mind my manners, that's for sure. That's royalty for you!'

Mungoo had shut his eyes and pretended to be asleep.

'By contrast,' Mirwais continued, 'I'm a typical Khalqi because I'm Ghaljai, that is to say, I'm from the Ghilzai tribal group. We fought the British when they invaded and we became the major rivals of the Durranis, and revolted repeatedly against Muhammadzai rule. Many Marxist-Leninist leaders are drawn from the Ghilzai, and also several leaders of the resistance. You see, Mungoo is a cautious bourgeois but I'm a working class radical. My friend here may be a Pashtun, but he speaks Dari. Like a bloody aristocrat! I speak just Pashto because I'm a hooligan. Yet we are best friends. Does that help, Mr Richard?'

'I think so. Thank you.' Brodick didn't think so, not really.

Mungoo opened his eyes. 'You might say, Richard, that we are united by our enemies. We are men trapped in the middle. We live every day in fear of the knock at the door by the ISI. I'm sure you know of them. We share nothing in common with the Islamists such as Burhanuddin, Hekmatyar and Sayyaf, and we are totally opposed to President Babrak Karmal and his Soviet masters. If there's one thing that will unite disunited Afghans, it's a foreign invader. Don't your people say *"My enemy's enemy is my friend"*? So what does that make us?'

'The very best of friends.'

Mirwais thumped the table. 'Precisely. We are also intellectuals, and you know what intellectuals really are? No?'

Mungoo was shaking his head, but it didn't deter unstoppable Mirwais.

'Permit me to explain. We are the "*Teaser Stallions*". Are you familiar with the metaphor? No?' Mirwais turned to Mungoo for his agreement. 'This comes from that wonderful Russian writer and critic, Viktor Shklovsky. Heard of him? No? Oh, dear. You must read him, Richard, really you must. He was a revolutionary and then a counter-revolutionary. He was an instructor in an armoured division. And a wonderful writer. Well, it's like this. You want to breed the very finest horses, okay, but your stud is huge and a little scary, so you introduce a little stallion, a friendly little fellow, well-mannered and neatly turned out, with a poetic soul, to the lady, and they make friends. She finds him perfectly charming. Just as that friendship is about to be consummated, our little gentleman is pulled off her much to his disgust and the big stud fucks her instead and the task is completed. Job done. You understand? We are Moscow's Teaser Stallions and soon we shall be Washington's. That's intellectuals for you, my dear Richard. Screwed and screwed again.'

Mungoo and Mirwais chortled over this like a couple of schoolboys over a dirty joke. It was an old joke, apparently—a Russian literary joke—and like all Russian literary jokes born of starvation, war and the firing squad, it was bitter.

*

41

He left first at around 9pm, slipping silently from the Mungoos' bungalow, anxious not to make any undue noise opening and closing the metal gate, and walking through the dark streets of University Town to the main road where he might find transport back to Dean's and Room 19. If not, he would walk all the way. It would take perhaps forty minutes on foot and, although it was chilly, he would warm up quickly.

There was little traffic. The night air was full of woodsmoke and dust, car headlights slid by like pale white discs and there were few streetlights, cloaking him in welcome anonymity. Brodick did not seem to be followed this time, but he could never be absolutely certain. He hoped he was right in thinking that his watchers mostly kept regular business hours and would be at home with their families.

He gave himself a pat on the back; he told himself he deserved it for the day's work. He'd cemented his friendship with Mungoo and set in motion a partnership in establishing the proposed newsletter. He sensed a turning point in his efforts. He had delivered on his promise to introduce Brodick to the Khalqi defector, and Brodick had built a tentative relationship with the enigmatic Mirwais. For once, he had managed to do so without pushing his luck and asking too many questions. For once, he'd exercised some measure of self-restraint. What was the man's real name? What appointments had he held in the PDPA government? How long had he been in exile? What could he say about what was going on now in the higher reaches of the Kabul regime? Was he under anyone's control, such as Pakistan's dreaded ISI? Brodick was sure Mirwais would be a fund of intelligence once he could be persuaded to speak freely, and provided he was not already somebody else's asset.

He'd hang an entire network of sub-agents on Mungoo's undertaking, and with any luck another on Mirwais. Maybe two or three networks eventually. It helped that Brodick and Mungoo liked each other and were comfortable in each other's company, or at least it seemed that way. Brodick felt he had a special bond with these two Afghan intellectuals.

It was a comforting thought for a man alone among strangers.

But he told himself he wouldn't hesitate to exploit his new friends, to use them for his own purposes and those of the Firm. SIS officers were nothing if not effective users of men and women, and he was determined to become one of the best of them.

His intelligence work was already expanding faster than he had ever imagined.

They'd agreed on a time and place for their next meeting. Mirwais had made it clear that Dean's was out of bounds—it was too easily watched, and he said it was monitored by several agencies, domestic and foreign. He wouldn't go anywhere near it, day or night. Mirwais had advised Brodick to get out, to rent a house, preferably on a corner where it would be harder for watchers to monitor, or with a back door to another street. A house that wasn't overlooked, also. These were the very characteristics required of an SIS safe house, in fact.

Just who the hell was the real Mirwais—the man behind the smokescreen of words and the fake name?

6

'How are you settling in?' Hermitage sucked on his log of a pipe and squinted at Brodick through the smoke. His long legs were stuck out under the table, ankles crossed. He wore brown suede ankle boots known as *Veldskoen*—without socks, apparently—threadbare yellow cords with turn-ups, the pants held up by what looked like a club tie, and a rumpled linen jacket stained by the sweat of several summers. A silk cravat in what Brodick assumed were regimental colours spilled from his frayed collar. He resembled a well-off weekend sailor slumming with the locals in Cowes Week. Old money. All he needed to complete the flâneur look was a battered Panama hat.

'Settling in' was an odd phrase. Brodick had been in place for almost five months.

'Slowly. I've only had five cameramen return so far. I debriefed them, took their cassettes, gave them money and sent them home. I've a new recruit due for training tomorrow. Whether he turns up is another matter.' Brodick reached over and handed Hermitage thirteen Super 8 cassettes and ten typed CX reports—otherwise known as human intelligence or *humint*. He thought they represented a solid intelligence contribution, and he was disappointed that Hermitage simply glanced at them before putting it all away in a battered leather briefcase. After all, Brodick had put so much time and effort into them. He felt a twinge of resentment. Perhaps the cavalier handling of his work was deliberate, some kind of psychological game, a test of character.

'How's the cover coming along?'

'So far, a couple of dozen brief reports for *Voice of America*, maybe ten for the *BBC Eastern Service*, a dozen newspaper stories—very short for the *Telegraph* and something similar but longer for the *Inquirer*. And for *The Orient* I have another 2,000-word feature, my third, this time on refugees which I'll send from the Reuters bureau in Islamabad when I fly down again in week or so.'

'Would you say that was sufficient for a freelancer trying to establish himself in what, four, five months?'

Shit, what did the bloody man expect?

'These things take time. I need to develop contacts, sources.'

Hermitage watched him, said nothing. Brodick thought he knew what Hermitage was thinking: that he needed to make enough money—or be seen to make enough—to pay his bills as a freelancer. His freelance income, however notional, had to be visible in column inches, airtime and by-lines. Brodick understood that, but he also thought that no journalist settling into a freelance role in a foreign country could hit the ground running. Unless he or she was some sort of celebrity. He wouldn't say it, though; it would sound too much like an excuse and, if he knew anything at all about Hermitage, it was that his case officer would sense it at once and it would be set down as a mark against him. Hermitage was not someone who tolerated excuses. It was better to keep quiet and keep things straight. He would elaborate at his peril. These questions were just boxes that London wanted ticked, or so it seemed to Brodick. Don't take it personally, he told himself. It was just SIS bureaucracy at work. In this instance, they were probably concerned that Brodick might fall back entirely on his SIS salary—the equivalent of a middle ranking intelligence officer's pay—deposited into a private bank most people had never heard of and located just off Trafalgar Square.

They were meeting—in spy jargon a meeting between operative and case officer was a *treff*, from the German—in the basement dining room of Green's Hotel, a stone's throw from Dean's and somewhat cheaper. Breakfast having ended and lunch not having begun, they had the place to themselves. Brodick had spotted Hermitage's white, long-wheelbase Land Rover Defender with CD plates parked around the back of the hotel, though he didn't believe Hermitage, a senior diplomat, would actually stay there. That in turn led to the thought that the SIS must have other assets and resources in Peshawar or close by, and that Brodick would never know what they were. Not that he wanted to. Who cared where Hermitage stayed? It was better—safer—not to know anything he didn't need to know.

'And have you? Developed sources?'

'We'll have to see. It's early days.'

Brodick had dug in his heels; they both knew it. He sensed his recalcitrance disappointed Hermitage. It felt very much like an interrogation and one that was neither friendly nor hostile. It was all work, no pleasantries, no banter, nothing personal. Not even a cup of coffee or tea to ease Brodick into it, certainly nothing harder. No pints of Tennent's on a picnic rug this time around.

He was being pushed, tested, and he had the feeling that that was going to be the nature of all his meetings with Hermitage— one long examination and no frills. Lots and lots of box ticking. Had Hermitage worked as a junior intelligence officer with his father? Perhaps there was a smidgen of hostility behind all this. Brodick tried to work out their respective ages and career paths and gave up. Was it possible that he was resented because of his father's legendary reputation in an SIS that in his dad's day had had the air of a gentlemen's club: its members eccentric amateurs slouching about in tweed, trout rods and gold clubs in office corners, chums from school and Oxbridge, rather than professional spies? Perhaps he was just imagining it.

'But you've met new people.'

'Yes. of course.'

Brodick wasn't going to volunteer; he would wait until Hermitage asked, which he would of course. He was beginning to dislike the man.

'Anyone I should know about?'

No, Brodick decided, I am not going to tell Hermitage absolutely everything even if he is my case officer.

'I paid a courtesy call on the Red Cross, the ICRC. As you know they don't generally have much to do with journalists. They keep things close to the chest, confidentiality being part of their approach, but they did ask if I'd met any Soviet prisoners or defectors, and that if I did so in the future, would I let them know. I said I hadn't, but would happily pass on the ICRC's contact details to both captives and their captors, but that it wasn't my role to act as an ICRC informant. It has to be a two-way street or none at all.'

Brodick was conscious of talking too much in an effort to cover his tracks.

It was bluster.

'Who did you talk to?'

'An Afghan named Mungoo. Fawzi Mungoo. Educated, a posh boarding school in India or Pakistan would be my guess. Influential family, in his early thirties, English fluent with a north American accent. Probably a U.S. university degree. Certainly a cut above most Afghans I meet, but a little spoiled from spending too much time behind desks in airconditioned offices. He had the hands of a paper-pusher.'

Brodick regretted that last remark. Hermitage would think it was aimed at him.

What Brodick had been planning to say—to boast, in effect—was that he'd met Fawzi's father, and that Mungoo senior had struck him as not only impressive and likeable, but a potential intelligence source, an agent of some importance, a man on whom Brodick would be able to build more than one network of sub-agents. But he wasn't going to share, not now. He would wait. He would let the relationship develop, see where it went. He was onto something with Professor Mungoo and if he did show off about it, he was sure Hermitage would just move in and take the credit, and Brodick would end up as a glorified messenger. So Brodick put up Fawzi as a diversion, and it occurred to him while he was speaking that he might actually use the son as natural cover for his interest in the father. He liked the idea; he almost smiled at his own cleverness.

'You think this Fawzi Mungoo might be agent material?'

'Possibly.'

'Let me know how it goes.'

'Of course, Colonel.' Brodick told himself not to seem too emphatic. Hermitage would spot a lie a mile off.

'Call me Tim, please. Anyone else?'

Brodick shook his head. 'No. No one else.' It was a lie. He was certainly not going to spill the beans about the meeting with Mirwais yet.

No, he wasn't about to say anything to Hermitage about it. Brodick would let Hermitage think whatever he liked. Let Hermitage underestimate him, think him a bit slow, a bit dull, lacking in enterprise, lazy. He'd not steal Mungoo and Mirwais away from him. Brodick's time would come when he was good and ready. Very rarely had Brodick senior ever discussed his SIS work with his son, but just occasionally he'd let his guard down. It was as if his father had forgotten who it was he was talking to. Once, during a walk together not long before the old man's death, he had started speaking of tradecraft, though it wasn't clear why. Brodick Senior had compared agents to magpies, seekers of bright objects, but in this context he had meant nuggets of secret information. Agents were out there in a hostile world on their own, he'd said. You couldn't not sympathise. Paranoia was the inevitable partner of loneliness—a lesson Brodick had certainly learned to his cost in recent months—and agents always salted stuff away that might come in useful later, from secret information to fake passports and identities. They invariably fiddled their expenses. It was to be expected. It gave them a sense of significance and power—and illusory safety in a hazardous environment.

'Great hoarders, agents. Secretive. The best of them will never show their real hand, always keep their best cards hidden.' William Brodick had stopped, turned, looked strangely at his son as if surprised to find him there. 'Which is why you can't fully trust them. When they should be spilling the beans they hold back the good stuff. They always want to be one up on the case officer. Can't blame 'em. It's a survival instinct. You have to know how to winkle it out of them gently, seemingly without effort. They crave praise. They want to be recognised for their skill, even loved, though they might not even know it. Charm and flattery can work wonders when dealing with a man or woman in fear of death. Bullying does the opposite. Drives them away. They clam up.'

How true, but charm and flattery were not, it seemed, in the Hermitage arsenal.

'If you're ever foolish enough to take up my trade,' his father had told Brodick on another occasion, 'you'll find they talk a lot about trust, especially at the start when you're both green and keen. They'll tell you that trust is what holds the Service together. As you scramble up the slippery slope, you'll discover how treacherous it is, that it's a lie, one of many myths they like to bandy about. SIS officers don't trust their colleagues. They can't afford to. They don't trust Whitehall or those corrupt fellows at Westminster. They don't trust their allies, and they certainly don't trust their own agents. They'd be mad or stupid or both if they did.'

Not that his father had ever hinted that his son should follow him into the intelligence racket: *"racket"* being his word, not Brodick's. Rather the contrary.

Hermitage uncoiled himself, stood, took the pipe out of his mouth and almost smiled. 'By the way, Richard, I thought you'd be pleased to hear London has no objection in principle to your proposed trip across the border. You've got the all-clear.'

7

The heat of late summer was making Brodick sweat as he sat at his table and he had to take care not to let perspiration drip from the end of his nose, chin or his fingers onto the latest harvest of eighteen intel reports for Hermitage, whom he expected to see the next day—their first meeting in two months. He used a small towel to wipe his face, neck and hands frequently, notwithstanding the floor fan whirring away and threatening to blow his papers all over the room. He used books to hold them in place.

He gave the last report a final read:

KHAD AGENTS SAID TO PLANT BOMBS IN PAKISTAN'S FATA

27.9.81

Source: Deputy Director General (DDG) North West Frontier Province (NWFP) Special Branch, Taleb Gul Achakzai.

1. Agents of Afghanistan's secret police, the *Khidamate Aetilaate Daulati* (State Information Service) or Khad, have planted and detonated three improvised explosive devices in Pakistani's Federally-Administered Tribal Areas (FATA) during July this year.

2. The explosions killed two people and wounded five. One of the dead was a plainclothes Special Branch officer. The remaining casualties were civilians, including a woman and her ten-year-old son who were wounded.

3. The targets were bus stops and petrol stations on well established routes used by smugglers and Afghan resistance fighters entering and exiting Afghanistan, and in the view of the Deputy Director-General, the aim of the attacks was, firstly, to discourage the passage of men and arms over the Durand Line and, secondly, to drive a wedge between local civilians and the Afghan resistance.

4. Seven people have so far been arrested and in one case an individual carrying an explosive device was intercepted before he could detonate his bomb. Another device was found after it had apparently failed to detonate. The DDG believes this is the start of a bombing campaign, and represents a new strategy on the part of Afghan authorities frustrated that the Soviets have not themselves taken offensive action in the tribal region. The agents—recruited and equipped in the Afghan towns of Khost and Gardez—were paid for their services, and promised that their families would be taken care of in the event of the agents being captured or incapacitated.

5. Security in and around Peshawar as well as the FATA has been tightened in recent weeks in anticipation of a fresh round of fighting in Afghanistan during the spring and summer months, with an increase in frontier militia border patrols and checkpoints.

NOTES: The above was provided to the author in his capacity as a journalist 'off the record' and for background purposes only and not for publication. It is not clear however whether the DDG (NWFP) intended this as a message to Western intelligence services or hoped that it would find its way to diplomatic channels. The source is clearly preoccupied by the matter of security of the frontier and concerned whether this is the start of a wider campaign. The information was disclosed as part of a friendly and wide-ranging conversation and it marked the author's first meeting with the DDG. The author had been invited to tea at the DDG's official residence in PESHAWAR. No one else was present.

Then the thought struck him: was this last intel report going to expose Brodick for what he really was: a spy working under journalistic cover? There was only one of his ilk in Peshawar that he knew of. It wouldn't take an allied service on the circulation list very long to figure it out. There wasn't a lot of choice: the city wasn't exactly brimming with foreigners all pretending to be something they weren't. After all, if SIS shared this with the CIA—and one had to assume that the Firm did so as a matter of course, albeit via the filter of intelligence liaison and with the usual redacted sentences dealing with Brodick's identity, especially in the notes—and if the CIA then passed it on in turn to Pakistan's ISI, removing the identity of the original source, then ISI would still be able to work out who it was behind this particular titbit of CX intelligence. The ISI may be many things, including murderous and vicious, but they weren't stupid.

Would the CIA be so careless, so irresponsible? Yes, of course it would. The Agency wasn't in the business of protecting the identities of British head agents; and why should it, after all? All it wanted was product and yet more product. It had a voracious appetite for product, all the more so because its record on Afghanistan was worse than lousy. It was hopeless. The Agency had no humint, no flesh-and-blood assets. It was all gizmos too advanced for the medieval nature of the place. Sure, they could read a newspaper from 120,000 feet or whatever it was, but what good would that do? They relied on second-hand product from ISI, skewed to suit Islambad's policy aims, naturally—and the British material. Why would the Agency share with Pakistan intelligence about Pakistan? Well, for one thing, Brodick reasoned, the Agency might ask the ISI for more detail, or seek confirmation of the details already contained in the SIS report.

Listening to the mosquitoes as he lay under a sheet in the dark—the kamikaze flying bugs having decamped or died—Brodick worried at this. Both the CIA and ISI would then know him for what he was, and eventually that would mean everyone knew. It was a horrible thought and it made Brodick sweat into his already damp sheets. Depending on Hermitage to protect him wasn't going to do it. He wished he knew more how SIS and "Five Eyes" intel sharing worked; but then again, perhaps it was a good thing he didn't know.

His father had been right: agents were paranoid.

Right before the end, weeks before his father died, they'd sat out in the garden side by side on an old bench that was beginning to fall to pieces after several winter frosts, staring out at the fields on the hill opposite. The old man had said something then that only now made any real sense to him.

'Every intelligence agency has its flaws, and they all in my experience have one important weakness that can be exploited by an adversary, and that's the relationship between a case officer and his or her agent. The agent runner is invariably the last to recognise that his cherished agent has been turned, just as the husband or wife is often the last to know when a partner has taken a lover—even though everyone else knows. Think of it as a love affair. The case officer has lavished time, attention and money on courting this particular agent. They become friends. Close friends. The agent does so well, too. Trust raises its traitorous head. Even when all the objective evidence points to the agent's betrayal, the case officer still refuses to accept the obvious. It's human nature, Richard.

'If you do make the grievous error of drifting into your father's trade, don't forget it. Make use of it.'

Brodick was expecting two new camera recruits to show up for training early the next morning. He now had twenty-one cameramen in the field and his trunk was almost empty; he was running low on cameras, cassettes and batteries. Then he was off to

Mungoo's place to watch in person as the second-hand Xerox—a gift courtesy of the Swedish ambassador, Ahlberg—produced the first edition of the *Bulletin*, and receive his own copy of the English version. He deserved it, after all; he'd spent an inordinate amount of time writing and editing it. He would then meet Hermitage for lunch.

Brodick was feeling more confident. He was pleased with both the quantity and quality of the material he had for his SIS paymasters, and he hoped he would surprise them with the contents of a couple of the reports. He was satisfied, too, with progress in consolidating his cover. He'd had two more substantial features published recently—one in the *Inquirer* on the issue of Soviet air power in Afghanistan and the restraint Moscow had so far shown in not bombing the guerrillas in FATA territory, presumably in order to avoid pushing Pakistan further into the clutches of the United States, and the second in *The Orient* on the way in which civilians were increasingly caught up between the Red Army meat grinder on the one hand and Islamist guerrillas on the other. There were also a couple of dozen short news items he'd placed in the *Telegraph*, the *Economist* and which had been broadcast by the *BBC Eastern Service* and *Voice of America*.

After the session with Hermitage, Brodick planned to visit Abdul, a tough young resistance commander reputed to be of growing importance despite implacable ISI hostility, and someone Brodick had commended to Hermitage as deserving of British assistance, such as it was: including a handful of Blowpipe shoulder-fired anti-aircraft missile systems.

Yes, he was doing pretty well, and with that comforting thought he felt himself carried off gently into the great ocean of sleep, the strong stench of DEET mosquito repellent in his nostrils.

*

It was shortly before dawn that he woke again.

Perhaps he'd dreamed of her. Whatever the cause, Marion was

on his mind and that was unusual. She didn't write, and neither did he. Presumably the Firm stayed in touch with her to ensure she was still on track for an eventual reunion in Peshawar in another year or so, not that Brodick believed it would ever happen. He didn't want to believe it. So far, Hermitage hadn't mentioned Marion or her plans. Had she already taken up with someone else? Was this someone among their friends, someone he knew? Did it bother him? No, to be perfectly honest; not as much as it should at least according to male pride. Not nearly as much. He should be angry, jealous, outraged, nauseous at the thought—but he wasn't any of those things. He was pretty much indifferent. He didn't care and he would be ashamed to admit it—to her or to anyone else. After all, it wasn't as if they had been good together even at their best. She knew that. If she was indeed "seeing someone", then it was all the less likely that she would turn up at his door, and in that case he should be relieved to be cuckolded, whoever the culprit was. He certainly couldn't blame her. Go, girl. You have your needs.

As for him, he was no longer sure what they were. He longed for female company, it was true. He was also just lonely, but he would get used to it. He would have to.

Outside in the pale morning light the gardens were swathed in mist, the grass drenched in dew. A mistle thrush trilled somewhere close by. Brodick decided to go for a walk before the daily eruption of traffic, crowds and the blast of a furnace-like sun. The exercise and the cool air would do him good.

Then he'd drop by Mungoo's place unannounced, hopefully in time for an Afghan breakfast with his pal the professor.

8

Brodick tried to keep his new students apart, but he didn't make allowance for the fact—something he should have known only too well by now—that Afghans were strangers to the notion of punctuality. The first trainee, a tall young Pashtun named Hamza from the city of Kandahar in the south, was due at 8am but arrived at 9:10am and the second, a sturdy Uzbek farmer's son from Mazar-i-Sharif, in the north, Abdulaziz, was expected at 10am but walked into the grounds at Dean's at 8:40am and hung about outside Room 19 until he was noticed.

Brodick was all too aware that crouching among the early Spring glory of salvia, strelitzia and zinnia and staining his pants on the neatly cropped grass while videoing passing cars through the shrubbery wasn't going to match being under fire in a ditch, but it was the best he could do in the circumstances. He'd thought of taking his students out of town and training them away from built-up areas, but that would have seemed highly suspicious to any passing locals, and the police or frontier militia would have come around asking questions.

He forgot about lunch. The prospect of holding the first English-language edition of the *Afghan Information Bulletin* in his hands excited Brodick. It had taken months of talking and planning to bring to fruition. He couldn't wait to congratulate the Professor.

At breakfast he hadn't said precisely when he next planned to visit Mungoo, only that he would do so. So he walked briskly into town, watching his own back as best he could, then clambered into a rickshaw, changed to another, and arrived at Mungoo's just after noon, halting at the corner and walking the last two blocks, working up a sweat as he strode along, the sun right overhead.

Every day now seemed hotter than its predecessor. Summer was upon them. He imagined congratulating Mungoo, sitting down and having a long chat about their future plans for the newsletter. He was surprised to see he was not alone. People were walking in ahead of him, all Afghans. There were cars parked outside. The guest room was packed. Mungoo was the man of the hour; he was on his feet in the centre, a broad smile on his face, welcoming his exclusively male guests. Mungoo himself wore a clean, crisp outfit, repleted with waistcoat and, over his shoulder, a neatly folded *potu*. His wispy hair and runaway eyebrows had been trimmed, and his white stubble was gone. He was talking, veined cheeks quivering, smiling, performing, telling jokes. He looked, at least to Brodick, a decade younger. This was no forlorn old man subsisting in genteel poverty, his world in ruins.

He was a celebrity and he was loving it.

A table had been laid with food and plates along with rows of the inevitable bottles of Fanta, no doubt bought with SIS funds. Brodick realised at once that he was an intruder. This was not his place. The glory was Mungoo's and the *Bulletin* was his creation— the Professor wouldn't want to be seen to have a Briton at his elbow. Brodick sidled around the walls, found what he was looking for: three neat piles of the first ANB in Dari, Pashto and English, still smelling of the Xerox copier. Helping himself to three English-language copies, he backed out quietly, unnoticed hopefully, and without greeting Mungoo. Brodick told himself it might not be polite, but it was discreet. He noted that Fawzi was there at his father's side, distributing Pashto and Dari editions. There was no sign of Mirwais—but then the defector would not want to appear in daylight and in public. It would be far too risky. There had to be at least one person present among the guests reporting back to ISI.

*

'There's something we want you to do for us.'

Hermitage pushed a sheet of paper across the table.

'I wasn't expecting to visit Peshawar so soon, but I've a few important matters to bring up and it's been quite a while since we met.'

Their plates, bowls and chopsticks had been taken away and small cups of tea served. Having eaten their spring rolls and sweet and sour chicken, they were ready to talk shop. Hermitage produced his pipe and looked around to see if lighting up was going to offend anyone. There were no other customers in the Chinese restaurant—one of two in Peshawar, oddly located side by side in the same street, and both waiter and owner-manager had left them alone.

Brodick read it through quickly.

'Could you place it in *The Orient*?'

Brodick cringed inwardly as if struck. He almost said it out loud: *Oh, shit.*

He went through it again, this time with greater care.

'Who's the source? What's his name?'

Hermitage filled his pipe. 'I'm sorry?'

'This is Agency material, isn't it?'

Silence.

Brodick wasn't going to give in easily. 'It's really not credible as it stands. It needs a named source.'

'The source is an Afghan army colonel of artillery, but I can't give you his name.'

'Okay. But perhaps some more detail on the man and his background? That would help give this at least some credence.'

'His identity is protected and I don't have details in any case.'

Brodick read it through a third time. This was bad.

'May I be frank? There's really not enough here. It stinks of

CIA wishful thinking, something designed to produce a particular effect or fit a particular policy. I see now this is labelled *"liaison"*. I think that confirms the origin, wouldn't you say?'

Hermitage wasn't interested in Brodick's suspicions.

'Can you do this, Richard? Will you do it?'

Oh, yes, Brodick told himself, I can. Of course I can. But do I want to? Is it in my interest to do so? And do I really have any choice in the matter? Not really. If they are bent on planting this in the media, they'll find a way. There's always someone else who'll be willing. What had Wolfe said about journalists and bribery?

*You cannot hope
to bribe or twist,
thank God! the
British journalist.
But, seeing what
the man will do
unbribed, there's
no occasion to.*

The BBC and *Financial Times* wouldn't touch something so meretricious. The Agency was farming it out to the Brits no doubt because they wanted to distance themselves from such a dubious report, and they thought that if they did succeed in planting it elsewhere, they could point to their European ally and say, *'See it's not just us —our British pals think so too!'* Or maybe, for some inexplicable reason, they wanted it to appear in Asia first, hence the interest in *The Orient*. They were sending a signal of some kind. Brodick looked hard at Hermitage through the pipe smoke. It was crap. Anyone could see that. Hadn't the former US Secretary of State, General Haig, publicly accused the Soviets of using chemical and biological agents in Afghanistan and southeast Asia, and hadn't he done so without a shred of hard evidence? It was a hot topic for the United States; Washington wanted to convince the international community and the American voters that Moscow wasn't to be trusted with SALT II or the Mutual and Balanced Force Reduction Talks. This was all about scratching around for facts to fit a particular worldview, one deeply hostile to Moscow.

Intelligence by numbers.

'May I be frank? I can do it—but I'd rather not. It doesn't ring true.'

Hermitage smiled without showing his tobacco-stained teeth, a widening of thin, bloodless lips, a smile without humour but one which Brodick thought was intended to signal tolerance for the bloody-minded obstinacy of the erratic head agent in the field, or perhaps for his youthful naivety.

'It's pretty detailed, Richard. The defector says chemical and biological agents are being used by Afghan Army units. He says,'—Hermitage took back the report and consulted it—'that gas companies of the 18th division at Mazar-i-Sharif and the 20th division at Nahrin are responsible for chemical warfare in the north of the country. He says these units are up to full strength.'

Brodick interrupted. 'Odd, don't you think, in an army with front line units grievously short of manpower? Seems to me they need more infantry and aircraft above all else.'

Hermitage ignored the comment and pressed on, reading slowly and exercising what for him amounted to great patience. 'The defector says the Soviets have deployed the 234th Gas and Chemical Department in Kabul, that the staff number 2,250 men and that Qal-e-Jangi, near the Soviet residential compound, is the location of the Department's headquarters. Now this is where it gets interesting,' Hermitage put a forefinger on the next line and his voice slowed further, emphasising each word. 'A chemical field battalion under the Qal-e-Jangi HQ is based at Hussein Khot near Bagram airbase, just to the north of the capital. The officer states that elements of the 234th Department have been involved in joint Afghan-Soviet operations in Parwan Province. Afghan officers and other ranks have been flown to Kabul for training, and chemical warfare munitions in the form of artillery shells, warheads for rockets or missiles as well as helicopter-borne gas canisters and grenades were all supplied to the Afghan Army.'

Hermitage sat back in his chair, puffing away, one foot waggling: his sign of irritation.

'I'd say that detail was pretty convincing, Richard. Wouldn't you?'

Brodick would have none of it and struggled to stay calm.

'Maybe. But isn't it a trifle strange that no defectors from the 18th and 20th divisions have mentioned any of this? Isn't it also strange that, despite my having good Parwan sources, this has never come up in conversations and interviews? Isn't it odd—most odd, in fact—that these weapons and operations are delegated to Afghan units, whereas in eastern Europe, Soviet CBW munitions and operators are kept under the strictest political control by the Politburo? Chemical and Biological Warfare in the Warsaw Pact is treated very much like the Soviet tactical nuclear arsenal. Centralised, in other words. And when you consider that the Afghan regime has to pay—at least in theory—for Soviet military assistance, you'd think they'd baulk at having to take on the luxury of CBW weapons and training while their conventional forces are in such a bloody mess. They don't even have enough ammunition. Their soldiers are sent to the front line with three or four rounds each.'

To Brodick, the logic seemed incontrovertible.

Hermitage fiddled with his pipe and matches. The foot wiggling intensified.

'My question hasn't changed, Richard. Can you—will you—do this?'

Fuck.

Brodick took a deep breath and raised his hands in mock surrender, only there was no such thing on his mind. He was going to fight this in the only way he could. 'Okay. All right. I'll do it. But please bear in mind it will not be a straight news story but a 2,000-word feature which will look at the whole question of chemical and biological warfare in Afghanistan, the US accusations, and the so-called first-hand witness accounts from Nangarhar, Badakhshan and elsewhere. I'll refer to the issue as it applies to southeast Asia, too. My conclusion will be that we're still a long way from establishing proof, and I'll mention that old saying: in war, truth is the first casualty. Washington has its own reasons for pushing the issue.'

'Well, you're playing the role of journalist. You tell it the way you want.'

'One more question.'

'Fire away.'

'Let's assume the article appears under my by-line in *The Orient*. Your friends in Washington read it. What do they conclude? The obvious. That I'm an SIS agent, one of your assets in Peshawar. That's how every intelligence agency will read it. In effect, you're blowing my cover: at least as far as the intelligence world is concerned, from the Czechs and Cubans to the Indians and the Chinese. My question is: do you really want that? Quite aside from the issue of my future usefulness. Is this story really worth it?'

'I don't think that's necessarily true at all. The defector's information could have come from a third party, or from research you've done for the article.'

Why did Brodick have the feeling that Hermitage really couldn't care less if he was blown?

Brodick looked away, took a deep breath. 'In that case, I'm not sure which is worse: a spy's identity uncovered by dubious material, or a journalist who accepts second-hand material planted on him without checking it himself or admitting that it's dubious hearsay from an interested party, namely the Agency.'

'Richard, you can simply refuse. This is a request, not an order.'

Hermitage was furious but doing his best to hide it. They were both furious and trying to hide it; Brodick somewhat less successfully.

'I'll do it, I said I would, but you might not appreciate the outcome. In fact, I'm pretty sure you won't, and your Agency pals will like it even less.'

If this was how he truly felt, why was he working for SIS? But then he knew the answer. If he was perfectly honest with himself, he relished the double life. He was good at the spy game and getting better all the time. This was his journey, he'd chosen it, and he was going to go all the way. And, with the help of Mungoo and Mirwais, he had every intention of cornering the market in intelligence in both quality and quantity. He was going to make his reputation as an intelligence operator and agent handler. He would make his father proud, not that the old man ever suggested he should work in intelligence. On the contrary, Brodick senior had hinted more than once that his son should go into business. That had a future, he'd said—not espionage.

Best of all, he would surprise the disapproving Hermitage and the bureaucrats of Century House. He would make this work. He had to, even if Hermitage—for all his derring-do in the military—was turning out to be an anally retentive civil servant.

*

They sipped more Chinese tea without really wanting to, for something to do.

Brodick handed over his eighteen reports and another baker's dozen of video cassettes. He gave Hermitage a copy of the first *Bulletin*.

'You wrote the English version?' Hermitage leafed through it, pausing here and there.

'I edited it and rewrote most of it to conform to the usual news format. I contributed the lead story.'

'You have been busy. I'll read it as soon as I get a chance. I have some cash for you to hand over to the Professor. The amount we agreed. It seems a worthwhile project, but the son—'

'Fawzi.'

'Fawzi doesn't seem to have produced anything in the way of intelligence.'

'So far, no. But I think he will.'

'The father, Professor Mungoo—he's pretty left-wing in his

views, wouldn't you say?'

Brodick shook his head. 'Not really.'

'Is he a socialist?'

'No more so than a Labour Party voter in the UK is a socialist.'

'So, a leftist.'

Hermitage was turning out to be a real disappointment, always seeing the worst in everything and everyone.

'Centre left, I would say. Maybe a social democrat. It's been years since Labour aspired to socialism.'

'You sound as if you're sorry about that.'

Brodick shrugged. So what? Ideology didn't really concern him. And yes, perhaps he was a "leftist", however such a vague term was defined.

'Perhaps I am sorry.'

'Some people say Mungoo is a leftist and sympathetic to the regime in Kabul. Our friends in the Agency are concerned.'

'Some people? Sympathetic to the Kabul regime? Oh, no. Absolutely not. I don't believe that. To some Afghan leaders, Colonel, anyone who doesn't agree with them is a Communist. And anyone who doesn't pray five times a day, of course. ISI does its level best to discredit anyone influential or effective it can't control by defaming them. They've developed it into an art form. I shouldn't wonder if ISI has been feeding the CIA this nonsense.'

'Please stop using my military rank and call me Tim. You're friends, aren't you, you and the Professor?'

'I suppose we are, yes. Why? Is that a problem? He's extremely useful, a first-rate supplier of intelligence on both the Kabul regime and the resistance, whether he knows it or not. He's good company and I'm learning a lot from him.'

Put that in your damned pipe and smoke it.

'I would urge caution, that's all. I hear he drinks vodka and enjoys listening to Russian composers. Is that true?'

'I don't think a taste for vodka and Shostakovich proves anything. He likes Mahler and Schubert, too. Neither is a crime and as far as I know they're not yet the defining characteristics of a

Soviet fellow traveller or sympathiser.'

Brodick silently reprimanded himself for his sarcasm.

'I didn't say it did.' Brodick could almost hear Hermitage grinding his teeth in frustration.

Brodick took the envelope stuffed with Pakistani rupees.

'I have two news items for you, Richard. The first is that we've decided to rent a house for you. We want you to move out of Dean's. It's not secure and too easily watched. I'm sure you've come to the same conclusion. I think University Town would be best: it's not too far from the centre and the houses are fairly modern.'

Brodick recalled similar advice from Mirwais.

'I'll be sorry to leave Dean's. I've grown quite attached to it.'

'But you do agree it's unsuitable given your role?'

'It is, yes.'

'In fact, we've been discussing your workload with London. Your cover seems stronger, and you're producing much more intelligence, and of higher value. In fact, congratulations are due. You've made it into Mrs T's Green Book more than once—'

Hermitage's mention of congratulations seemed flat, unenthusiastic, as if he didn't share London's view of Brodick's success but was under orders to pass it on.

'Green Book?'

'The prime minister's weekly intelligence digest, produced every Friday morning. London is pleased. We're wondering whether to pass the camera operation onto someone else and encourage you to concentrate entirely on intelligence gathering as you seem to have a natural talent for it.'

Duly noted: London was pleased but that didn't necessarily reflect Hermitage's view.

Brodick's last CX report had been more than interesting and Brodick wondered if London could confirm it: not that he would ever be told. According to Mirwais, who was the source of the report, the Soviets were deploying undercover counter-gangs— along the lines of British counter-insurgency tactics in Kenya and the Selous Scouts in Rhodesia—these were units comprising

KGB troops operating at company strength, posing as guerrillas under the code name KASKAD or CASCADE. One such unit had proved devastatingly successful in western Afghanistan, aligning itself with genuine guerrilla groups and then wiping them out, village by village, valley by valley, unit by unit.

Brodick hid his pleasure at Hermitage's proposal with a frown. Nothing would please him more than to drop the propaganda campaign and concentrate on intelligence collection. He'd be a real spy, doing real good, expanding his sub-agent networks.

London is pleased.

Brodick was careful to rein in his enthusiasm. 'I wouldn't say no. I think the *Bulletin* will provide good cover for gathering intel and for recruiting more sub-agents. The volume will hopefully increase substantially over time.'

'That's our thinking, too, although as I say, we think you should be careful where Professor Mungoo is concerned. Don't let your guard down, even if he and his pals are good company. Anything else you want to mention before I go?'

'It's starting to get cooler at night. I think it would be wise to organise a trip inside before the fighting season ends and it gets really too cold for a long walk—and before I become too busy with the *Bulletin*. Sometime in the next few days if I can arrange it.'

Without telling his case officer, Brodick had already set things in motion.

'Where?'

'I'm not entirely sure. I can't be away long. There's too much to do on the *Bulletin*. *The Orient* won't like my being away for longer than that, either. They won't like me being away at all. So that means a border area. I won't have the time to go deeper inside.'

'Fine. Let me remind you that if you come across any physical evidence of chemical and biological weapons or equipment, we want to know about it. And that goes for that helicopter gunship shot down in the Hazarajat or any others you may discover on your hike. We're interested in the mini-gun especially, and we're willing to pay if it's intact—within reason. Seven thousand U.S.

absolute tops.'

Brodick had seen Hermitage park his white Land Rover with its CD plates under the trees and alongside the neighbouring restaurant. As if that would make any difference to anyone watching them. What he resented was Hermitage's rather cavalier attitude towards Brodick's security; being openly associated with Hermitage, a senior British intelligence officer no doubt declared as such to the host government, Brodick would be immediately earmarked as his agent. Why couldn't the bloody man use a local, civilian registration when meeting an agent? It seemed so unprofessional—as if Hermitage couldn't really care less about Brodick's cover despite all his assertions to the contrary.

'This came for you from London via the diplomatic bag.'

Brodick recognised the handwriting but said nothing. Presumably Hermitage knew too. Brodick folded the envelope in two and pushed it into a shirt pocket.

Having paid the bill and left a tip, Hermitage exited first. The two Britons didn't shake hands. Brodick stayed seated at the table, waiting the standard ten minutes, then went out back through the kitchen. By the time he'd sauntered around the building to the street, the Land Rover had gone.

It was time to visit Abdul: possibly one of Afghanistan's two most effective guerrilla leaders.

9

There were resistance groups and resistance groups: the good, the bad and the worse-than-ugly. Brodick had his favourites, though "favourites" was probably the wrong word—it wasn't a colour or a flower or a dish of pasta—but after the mainly Tajik Jamiat-i-Islami, the organisation he respected more than any other and visited most often was the Yunis Khalis faction of Hezb-i-Islami because it was compact and had an emphasis on fighting rather than on schmoozing the great and the good in the salons of Paris and New York. It had what the Ministry of Defence in London liked to call a *"high tooth-to-tail ratio"*.

Outside, the dusty compound with its yellow mud walls and high wooden gates was watched by more than a dozen Pakistani security and intelligence personnel, monitoring the constant stream of comings and goings. Inside, the place was grubby, noisy, crowded and cheerful. The narrow flight of stairs Brodick now climbed led to a simple room where Yunis Khalis himself held court from a broken armchair. He was reading from a stack of papers. Occasionally he scribbled something, perhaps a signature or a command, handing it to a messenger, or called someone over and muttered something in his ear. Khalis seemed to be the only Afghan present who was literate. Indeed, he counted himself as a Pashtun poet of some repute. He was in his late sixties, his long beard henna'd, his eyes blue, his bald head concealed by a large turban. He was known to have several wives and numerous children. To a man like Khalis, marriage was a means of widening his network, of cementing alliances. It was all about power.

Around him sat his commanders, backs to the wall, squeezed together on cushions and ancient sofas: fierce, sunburned men with ragged hair and massive black beards, turbaned and talking to one another in a rumble of low voices while sucking on their tea. Khalis led by consensus—these commanders formed a loose coalition rather than a military structure, straddling the political ground between Islamists and traditional tribal loyalties, with a strong base in the border province of Nangahar. There was no clear line of command as Westerners would understand it.

The commanders were also clan leaders, not unlike Scottish Highland lairds, and they were smugglers, too. Family, clan, tribe—and profit. The state—Afghan or Pakistani—meant little or nothing to these people other than something to be fought, resisted, manipulated and milked.

They made space for Brodick. He pushed in between two men he didn't know and accepted a glass of green tea, sipping it slowly and taking in who was there and who wasn't without being seen to stare at anyone. He noted that the fierce North Waziristan chieftain, Jalaluddin Haqqani, renowned for his skills as guerrilla and smuggler, was sitting in a corner, an AK-74 across his lap, a weapon much prized because it was the latest Soviet sub-machinegun. His possession of it indicated it had been taken off a dead, wounded or captured Red Army soldier, and not merely a Chinese or Egyptian AK-47 supplied by Pakistan's ISI, the military agency that reported to the Pakistani chief of staff.

After what seemed to Brodick to be an hour or so, Khalis peered over the top of his reading glasses and nodded at the foreigner as if noticing him for the first time.

They went through the usual ritual of greetings in Pashto, Brodick careful to show his respect for the old fighter, placing his right hand over his heart.

'What do you want?'

'Abdul Haq. Is he here?'

'He's at home. You can see him there.'

'Thank you.'

'You have driver? I will send someone down with you to give him directions.'

Pulling up at the bungalow a few minutes later, Brodick saw the metal gate was ajar. And there was Abdul himself, holding a male toddler off the ground by the arm. The toddler made no complaint and didn't cry, though being carried that way could not have been anything but uncomfortable. Abdul put the child down, none too gently, and watched him scamper away.

Abdul's greeting was limited to a nod. 'My son,' he said, referring to the child. 'I got back yesterday.'

'How was it?'

There was something brutal yet principled about this human bulldozer. Though little more than five eight, he had the build of a weightlifter and the face and head of a gladiator, his curly black hair cut close to the scalp, his beard neat and short. The eyes were small, black, unblinking, hands massive. He was a killer: had killed. It was said Abdul carried so much metal around from his several wounds that he set off the metal detectors at airports whenever he travelled, though the tale was probably apocryphal. At twenty-six, he'd been fighting since 1973, the year the left-leaning Daoud came to power in Kabul. Abdul had begun his activism while still a schoolboy, leading a protest against a teacher he had considered a communist. For leading the school strike, Abdul had been arrested and imprisoned in the infamous Pol-e-Charkhi jail in the capital, and had freed himself and his fellow students by killing a guard, strangling him through the bars of his cell.

He had been fighting ever since, and his distinctive leadership and cunning meant that he was now reputed to have about 4,000 Afghans under his command in Kabul and surrounding areas, some of them members of the PDPA armed forces, up to and including the rank of colonel. For this accomplishment he'd earned the enmity of ISI. For although he'd begun the war along with the likes of Burhanuddin, Sayyaf and Hekmatyar, unlike them he'd refused Pakistani "help" in the form of money and arms. He'd kept his distance from Islamabad. He would not submit. Abdul could not be bought and for that he would never be forgiven. He'd also moved beyond the border areas in which the Yunis Khalis fighters usually operated, and had forged military alliances with non-Pashtuns, notably Jamiat-i-Islami's Panjsher Valley commander, the Tajik known as Engineer Masoud, allowing for real coordination to take place on the battlefield. He was not only a threat to the Soviet presence, then, but also to Pakistan's strategic aims in Afghanistan.

Abdul's eyes were fixed on some point over Brodick's shoulder as if picturing again whatever he'd just experienced over the frontier. Finally he answered Brodick.

'Kabul has no light now. That's good, no?' He followed this with a thin smile.

'What happened?'

'You know Sarobi?'

Brodick wasn't going to be invited in. He saw sudden movement, a flurry of activity; through the partly open front door people—men in white—were hurrying out. Someone was urging them to leave, ushering them into another room. Arabs, Brodick thought. Abdul's hosting Gulf Arab volunteers. Not that he had much choice; accept Wahhabi money, and the recipient had to accept Wahhabi 'volunteers'. Saudis and Egyptians, mostly. Their reputation as fighters was poor.

'I know of the hydroelectric dam at Sarobi, yes.'

'I warned them last time.'

'Warned who?'

'Harakat. Harakat commanders. They were guarding the pylons.'

'Why would they do that?'

Abdul gave a bark of laughter, but there was nothing funny in the sound. He rubbed fingers like truncheons together under Brodick's nose. 'Money, my English friend. Lots of money. They were taking the communists' money every month not to attack the pylons. From the government in Kabul. You understand, Mr Richard? I warned them. I gave them, what do you say, a—'

'Deadline?'

'Yes. Deadline. And warning. Two weeks.' Out of a pocket Abdul produced a small black notebook and the stub of a pencil.

'How you spell this "deadline"?'

Brodick spelled it out and Abdul wrote it down in capital letters, sounding the letters as he did so, frowning with the concentration of a child, even the pink tip of his tongue showing. He was teaching himself English and clearly making excellent progress.

'They didn't listen. I had to go back and teach them, what do you say, a lesson? Yes? So now Kabul has no light.'

'You fought Harakat?'

'Fought? No, no. They ran away, most of them. Just a few stayed. We attacked them. Three died. One bad commander we shot. As example. He dug his own grave, stood in it and we shot him so we didn't have to touch him.' There was satisfaction in Abdul's recollection. 'Then we blew up the pylons. Understand?'

Brodick had another lead story for the *Bulletin*. Or maybe he'd sell it as a news story first. The BBC, *VOA*, the *Telegraph*. A Kabul blackout as the result of resistance infighting was indeed news. Taking the war to the enemy. He was now in the enviable position of being able to back up his own stories, using the *Bulletin* as his source, though it was hardly ethical. 'How much of Kabul is dark?'

'All.'

'All? Really?'

'Except generators in the Russian bases and some government offices, yes.'

'How many pylons did you destroy?'

'Eleven. I think eleven.'

'But there are twenty-three pylons in total, or at least that's what I've been told.'

'Eleven carry power to Kabul. Those we destroyed.'

'People in Kabul will suffer, Abdul.'

'In war, everyone suffers, Mr Richard. Better communists suffer, no?'

If this guerrilla chief was beyond Islamabad's clutches, it was true also for Brodick and his SIS masters, something Abdul was keen to make clear. 'You want us Afghans to fight and die in your Cold War,' he lectured Brodick, standing face to face in the driveway, waving a stubby forefinger in Brodick's face. 'I'm sorry, okay, but we are not fighting Russia so you can once again become our masters and steal our land. We know the English.'

Abdul hadn't finished.

'You know Professor Mungoo? I think you visit him often, yes?'

'He is a friend and I do visit him. What of it?'

'He's a bad man. Communist.' Abdul turned his head, spat.

'He's no communist. Do you really know what a Communist is, Abdul?'

Abdul would not be deflected. 'He has communist friends, people in the People's Democratic Party of Afghanistan. They are not Muslim.'

There was nothing worse than being condemned as a nonbeliever.

'It's a lie and it's being spread by ISI, the same people who are trying to discredit you, Abdul. They call you a Western media star. I'm surprised that you fall for the same trick.'

Abdul was unimpressed. 'That's my business. But let me tell you this: your friend Mungoo is working with a man who calls himself Mirwais. You know? No? You met him? This Mirwais is very senior officer in Afghan secret police. The Khad. You know Khad, I think. He says he is refugee, but not true. And Mirwais is not his name. He is dirty spy.' The finger started wagging again and Abdul moved closer to Brodick, so close that Brodick could smell the onion on his breath. Abdul's voice dropped to a whisper. 'Mirwais is danger for everyone. You be careful, Mister Richard. Tell your friend Mungoo. Tell him you know about this Mirwais, yes?'

'Is this a warning, Abdul?'

'You are watched. You don't know this? Always you are watched. You are seen as part of their little—how do you say—group? You go to Mungoo's home nearly every day, no? You are Mungoo's foreign contact, Mungoo is a friend of Mirwais. ISI knows this. Of course. Maybe safer for you in Islamabad. Stay away from Peshawar. Not safe here—not for you.'

This diatribe of Abdul's lodged in Brodick's mind. What were the British, and SIS in particular, doing in Afghanistan? How was the "national interest" being served? By trotting along in Washington's wake, performing tricks for treats, gaining favours inside the Beltway? Was it simply Mrs T's global war against Communism, yet more of the old nonsense about Asian dominoes falling to Moscow and Beijing?

Was the war in Afghanistan really intended to bleed the Soviets dry, to bring the Soviet Goliath crashing down, tripped up by the minor inconvenience of Afghanistan? Moscow's Vietnam, the U.S. media called it. But never mind whatever it was that London was up to. What was he, Brodick, doing? What did he think he was really up to in Peshawar with his *Boy's Own* dreams of glory? Was it worth the risk? And there was risk, certainly. Was it a cause worth the loss of his own life to say nothing of the lives of thousands of Afghans?

Yes, it was true that he'd wanted to escape a dull job, a bad marriage and a damp basement flat at the wrong end of Chelsea. He wanted to prove his worth. He wanted his place at the metaphorical top table, a perch in the Establishment. He wanted to belong. And yes, he did seek his father's approval, of course he did. He wanted to live up to the previous generation's war against the Nazis, what Hollywood portrayed as an exhilarating contest between good and evil; his father, his mother, his maternal aunt and three paternal uncles having all served in uniform. It was a continuation of the same existential struggle, wasn't it, just with different flags and different rules?

But the Great Game somehow lacked the allure he'd felt just a few months ago.

Try as he might to persuade himself of the rightness of the cause and his own singularity, it was beginning to ring hollow. As the cynics said, the British and Americans were willing to fight the Soviets down to the last Afghan. Maybe down to the last head agent, too. Maybe Abdul was uncomfortably close to the truth— but not about Mungoo. Mungoo was a decent sort. Abdul was totally wrong about that; Abdul was a simple man, uneducated, a practising Muslim and warrior peasant who had no idea what it was to be a liberal and a democrat in a secular society.

Anyway, they were friends now: Brodick and Mungoo. That had to count for something.

*

It was only when he tossed his sweaty shirt in the laundry basket that night that he felt the edge of the envelope and remembered the letter. He sat on the edge of his bed and tore it open with his thumb, feeling apprehensive.

Dearest Richard,

I do hope everything is going well for you. I've missed you, of course, but have set my mind on concentrating on my work, on my family and friends. I did say to you before you left that I would follow you out there because I thought then that I had to, that it was somehow my duty as a faithful and loving wife, that it was expected of me by even my own family.

I know I promised to join you.

After much thought I have decided that it wouldn't work for either of us. Please try to understand. I'm not prepared to give up everything here. I would only feel resentment and blame you if I did. I love my life in London. I don't want to walk away from it. I'm truly sorry, I really am, and I hope this hasn't reached you at a bad time, but the truth is that I want a divorce.

Please think carefully about it, Richard, as I have done, and I believe that on reflection you will agree with me. I hope we can do this

without animosity and that we will always be friends.
   Please let me know when you have had time to consider.
   With fond wishes,
   Marion

So that was it.

He read it through twice.

It made him feel strangely tense and disconcerted.

Brodick told himself he should be relieved, even pleased. He had feared she was going to say she was preparing to join him. He hadn't wanted that at all. He recognised that she had chosen her words carefully, making an effort to be reasonable and displaying neither bitterness nor anger.

Yes, of course she could have her uncontested divorce.

He told himself his loneliness was preferable to maintaining the fiction of a marriage that had already failed. She was right—but then, she usually was.

*

Brodick recalled one particular exchange in June with the local Special Branch chief as they drank tea and ate cake on the latter's lawn, and watched monkeys gambolling among the trees. His villa was on a hill that allowed him and his family to escape the worst of the summer heat.

The issue of safety had been the main topic.

'We can't protect you here in Peshawar, Richard, I'm sure you realise that. I don't have the resources and it's not in my brief, not officially.'

'Protect me from what?'

Taleb Gul, the deputy director in charge of North West Frontier Province, offered Brodick a slice of homemade cream cake, but Brodick declined. 'This is a heavily armed community. You know that much. We have millions of refugees on our doorstep. We have competing Afghan resistance organisations with various affiliations. We have foreign powers involved in the war across the frontier and trying to destabilise our borders. The tribal areas are semiautonomous and rely on smuggling to make ends meet. That means weapons, drugs, sports utility vehicles and the rest of it. It's an explosive mix. At the same time people are very poor, and easily manipulated with the promise of money. One reason why we have regulations stipulating that all foreign correspondents live in Islamabad is that they're safer there. You are not safe here, Mr Richard.'

'You're also able to keep better track of us if we're all in Islamabad.'

Gul smiled. 'Of course. It works both ways. But it isn't secure here, not for a foreigner, especially a Western journalist. Please. I mean that sincerely. I want you to think about that very carefully. Consider your options. Certain quarters will be taking a close interest in your activities. Please understand. I am concerned for your safety. I don't want anything unpleasant to happen to you while you're on my patch.' Gul waggled his head from side to side in emphasis.

Brodick had decided then and there he would not tell his SIS employers about that particular exchange, or Hermitage might well order him out of the country.

*

The nights were always difficult, and as the weeks and months passed, they became more so. A dutiful Brodick wrote up his intelligence reports, of which there was always an increasing number. He wrote his news stories and features, too, and typed up the English-language reports for Mungoo's newsletter, but the hours of darkness were a time of restlessness and loneliness in Room 19. The bottle of single malt was still untouched, but it was a struggle.

Occasionally he bought a Pakistan Airlines return ticket and flew to Islamabad in a little Fokker turboprop, a fifty-five minute trip, filed his features through the Reuters bureau—most "specials" had such an arrangement with one or other of the wire agencies—and managed to get tipsy if not falling-down drunk either at the small and dreary British high commission watering hole where a sad, solitary and sweaty freelancer working for *The Guardian* and BBC had taken up semipermanent residence at the tiny bar, or at the much larger and lavish American embassy club with its cold beers and burgers. But access to the latter depended on Brodick being invited by a U.S. correspondent, alternatively tagging on to a group of Brits and their Canadian and Australasian buddies, one of whom might have a club pass: and that had happened only once during a visit by the U.S. Secretary of State. The Reuters man, Cowley, was good company, but he was almost as busy and hardworking as Brodick and had little time for socialising.

Lying in his iron bed and thinking about helicopter gunships and whether he could contact the Hazaras and negotiate a price for the minigun, he heard voices outside Room 19. Brodick jumped up, pulled on his clothes and went to the door, throwing it open and walking barefoot out onto his stoep, ready to reprimand whoever it was for making a racket so late at night. His nagging fear had made him brazen with anger. He knew he was overcompensating. How dare they!

'Mr Richard.'

A bearded stranger stepped out of the gloom, wrapped in his *potu* which also hid his Kalashnikov rifle, and mounted the steps onto the stoep.

'Who the hell are you?'

'Jamiat-i-Islami, Mr Richard. You come. Now.'

There were three more of them out there in the darkness, draped in their shawls.

He'd been waiting for this, and now it had arrived all Brodick felt was that the dull ache of fear that was his constant companion had sharpened into a cold sliver of terror tinged with excitement. He went back inside, sat on his bed, pulled on socks and boots and grabbed his pack, *potu* and turban. He put off the lights and locked the front door behind him. Brodick was going to war.

10

His companions pressed up against him, herding him on board the bus, a human sheep nudged to slaughter. They didn't look at him directly, or speak, but they seemed anxious to shield him from other passengers, and to ensure no one got a good look at him.

Brodick was struck by their smell, a distinctive pong he would get to know all too well over the next year or so: a pungent mingling of mutton fat, sweat and dirty feet. There were three escorts; the first leading the way and then pausing at the seat where Brodick should sit, pointing his beard at it. As Brodick took his place, the first man turned away and took a seat two rows back, directly behind him. The second sat opposite, on the left, two rows forward. This second man—with an immense aquiline nose and in his early twenties with the eyes of an assassin—sat sideways so he could see his two companions and Brodick. The third—both tall and burly—sat at the front, his back to them, right behind the driver and opposite the only door. They did not appear to be armed, at least not with the ubiquitous AK-47, but perhaps one or more of them had a pistol hidden under his loose clothing. They looked poor, their *shalwar kameez* threadbare and stained, their turbans little more than ragged cloths, their beards thick and tangled. Perhaps their lowly appearance was deliberate so they'd arouse no interest and they'd pass unnoticed—common folk of no rank or consequence and lacking any wealth worth stealing.

Brodick had taken the free end of his turban and wound it around the bottom of his face, hiding his mouth and jaw. The most foreign aspect of him, he supposed, was his hairlessness. It would take him at least two weeks to produce a decent growth of reddish curls.

The weekend hiker's pack he kept between his feet. Right now it looked too new, too smart, but that would change soon enough in the days ahead.

Brodick avoided looking directly at anyone, although he knew there were certainly some Pashtuns who, like him, had blue eyes.

At the first Pakistani checkpoint he sat forward and lowered his forehead onto his forearms that rested along the back of the empty seat in front of him, the sleeves of his shirt rolled down to hide his pale skin. Turning his head, he glimpsed police uniforms through the dirty window. There was a lot of shouting—well, it sounded like shouting but apparently it was just the usual banter—and it seemed to involve several police on the one hand and the driver on the other. The former didn't appear interested in the half dozen bus passengers and a solitary goat—but their attention was drawn by whatever goods the bus carried externally, lashed down on its roof.

Two hours later, as they rocked, rattled and bounced out of the Vale of Peshawar southwest into the first barren hills of stone, they came to the second checkpoint. This time a uniform stamped up the steps at the front of the bus and looked down the length of the interior towards the rear. The uniform clumped out again. There was nothing there to interest him. He didn't ask for papers. The passengers must have seemed too wretched to rob. The painted pole across the road rose and on they went.

There were three more checkpoints—but not police. Instead they were troops of the Frontier Force, a paramilitary organisation whose members dressed in dark grey with black berets. Brodick noted that their 1950s Canadian-made Long Branch .303 bolt action rifles and World War Two vintage Sten guns had been replaced with AK-47s. It wasn't just the Afghan resistance that was getting arms from somewhere: Pakistani border forces' weaponry was being upgraded, too.

No one paid Brodick any attention. He wasn't asked his name or for his passport. It was as if he didn't exist, a ghost invisible to other mortals, and this anonymity was something for which he was immensely grateful. His escort, notwithstanding their impoverished mien and peasant stench, knew their business. After the fifth checkpoint, their leader sitting behind him coughed and, when Brodick turned, he gave Brodick a thumbs up and smiled, baring startlingly white teeth in his immense black beard: apparently there would be no more halts or official inspections. His companions relaxed. The two nearest Brodick lit cigarettes and started an animated conversation. The big one up front removed his turban, stood to give his crotch a vigorous scratch, curled up on his seat and was soon snoring. The goat and its owner disembarked in what seemed to be nowhere, just a track of flattened stones glinting in the sun.

By mid-afternoon they found themselves in a different world. Brodick must have slept at some point because, when he pulled himself up and peered out from the bus, the terrain had changed; it was green and lush, almost tropical. They were trundling west along a dusty road between fields of wheat and maize. There were stands of trees. Cattle grazed in the middle distance. Ducks swam on a blue sliver of lake. Clusters of white buildings suggested a modest agricultural population arranged in small hamlets. They seemed to be crossing what appeared to Brodick to be a saucer, an amphitheatre many miles across, and rimmed by mountains capped with snow. Those along the western edge of this hidden Shangri-La—the Kurram Valley—were huge walls of rock arrayed in hues of blue and white like ragged stairs and leading up to the sky. They were the ridges and peaks of the Sufed Koh range.

The air was cool, clean and fragrant with orange blossom and jasmine.

He pictured the map—a rough mental version of it, anyhow—

and knew they were in the Kurram Agency, the largest of Pakistan's Federally Administered Tribal Agencies or FATA, a salient jutting into Afghanistan and one of several jumping off points for guerrillas and their supplies at the start of the annual fighting season. To the north-west was the Afghan province of Logar; to the west, Paktia. Brodick's escorts were on their feet, addressing themselves to him, all talking at once, jabbing fingers at something out there. From what he could gather, the bus was heading into Kurram's main town, Parachinar. According to Brodick's history books, this was the place where British and Afghan officials, including Sir Mortimer Durand, negotiated the boundary between British-ruled India and Afghanistan known thereafter as the Durand Line: a boundary, not a real border and never ratified as such.

Afghanistan was a day's hike away.

*

Stones and rocks appeared in the torchlight as glimmering ovals. It was like crossing a river in the dark by hopping from one stepping stone to the next. Trouble was, the rocks and boulders were unsteady and the torchlight was anything but steady; it came and went, flickered on and off and there were long moments in pitch darkness when all Brodick could do was stand still and hope whoever was behind him in the column didn't cannon into him and send him flying. At least, he told himself, they weren't climbing. They were in some narrow cleft in the mountains, using a dry riverbed to cross the frontier.

All the previous afternoon and night, from his vantage point on the roof of a village shack, waiting to leave, he had watched never-ending columns of men and mules heading into Afghanistan. The mules carried Chinese landmines—large, round, light green, plastic, ribbed objects—as well as mortar tubes and base plates and heavy 12.7mm machineguns of Chinese or Soviet bloc origin. The men carried Kalashnikov rifles, RPK light machineguns and rocket-propelled grenade launchers—and both belts and boxes of ammunition. The torrent of men and gear was constant, all day and all night, one detachment after another. Just after midnight, he'd been urged to his feet and had joined the march.

Where were the Soviets and their Afghan allies? Where were their aircraft and artillery? Why didn't they try to interdict the men and supplies before they crossed the Durand Line? What was holding them back?

Now, as the sun rose, they were climbing.

Oh, Christ. Here we go.

The mountain reared above Brodick and on the conquest of each ridge, yet another loomed only higher than its predecessor; they were a succession of stony waves, each bigger and steeper and more monstrous than its predecessor, from seven thousand feet to ten, from ten to twelve. The forest of pine and larch he'd left far below—only rock and scrub stretched above. Brodick felt infuriated as if played for a fool by this immense, lordly landscape that reduced him to a wee smidgen of tormented, insignificant life squirming on its broad face. He had done no training for this and he regretted it. He was no paratrooper or marine. He was an amateur reporter and an amateur spy; moreover one drenched in sweat, his face crimson, and his lungs and throat afire with the effort of sucking in air; his thigh muscles screamed bloody murder and, when he stopped, however briefly, they quivered and twitched. He sensed that he was the only one in the column gasping noisily, the only one whose *shalwar kameez* was sopping black with sweat, the only one who grunted and tripped and stumbled about like a drunk. A falcon swept out of the crags, then shot away at the sight of two hundred men climbing. The only sounds he heard were his own tortured breathing and the sandals of the men slipping, scraping and kicking the loose stones, the slings of their rifles rattling against their weapons.

'English.' A fighter put out a calloused hand, and Brodick was tempted. But fuck it: no, he shook his head, attempted a smile of thanks that was more rictus of pain and embarrassment. He wasn't English, there wasn't a drop of that stuff in his veins—so he liked to think—but the truth of identity was too difficult to explain in Pashto. Perhaps in their communal memory of resisting the imperial British, they had retained some image down the generations of the Scots as colonial troops in kilts, but this was not the place or time. Carrying his own pack was part of their unwritten code; hand it to someone else and he'd feel their respect slip away. The same went for his position in the van of the march; he could at any moment stand aside, let others in his group pass, fall back until the porters with their loads of heavy weapons and ammunition caught up with him at the rear. No one would stop him, but he knew that for every fighter who overtook him, his standing would slip a further notch. It was a high price to pay for a twenty-minute breather. He had to keep up.

A blessed relief, at first: squalls of rain struck in late afternoon, icy needles stung face and hands, blinding the guerrillas. From burning with heat Brodick shivered until the rain stopped and his body heated up once more, his clothing clinging to him and making it more difficult than ever to keep his legs moving. Then it snowed, feathery flakes floating into his face.

As night fell, they stopped at some sort of shelter and Brodick realised it was a bothy, or the Afghan equivalent, and stinking of goat; a mighty fire burned in the centre and the dripping, unwashed bodies formed a solid, foetid wall around it. That stench again of unwashed feet and mutton fat. The front of him burned, the back of him stayed icy. His eyes streamed from the smoke. He could feel vermin start to move out of the waistband in his cotton pants; the crab lice spread across his belly and abdomen, found the warmth around his testicles and anus and began biting, and when he lay down on the filth near the embers, wrapped in his *potu* cotton shawl, they continued feeding on his blood and were joined by cattle ticks. He chucked handfuls of insect powder into his voluminous pants, but it had little effect.

There was no point in asking how much further or how much longer, for the Afghans seemed to have little conception of distance or time. It was what it was and it had to be done if it took an hour or a month; they were walking someplace and walk they would until they reached it. They were a stoical lot. If Brodick did ask, they might say 'Over the next hill', or 'Three-four hours, maybe'. They'd say whatever they thought he wanted to hear, the way one quiets a child and suppresses his or her tears with a comforting but untruthful response. It was possible they themselves didn't know, that only the commander knew and he wasn't saying. Here Brodick was a child again, ignorant and naive, powerless, his life in their hands, his wellbeing a matter of their generosity and empathy. He did want to cry at times, his self-pity almost overwhelming. He was pathetic. Without them, and without their help and their humanity, he would die. He might of course do that anyway, but in the meantime he must try to earn their respect as their guest. It was the least he could do.

It took not one but three days to traverse the mountains and during that time he learned some important things about himself: that he could sleep on the ground, on rock, and entirely wet through. He learned that he would not catch a cold from simply being chilled or drenched, and he learned to walk with bloody blisters and feet so cold he couldn't feel them. All experience was useful, though he would never be able to say he would ever get used to any of it. He was no Royal Marine or paratrooper.

It was also a far cry from the adventure he'd dreamed of.

He stank like everyone else. His clothes quickly became filthy and torn. His sense of British exceptionalism—that he was in some ways not only very different but superior by virtue of education, language—evaporated. He was just a man, no less and certainly no more. It was one thing to know his life was worth no more than any other's, but another thing entirely to live it, to experience it.

It surprised him that the Soviets were still so predictable even now, more than a year after the invasion; they sent over reconnaissance aircraft before they attacked. The mujahedeen broke up into smaller parties when they heard the drone of the Soviet plane and they hid among the rocks. There was never enough sleep, so hiding was a chance for Brodick to catch up.

Under an immense boulder—he crawled on his belly into a sandy depression right under it—he slept until his companions pulled his legs; the English must wake up. The English did, just in time to drink a glass—two glasses, but very small glasses—of hot green tea with sprigs of wild mint. He ate, too, half an unleavened roundel of scorched bread. He wondered how it was that these rough peasants could carry small, delicate, bell-shaped tea glasses around the mountains without breaking them. For days that was all they ate or drank, and Brodick had the novel experience of replacing his dreams of sex with uninterrupted fantasies of food—invariably Italian—and drink—mostly Bordeaux and Burgundies and his favourite single Speyside malts. Not even his blisters or immense population of vermin could spoil these desperate dreams. Yes, he was pathetic.

Resting in an Alpine clearing, enjoying gentle sunshine and sitting on grass as rich as anything to be found in the Highlands, his back against a rock and surrounded by pines, Brodick's mind idled in a state between sleep and consciousness when he became aware that an elderly, tall Afghan with a neat white beard was trying to get his attention by smiling and nodding. The fellow had been admiring himself in a pocket mirror. Afghan men liked to look at themselves, apparently, and carried mirrors for the purpose. Many used kohl as eyeliner. This one did not appear to carry a weapon, and his clothes seemed unusually clean. He moved closer to Brodick and by means of gestures, indicated that the foreigner's leg muscles must be stiff—which indeed they were—and that he would be happy to give their foreign guest a massage.

Brodick never liked being touched by strangers. In any case, he noted that some younger Afghan fighters were grinning at them, nudging one another and pointing. He declined the offer as politely as he could, given that he had little Pashto; shaking his head, smiling and showing the palms of his hands. No. Thank you, but no.

A week after leaving Peshawar, capital of Pakistan's North West Frontier Province, Brodick and his companions were lying up in wooded foothills overlooking a village on the edge of a wide, stony plain that the Afghans said led to their capital, Kabul.

'English, you stay. Too much danger. You wait here.'

Brodick disagreed. He argued; he refused to stay. In truth, he was afraid; he could hear his built-in alarm sounding shrill in the back of his head. He knew they were testing him. He also knew that he hadn't walked for a week across the Hindu Kush into Afghanistan, starved himself, gained blisters on both feet, learned to use a stone to clean his arse having shat something as hard and painful as a brick—he half expected it to bounce but it didn't—and become lousy with vermin, merely to turn away when at last he had a chance of seeing action.

The little Soviet monoplane interrupted the argument. It buzzed up the valley, turned in a leisurely half-circle over the village, flew back. Don't mind me, it seemed to say.

Early the next morning after prayers, they walked down to the village, Brodick among them. It was still dark. There were twenty-three Afghans, young and old, armed with Kalashnikovs of one kind or another, from Czech to Chinese and Egyptian versions. They walked through the cool, mud-walled alleys through to the other side, then sat themselves down on a small rise just beyond the hamlet as the sun rose. They ate a kind of scrambled eggs—Brodick wolfed down his share—with the flatbread; it was very oily, but the first protein he had enjoyed since the journey began. They drank heavily sweetened green tea, smoked Brodick's Lucky Strikes and chatted with the village elders and admired the sea of gravel. It was going to be a beautiful day. They were waiting for dusk before moving across open ground. Brodick felt sleepy with a nearly full belly. He told himself he and his throbbing blisters had the entire day to rest; he could feel afraid again later if he had a mind to.

They heard the enemy before they saw them.

Helicopter gunships, the formidable Mi-24s, were at this distance tiny insects, flying low, back and forth, back and forth, buzzing busily. Now Brodick saw the dots, a string of them, raising billows of brown dust. The two gunships fussed over them like a couple of overzealous collies nipping at the heels of recalcitrant sheep.

The dots grew and so too did the aircraft.

It was only after perhaps ten or fifteen minutes that Brodick's companions showed signs of unease. The dots were turning; yes, they turned east, line abreast, heading towards Brodick's companions and the village that lay directly behind them. The predatory outlines of the gunships and distinctive whack of their rotors were unmistakable. Another minute and the vehicles were no longer dots but clearly BMP-1s, tracked and armoured fighting vehicles that were fast and low, armed with both coaxial machineguns and 73mm smooth bore cannon. They were accompanied by more mundane troop carriers, the wheeled BTR-60s, the workhorses of both Warsaw Pact and People's Democratic Party of Afghanistan (PDPA) infantry.

The BMPs fired. Shells fluttered overhead and struck somewhere in the village, each detonating with a flash, a dull thump and a plume of dust and smoke.

Serious shite, this. Brodick spoke out loud; in his time among these people he had begun muttering to himself. He turned; he was quite alone. Brodick had been so absorbed in what was unfolding to the west that he hadn't heard his companions shouting, or noticed that they were fleeing in some disorder, their loose clothing and *potus* streaming behind them, billowing in the morning breeze. They didn't fall back. They didn't retreat in stages, facing the enemy. They turned tail, scattering like kids who've been spotted stealing sweets from the corner shop.

They called to him, turning around momentarily, but they turned back again and kept running towards the village and the hills and mountains behind it. Brodick caught up, but he was still Tail-End Charlie as they ran through the village; they had no intention of defending the place or its inhabitants, and they wouldn't slow down for him.

With the mud-walled village now between the guerrillas

and the Soviet/PDPA attacking force, a red, single-decker bus appeared, apparently summoned by the commander. Where it had come from Brodick had no idea. Its engine idled while the two dozen fighters scrambled on board; two Afghans grabbed Brodick and pushed him on, too. He had no option, unless he wanted to throw himself out of a window, for the windows had no glass so it wouldn't have been difficult. The bus might be ancient, but the paintwork was new; on this drab landscape it must have stood out for miles.

The Afghans gave vent simultaneously to their opinions as to the best course of action. Yelling at the driver, they jumped up and down and hammered feet and fists on the body of the bus and its floor, cocked their weapons and pointed them at the driver's head. With a grinding of gears the bus bumped along a track, swaying from side to side; progress seemed excruciatingly slow. The mud walls fell away and they were in open country; the sound of the gunships overrode everything else, drowning out the shouts of the panicky passengers, and Brodick glimpsed the shadow of one of the predators as it sped overhead.

A single burst from the mini-gun jutting from under the nose of the "Hind" would tear them to pieces, all of them.

The bus halted. The driver leapt out of his seat.

They all got out, or fell out, leaping from doors and windows. They ran.

They loped through fields of melons, they skidded through fields of opium poppies. They raced across what seemed to be fields of watercress or clover and jumped over irrigation ditches; they climbed over mud walls and sprinted through openings from one field to the next, dodging the trunks of apricot and plum trees like downhill skiers navigating moguls. The egg-beater whacking of the gunships thudded in Brodick's brain. There was a great deal of firing behind him: the attackers were shooting up the village.

Brodick dared not look back or up; it would only slow him down. He did not know how far or for how long he ran: he sprinted for his life. His grandiose turban was beginning to come undone and to wind itself snake-like around neck and shoulders. Such vanity! Constrictor-like, it would work its way all around him and eventually trip him up and he knew that if he fell he might very well not get up again.

Two thousand pounds of education
Drops to a ten-rupee jezail —
The Crammer's boast, the Squadron's pride,
Shot like a rabbit in a ride.

A hand grabbed Brodick's shoulder, pushed, gave one final thrust; a gruff voice gave orders, and he realized the iron fingers digging into his flesh belonged to the commander. Driven forward, he bent, waded in, following others, away from sunlight into grey gloom; icy water cascading over his ankles, his knees, his thighs, the snow melt shocking, numbing his joints.

They stood in line, snaking along the *kerez*, the almost horizontal, underground irrigation channel that carried mountain snow melt under the road to the fields below. Some Afghans prayed, reciting passages from the Koran; some drank the water; some lifted their *shalwar kameez*, fumbled with baggy pants and urinated. Urgent prayers for deliverance ceased as a new danger reached their ears from the vertical shafts every fifty meters or so: these provided not only sounds from the surface above but also a thin, dusty, cone-shaped cathedral light to reach those standing nearest to them. The noises told Brodick the BMPs and BTR 60s had left the village and were coming up the track in the wake of the bus; their tracks squealed, grinding away like steel teeth, hungry for prey. Brodick cringed; he imagined that at any moment a PDPA or Soviet soldier would jump down and stroll over to one of the shafts, pull the pin on a grenade and drop it. Fire in the hole! Anti-personnel, fragmentation, phosphorus: whatever took his fancy, whatever he had on his belt.

They were overhead.

Brodick held his breath.

The noise of the enemy receded.

It was late afternoon when Brodick and his companions emerged; the shadows were lengthening as they walked back to the village. When they reached the pink-beige houses he saw that the attackers had rolled along the main street, firing into the homes and sun-baked mud-and-straw walls. Several people had been injured, mostly women; two village men had died in honourable but futile defence. Their bodies were laid out on their backs and wrapped in their *potus*, awaiting burial. They hadn't been washed, there was still blood on their waxy faces. Their expressions seemed surprisingly calm, even serene.

It was expected of Brodick that he would do something to help. To his surprise they didn't object when he cleaned the wounds of the women: a head injury, a puncture in an elderly woman's breast, a strangely bloodless hole in the upper arm of another. He did his best; he used up his iodine, antiseptic cream and dressings. When he was done he asked a village youth—the lad spoke some English, seemed to be about fourteen and was therefore considered an adult—what they would do with their wounded.

The boy seemed surprised. 'Oh, they'll take the bus to Kabul tomorrow. There's a Russian hospital where they can get help. They'll say they were wounded by the *mujahideen*. They'll come back in the evening.'

For the first time Brodick—until now unwitting victim of his own and others' propaganda—saw clearly that the peasants were caught in a vice, squeezed between superpowers and their proxies. It occurred to him that the red bus provided a regular, twice weekly, service between village and capital and perhaps that was why the gunships had not destroyed it. Perhaps the *mujahideen* were counting on Soviet / PDPA restraint. Would U.S. or British or French aircrews have held back in similar circumstances?

He thought he knew the answer.

Brodick was elated. Every fibre, every nerve was joyously alive; the bliss was intensely physical. He talked a lot, loudly; he couldn't help himself. He was mad, certainly. He had learned an important lesson of war: survival in the face of others' violent death brings intense pleasure. He forgot his blisters, his hunger, the vermin; he felt more alive than ever.

He had to return to Pakistan. Kabul would have to wait. He had been away two weeks, and *The Orient* would sack him if he delayed any longer. The Jamiat-e-Islami *mujahideen* commander arranged for Brodick's return to Pakistan by providing a guide and a donkey. The donkey belonged to the guide, a sullen youth with acne and an AK-47 rifle. Brodick wasn't sure if he'd bought it or simply rented it but either way, he had no intention of riding the animal; he told himself it wasn't much in Pakistani rupees and, although he suspected he was being overcharged, Brodick didn't object. He was in too much of a hurry.

If he started early and walked hard by the most direct route, he could make the border in a day, albeit a very long day; eighteen hours should suffice. Brodick would write up his experience in several different ways, tailoring each version in style and length for each outlet to maximize the return. It never occurred to him until very much later that his tale of hiding in an underground irrigation channel would have consequences, that a party of Afghans would be slaughtered in a similar *kerez* the following year and that Jamiat-i-Islami would blame him for the loss of life.

Only a handful of mostly French and British freelancers covered the Afghan war on anything like a regular basis, and some ventured deep into Afghan territory for weeks or even months: especially five freelance cameramen and photographers, two British, two French and one American of French origin. They had enviable stamina and courage. How they could justify the amount of time they invested in the conflict in terms of financial return, Brodick had no idea. Perhaps they didn't try. Maybe they did it for the love of the place, of the Afghans, of the cause of so-called freedom, or to build up their own career prospects; maybe they paid for it from the proceeds of other assignments. It certainly wasn't the American notion of war reporting: there were no helicopters to take correspondents to the front—or anywhere near it—then back in time for a hot shower and cold lager at the hotel bar. There were no real briefings. The news wasn't neatly wrapped and packaged. The American vice-consul in Peshawar gave 'off-the-record' briefings based on what a single, unnamed carpet dealer or simply 'a traveller' had reportedly seen in Kandahar or Kunduz, and this was also provided the same day at the U.S. embassy in Islamabad. But no one could take that State Department drivel seriously, except for the *New York Times*—which could never resist, then or later, the temptation of publishing highly dubious stories based on "Sources that spoke on condition of anonymity"—and the ideologically-driven *Wall Street Journal*. The only way to be sure of anything was to get to the fighting on foot, with no guarantee that at the end of it there would be action; the reporter was limited to line of sight. Then there was the return hike to file copy by telex, by which time any news would be stale. There were no phones, of course. The enemy wasn't Soviet; it was exhaustion and it was time itself, for there were vast tracts of Soviet-occupied Afghanistan—and indeed, even larger tracts that weren't occupied by anyone—that went unreported for years, maybe decades.

All went more or less well until Brodick and his guide reached the mountains and hit snow fields on the western slopes from the previous winter. The donkey carried nothing but was still slow. In the drifts it came to a complete halt, its front legs sinking deep. It made no headway at all and looked to Brodick pretty pleased with itself for its wilful act of civil disobedience. The guide refused to beat his charge or insert the muzzle of his AK-47 up the animal's backside, as an increasingly ravenous and ill-tempered Brodick insisted.

Brodick practiced what Pashto he had learned.

'Your gun.'

'Huh?'

'Give.'

'What for?'

Miming the action: 'I want to shoot the fucker and eat one of its legs'.

Guide, sniffily: 'Ha! Only a Russian would eat a donkey.'

Brodick pressed on; after twenty minutes or so he turned and looked back. The guide was far below, pulling the donkey after him and trying to catch up, but it was a losing battle. All Brodick had to do was keep heading east, for eventually he would be in Pakistani territory, or more accurately, in one of Pakistan's semi-autonomous tribal agencies. Somehow the climb seemed easier this time. He panted with the effort, and he used his hands to push down on his thighs, but he felt pretty good. He was stronger, fitter than he had been at the outset. He was quite alone. Guide and donkey were out of sight; maybe they'd turned back.

Brodick came upon a valley with a broad, shallow stream meandering down the centre. Forests grew on either side; above that the valley was rimmed with blue peaks and white patches of snow. There were no villages, no houses he could see; there was no sign of human habitation at all, though he had to assume he was being watched by someone, perhaps a shepherd. Afghans could tell a great deal about a stranger at a considerable distance, from the way he walked to the cut of his clothes and especially the way he wore his turban. Brodick knew that if there were watchers they wouldn't mistake him for an Afghan. He wore American combat boots, not sandals, and he was far from expert in tying his turban in the correct fashion. He didn't worry about it for there was nothing he could do: anyone watching his progress would certainly think it odd that he wasn't armed. In the meantime he enjoyed the scenery.

At dusk he was moving uphill from the valley when he heard voices and looked up. Ahead, on the same track but moving down towards him in the opposite direction was a group of Afghans, perhaps thirty or forty in all; they strolled along in a crowd, bunched up, chattering. Companionably, some held hands. They hadn't seen him because they weren't looking: they had no scouts out on their flanks, no advance guard. Apart from their weapons and ammunition, they were no more military in the way they carried themselves than football spectators heading to a match on a Saturday afternoon. In fact, they were youngsters for the most part; they were going in to fight. Brodick was tempted to move off the track and take cover behind some boulders, but he decided to act openly, reasoning that if he were caught skulking behind the scree it might seem as if he was hiding something, and it wouldn't go well for him, so he kept walking uphill in full view.

The Soviets were missing a great opportunity.

When they were no more than a dozen paces apart, one of the Afghans saw him and said something. A dozen AK-47 and SKS rifles were raised and cocked as the group parted and moved aside for him to pass; strangely, they made no physical effort to stop him.

'Russki,' said one Afghan as they drew level. It was more statement than question; they were close enough to see the colour of Brodick's eyes, his reddish-blond beard, and his foreign boots.

'Russki?' They'd stopped and turned.

Be friendly. We're all pals. Brodick forced himself to smile and he shook his head.

'*Assalaam aleikum*,' he said, placing the palm of his right hand over his heart in respectful greeting.

'*Waleikum salaam*', came the chorus of replies.

They stood around him in a circle, uncertain. While several weapons were pointed loosely in his direction, Brodick noted that the faces of their owners were more curious than hostile. For one horrible moment, Brodick realised he'd forgotten the word for "press" and "journalist" in Pashto; he raised his hands and tapped away as if at a keyboard. Then he made a scribbling motion with his right hand, as if holding a pen.

At last, someone got it. 'BBC?'

Brodick nodded. 'BBC'.

A long, drawn-out breath. 'Ahh. BBC!' That explained everything. The muzzles of the rifles dropped and in their place a hedge of brown hands appeared. Brodick, grinning, shook as many as he could. They patted him on the arm and slapped him on the back as the acronym was repeated again and again. 'BBC. BBC!'

They went on down the hill, still saying 'BBC' and turning

to wave to him. No Afghan, certainly no Pashtun, would let an evening go by without listening to the BBC's Pashto or Dari services on a shared transistor radio, its owner expertly switching from one wavelength to another as reception faded in and out. The *Voice of America*, or VOA, was the second choice. Still, Brodick could have been just about anyone walking up that hill.

Minutes before midnight, Brodick arrived back at the Jamiat-i-Islami compound in Parachinar. He banged on the metal gates until a guard woke and let him in. He was fed, and everyone who wasn't still asleep gathered round to watch him devour goat stew on a tin plate, using his fingers and bread to scoop it up. Brodick didn't mind the audience; he was used to it by now. He was shown to what he was told was the commander's bed, the commander being absent. It was inviting: it was a three-foot bed, with mattress, sheets, blankets, pillows in pillowcases and, to Brodick's amazement, it was clean—much cleaner than he was—and it stood against a wall in the main room where most of the others slept on the floor.

He protested as he thought he ought, but his hosts insisted.

'No, no, no, you must take it. You are our guest.'

The commander would be in for a nasty surprise when he got back to find his clean sheets soiled and his blankets infested with crab lice, but by then Brodick would be back home in Peshawar. Aside from boots and turban, he climbed into bed fully dressed. It was comfortable and warm and smelled good. Brodick stank like a zoo, even to himself, but he fell asleep at once, even before he felt the lice start to bite. Everyone else went back to bed, too. Or so he thought.

He was woken by someone shaking his shoulder.

'My bed,' said a voice. 'My bed.'

Brodick recognised the younger of two kitchen cooks, a plump, round-cheeked youth who'd brought him his stew and watched him eat it.

'Fuck off.' Brodick went back to sleep.

It happened again. It might have been five minutes or five hours.

This time the Afghan was trying to get into bed with Brodick, and was urging him to make room.

'My bed.'

Something in Brodick snapped. All the frustrations, the fear, the impatience, the loneliness, the discomfort of the previous ten days erupted in blind rage. Leaping up, he had both hands round the youth's neck. He drove him back and slammed him into the opposite wall, stepping on sleeping figures, ignoring protests. His fingers dug deep into the flesh of the lad's throat, his thumbs were on the boy's trachea and he was pressing into it. Hard. He was going to crush it. He was going to rip it out. He was shouting. He didn't know what he was shouting, but he wanted to rid himself of this pest. He wanted to obliterate this fat, soft creature. It felt good and right that he should.

Others intervened, forcing the two of them apart. Brodick broke out of the scrum, pushed his feet into his boots, grabbed turban and backpack and ran out into the forecourt. He hammered on the outer doors, demanded the guards unlock them.

'You can't go out there—the Pakistanis will arrest you. The police are watching us.'

Five Afghans had the cook by the arms and dragged him before Brodick. They handed him a Kalashnikov. 'Beat him. Please. Hit him. He has shamed us.' That was what Brodick thought they were saying, but he wasn't sure. To ensure he did understand, they performed a pantomime of striking the youth with the rifle stock and kicking him. He took the weapon and pushed the muzzle into the cook's cheek. He racked the slide. He pushed the safety off. Why beat him? He could and would shoot the bastard. A bullet was so much easier. The kid fell to his knees and started blubbering; he was sorry, please, mister.

There was no clip.

Brodick squeezed the trigger.

Click.

Damn thing wasn't loaded; there was no round in the breach.

The thought occurred to him that possibly—just possibly—

both cook and bed were regarded as amenities for the foreign guest to enjoy on his first night back. A welcome gift like scented soap in a hotel bathroom or a Belgian chocolate on the pillow. With Pashtuns you could never tell, even if they were members of an otherwise devout and morally earnest Jamiat-i-Islami.

So here was the romantic adventure Brodick had dreamt of; this was the Great Game of nations. And what did it amount to but exhaustion, filth, ignorance and the illiterate, a squalid, violent world without women? For what? Democracy? To improve the daily lives of the Afghan masses? And he, Brodick, no knight in shining armour but a wee man as malodorous and malevolent as the next and certainly no better than any of his companions.

The absurdity of it; the impulse to murder evaporated as swiftly as it had arisen. He laughed at his hosts and at himself; he walked back into the headquarters, giggling, weeping, hysterical, tore off his boots, dropped turban and backpack and fell onto the bed. He slept undisturbed for twelve hours. When he woke, Brodick staggered out into the yard and urinated, Afghan-style, squatting in the dust. He was relieved to find that he had not shot the assistant cook, after all. He was just in time to catch the public bus back to Peshawar.

11

In bed, in total darkness, alone, listening to large, flying beetles hurl themselves against the walls of Room 19, Brodick had plenty of time to think about how it had all begun. This time he recalled his training. To his surprise and relief, Marion had not only joined him on the three-week-long Fort Monckton course, but had charmed their handlers and never once let on that she wouldn't be joining him in Peshawar. For which he was truly grateful.

She'd excelled at report writing, too; unlike Brodick, who had to admit he was hobbled by his news writing style. It was hard to adapt. The two kinds of writing were totally different. The news story was a standard affair: the lead paragraph provided the *who*, *what* and *when* along with the source, and all within thirty-five words, tops. The second paragraph was commonly a quote that backed up the lead paragraph, and third was the "nut" paragraph, providing context and, in essence, explaining the importance of the report. The rest of it was an inverted pyramid, with the facts mustered in descending importance. The idea—as old as the first newspapers, presumably—was that the story could be cut by a subeditor's pencil to any length. Only one, two or three paragraphs and the story could stand on its own and still make sense to fit the available column inches.

As for intelligence reports, Brodick found the style a good deal more subtle. There was a headline, of course, and the paragraphs were numbered, but not necessarily in diminishing importance, unlike news. It was more of a narrative, and at first Brodick found it hard to master. Right at the bottom was an opportunity to make a comment: on the lack of details, perhaps, or the veracity or otherwise of the source. The comment was sometimes as long as the report, if not longer. It had taken him the entire course to compose intelligence reports good enough for his training officer—and even now he wasn't too sure of his own ability. It was going to take many more months of daily practice.

He found that journalism and espionage were very different. The journalist was, in effect, in the entertainment business. His or her "facts" were there on the page to sell advertising, to make the media barons their millions. The reporter did not slavishly note down everything a politician said at a press conference; instead he or she sat back, waiting for the catchiest quote, the snazziest foul-up that would make the most attractive headline, the best attention-grabbing first paragraph. Journalism was never about truth. It was about getting the reader's attention. It seemed to Brodick that there were only two things the two meretricious trades had in common: the need for access to those with influence or power, and the very nature of the reporter and spy at work. Both were observers. They watched, they listened, but they did not participate. They waited. They stood aside from the battles swirling around them. The spy tried to make sense of it and report back in secret. The journalist shouted it out from the rooftops, and got paid for his noisy over-simplifications, his headlines, brazen first paragraphs and by-lines.

The first might start or prevent a war, the second would bring in advertising revenue.

Even back then, though, Brodick knew it wasn't enough for him to be merely a passive observer. He wanted to take part. He wanted above all to create the news, not just report it.

During his training, Brodick spent days tailing people, and being tailed, on the streets and in the department stores of Plymouth and

Portsmouth. All too often he'd failed to shake off his tail, and had lost his mark within twenty minutes of beginning to follow one of his instructors. The memory of it still embarrassed him.

Brodick turned away from that embarrassment to something more agreeable: his high scores for agent handling. There were exercises in which various members of the Fort's staff would appear in disguise, posing as agents: agents-to-be, or established agents with information to divulge, some of it hidden beneath layers of deliberate obfuscation and prevarication. A double agent. A man afraid for his life. What Brodick and Marion had not realised was that they were being closely monitored throughout these sessions, not least by cameras behind pictures and one-way mirrors. The "agents" and "agents-to-be" were all tricksters—voluble, silent, offensive, aggressive, timid—but the information that mattered had to be winkled out of them somehow and the chaff they offered up at the outset stripped away and discarded.

Brodick had enjoyed firearms training, too, though it had been pointed out it wasn't really all that necessary. SIS operatives didn't—as a general rule—carry firearms. It was more a kind of therapy, a letting off steam. A giant paper screen on rollers was synchronised with a 16mm film projector while he and Marion took in turn to stand on a wooden platform to fire the 9mm Browning Hi-Power two-handed at targets as they appeared. These targets came and went singly or in multiples, on staircases, balconies, doorways, roads, in vehicles and in fields or behind trees. Some appeared to be going for a gun, but in fact were reaching for their car keys or a sandwich. The instructions were to engage each valid target with two rounds: a double tap.

'Fuck, fuck, fuckety-fuck.' To the ex-Parachute Regiment instructor's amusement, Brodick became so excited that he forgot to count his rounds and quickly ran out of ammunition, cursing and fumbling furiously to eject the magazine, replace it and resume firing.

They were told to aim for the target's thorax on the grounds that it was the biggest target area and contained several vital organs. But

Brodick didn't care. He wanted to make absolutely sure his targets wouldn't get up again, so he always went for the head.

He never missed.

At one point a young woman on a busy pavement looked at the camera, opened her handbag and put her hand into it as if getting hold of her purse. She was pulling out a pistol when Brodick shot her twice in the head—both rounds overlapping, right between the eyes. It was good shooting and fast. He didn't think anything of it at the time, but that evening when they were alone in the guest flat they occupied, Marion exploded.

'You bastard. You didn't even hesitate. You shot that woman twice in the head before she'd even got her weapon clear. Unbelievable! Jesus!'

'She was armed. What did you expect—that I wait until she gets a shot off at me before I return fire? This isn't cricket. It's not about gentlemen holding the door open. It's about bloody survival, for God's sake. And so far I haven't shot a single hostage or innocent passer-by.'

She wouldn't speak or look at him for two days.

*

'How big is this thing?'

'I'm not sure, exactly.'

'Is it the size of a bomb, you know, the kind of container—a projectile —that's slung underneath an aircraft's wing? Like a disposable fuel tank? No fins but pointy? Perhaps four feet long? Like one of those napalm bombs the Americans use?'

Mungoo shook his head with some impatience.

'No, no. Not at all. Smaller. Much smaller than that. Like a big bottle, how do you say, a flask. Like so—' He had put down his glass and now made several vague shapes in the air with his pale hands.

'Square?'

'I wouldn't say square exactly. More rectangular, but curved, with a screw top.'

'A screw top? So it's not designed to explode. It's not an explosive device with a firing mechanism, a fuse. What you describe sounds like an outsized hipflask. An oddly shaped bottle. Maybe a kettle.'

'I don't think so, but I'm not sure. I don't have the exact measurements and I don't have any pictures.'

'It's all rather vague, don't you think?'

'I'm sorry. Our people are simple. If you don't want to do this, it's okay. If you think it too dangerous, I quite understand. It probably doesn't matter.'

Brodick suspected Mungoo said this on purpose, to goad him into going, but he didn't need goading. Mungoo was doing his best to help him. The old boy had introduced him to all sorts of people over the past year, had taken Brodick under his wing, helped feed him material. Mungoo was doing his best—Brodick told himself he shouldn't be so critical. Hell yes, he would go, even if it proved to be a mistake. He'd already committed one deliberate error and that was that he hadn't informed Hermitage. He could have. There was nothing stopping him from doing so; the truth of it was that he decided not to in case Hermitage forbade him from making the trip, or tried to delay it. Hermitage would, as ever, want to seek London's advice, London's permission, and that would mean a pause of several weeks. Trips like this took a good deal of preparation, and when the opportunity arose Brodick had to seize it. Hermitage didn't seem to appreciate the difficulties of arranging a journey over the frontier; he wasn't willing to light his bloody pipe unless he had the green light from Century House.

Professional spies were civil servants when all was said and done, and they loved to find all manner of reasons to say no, or ensure the responsibility for making a decision was tossed into someone else's in-tray. Whitehall was all about buck-passing up the chain of command. Well, too bad. He would take responsibility for this. He would make up his own mind. He would fly to Quetta, make contact with Mungoo's friend, and go on to Kandahar. He would take the chance and grab the canister or whatever the hell it was.

'How will you bring it back?'

'Oh. I see what you mean.' Brodick hadn't thought that far ahead, but Mungoo had a point. He couldn't take the flight back to Islamabad. He realised now that it was too risky. What if the pressurised cabin burst the device? What if it exploded, or simply leaked? It could kill everyone on board, Brodick included. The Pakistan International Airlines Fokker could crash. Who could tell what the extent of the contamination would be if that happened, if the plane broke up in mid-air and it sprayed whatever was in this thingy over a wide area? It might be catastrophic, even in the sparsely populated wilds of Baluchistan.

'I'll take the train from Quetta to Rawalpindi.'

'That's three days. It's very slow from Quetta.'

And extremely hot and uncomfortable, too, even though it was again winter—it was freezing at night, then the temperature rose fast with the sun. Brodick wasn't looking forward to that part of the mission at all.

'It'll be safer for everyone, I think.'

They drank their tea, each man with his own thoughts. Mungoo offered his guest a biscuit.

'So you'll go?'

'I'll go.'

'Good. Very good. Arrangements have been made.' Mungoo looked relieved that they'd reached agreement.

'I'm grateful, Professor.'

'No need, no need. We're friends aren't we? Nothing is too much trouble for a true friend, right? As a matter of interest, what will you do with it once you have it?'

'I'll write about it, of course, if it is what we suspect it to be. First it will have to be properly examined, scientifically tested, to verify it. It'll be the first hard, physical evidence that they're using chemical weapons.'

Mungoo raised his hands, palms outwards. 'Forgive me. I know you believe this is very important and it goes without saying that I'm happy to help. It's my duty as an Afghan. But quite honestly,

Richard, I don't see what difference it makes to anything. If they kill us with Kalashnikovs or bombs or gas it matters little to the dead or to their grieving families. They're killing us—and that's what's important. The how doesn't matter. Or does it?'

Brodick nodded. He knew what Mungoo was getting at and, if he was honest about it, he agreed with him. 'If we prove it, then it will give your struggle extra moral force against a superpower using inhumane weapons banned by the international community against the civilian population.' Brodick felt rather proud of his improvised response.

'The United States used Agent Orange in Vietnam, didn't it? Yes? The suffering will be felt for generations. I don't recall howls of rage from the international community back then, do you? And even if there were, it didn't stop the Americans. I don't wish to offend you, my young friend, but I have to say as a former politician that your so-called moral force doesn't seem to count when superpowers compete for influence or resources in their colonial possessions. I seem to remember someone named Mr Churchill approving the use of poison gas on frontier tribes around the time of World War One. The idea being, apparently, to terrorise the tribes into submission. Isn't that what terrorism is? Am I right?'

Brodick had no answer. He did wonder why Mungoo had gone to all this trouble on his behalf if he, Mungoo, doubted the reasoning behind the search for CBW weapons. Was it simply the strength of their friendship, their shared cause? Or was Mungoo sending him off deliberately on a false trail if only to persuade Brodick that the hunt for CBW was a waste of time and effort and nothing but a fantasy dreamed up by the hawks in Washington and their obedient stoolpigeons in Westminster?

If so, he needn't have bothered. Brodick had already come to that conclusion.

*

Something had changed, but Brodick wasn't sure precisely when they started following him so blatantly. On leaving Mungoo's home he walked swiftly to the intersection in University Town and turned left, heading away from the tea shops and food stalls for a group of rickshaws and their drivers waiting in the shade. He signalled with his hand and one driver climbed into his seat, starting the engine in a cloud of toxic fumes as he waited for Brodick to climb in the back.

He couldn't help notice something odd. Usually people watched him pass by, and he was used to that. This time, though, three men in *shalwar kameez* had turned their backs and continued their conversation as if they hadn't seen the foreigner. Once settled in the rear of the gaily-painted rickshaw, Brodick glanced back. One of the trio had jumped onto the back of a motorbike, the second man headed for another bike and the third had jogged to a Peugeot 505, opened the door and slipped behind the wheel.

All three stayed with him all the way back to the hotel, the car behind, the two bikes just ahead of the rickshaw, only to peel away once he stopped and paid off the driver.

It was a crude message—another warning—and it seemed to Brodick that they wanted him to know that he was now a person of interest.

*

Brodick climbed onto the back of the waiting motorcycle.

This was going to be very different. Without mountains, the journey time would be much shorter—but once again, that speed would be essential in evading the numerous Khad informers that infested the villages and towns of Kandahar. Word travelled fast, too, and the secret police would know of Brodick's arrival at any location within twenty-four hours, according to Mungoo.

They were off in a burst of blue exhaust and beige dust. Brodick held on with one hand, primarily three fingers of his right, his left making sure his turban wouldn't fall off. It was a new turban, much cheaper than the first, less flamboyant and woven with some kind of artificial elasticated material that helped it stay in place in situations like this, riding pillion on an ancient 150cc Honda motorcycle. His chest touched the back of the man in front, a skinny youngster dressed in black with dark hair curling over his collar and ears. He didn't smell too bad. Brodick didn't know his name, and hadn't really seen his face, but none of that mattered. He drove fast, whoever he was, perfectly straight, obviously knowing exactly where he was going and how, only swerving to avoid deep potholes and gullies created by flash floods.

They left the two-lane highway behind and soon the road became a single tarred road, and that too turned to a macadam track, cambered with a ditch on either side until they left that behind, too. At first they moved through a market, then densely packed homes, clusters of UN refugee tents came next and finally they moved beyond all human habitation. They had avoided the border checkpoints entirely, but where Pakistan ended and Afghanistan began wasn't at all clear. The motorcyclist maintained his speed throughout. There was no other traffic. Not another soul, in fact: not so much as a single goat. They seemed to be heading in what Brodick thought was a westerly direction. The column of dust they made could be seen for miles, Brodick was sure. In such a featureless landscape it felt to Brodick as if they were both flying and at the same time remaining motionless, suspended above the land. There was dust in his eyes and mouth, and the roar of the engine in his ears. After an hour of this he felt stunned, numbed.

Day was rolling over into night, the temperature dropped fast and before them the sun was a flat white metallic disc dipping fast through thin, horizontal layers of grey cloud-like gauze. The land was pale and it reflected the dying light like a placid sea. The desert scrub was invisible. Only thin, straight pencil lines on the horizon indicated that low, flat-topped hills lay ahead.

At least he wasn't walking or climbing.

They sped through the deepening night. Brodick was not only numb but frozen. There were no lights. The motorcyclist had switched off his headlight. The sense of being disembodied, suspended in space, intensified. How did his Afghan know the way? How could he avoid getting completely lost? There were landmines out here, Brodick knew, but the dark hid any warning stakes and wire.

Brodick had almost fallen asleep when they juddered to a stop. He dismounted with difficulty, his legs stiff and cold.

'You stay.'

Two figures loomed out of the total darkness. They looked like extra-terrestrials, aliens, with their *potus* over their turbans and shoulders so they appeared to form inverted triangles.

'Come, mister.' They beckoned with their hands, the Afghan way, as if they were grabbing something in the air with their hands. The motorcyclist started up and sped off into the dark.

Brodick had no option but to follow, reeling like a drunk as feeling returned slowly and painfully to calves and thighs, and he staggered after the strangers. There were buildings ahead, he realised, quite unlike anything he had ever seen. As he reached the wall of the first, he saw they stood in a line, that they were whitewashed like Greek island cottages, but were rounded, domed. To Brodick they looked like beehives. A door was opened, he was ushered inside.

He stood in a small mosque, a single room with a few tattered prayer mats. A Koran. The dome overhead gave the place an immense, airy feeling.

'Sleep. Sleep.'

His escort carried Kalashnikovs. They stood watching as he removed his boots just inside the door—they insisted they stay inside and eventually Brodick realised why; they were obviously a foreigner's boots so could not be left outside where they were sure to be noticed—and they waited just long enough for him to lie down fully clothed on a foam mattress with a thick bedcover. Satisfied, they turned away abruptly and left him, pulling the door shut behind them. He heard their low voices outside, gradually receding. Had they locked him in? He could be a prisoner, and he might be in the hands of Khad agents, but Brodick didn't care. He would worry about it later if he had to. Right now all he wanted was sleep.

It seemed only moments later that he was shaken awake. Someone had him by the shoulder and was rocking him back and forth with increasing force and hissing in his ear. It was still dark. Brodick understood the general thrust if not the words themselves. He had to get up, go. Now. Quickly. One of Brodick's eyes, his left, seemed glued shut. He threw off the quilt, clambered to his feet and leaned against the wall, using his one good eye to see that the origin of his brutal awakening was the mullah himself: a small, wizened man with few teeth but a broad smile. The preacher was really quite friendly, in fact; by the time Brodick had managed to open both eyes fully, arrange his turban and *potu* and shoulder his pack, the old man in the black turban had returned, bringing with him a boy—his teenage son, perhaps—bearing a tray with a glass of steaming hot tea and a saucer of biscuits and more dried fruit. Breakfast! Brodick bowed and said thank you. He began to feel almost alive again.

Outside he was helped—manhandled with some difficulty— onto the back of a donkey. Or perhaps it was a mule. There was no saddle, just a folded blanket. Brodick used his feet to feel for stirrups but there were none. There was a lead rein held by another man on another donkey. Or mule. Brodick thought they must be moving him before the dawn prayers to avoid him being seen by villagers converging on the mosque. Though he craved more sleep he nonetheless appreciated their caution: curiosity and loose talk would only speed news of his whereabouts to Kandahar's Khad headquarters. He held on as best he could to the animal's withers as they plodded, rocked and stumbled forward into total darkness. There was no moon. Occasionally the animals broke into an uneven trot, nearly unseating him and jarring his spine. Brodick could see absolutely nothing. His eyes, even rubbed clear of sleep, were useless. He was aware at one point of passing through a village: high, mud-walled compounds took shape up on either side of a deeply rutted path as intense black shapes loomed out of the murk, black on black. They trotted painfully all the way through to the open country on the other side. Dogs barked at their passage but Brodick, glancing back over his shoulder, saw no lights come on. Then they were alone again.

Noon found Brodick squatting in a cave above a dried-out stream, the sort of gully that would channel a sudden flood down to the beige-pink plain beyond. The entrance was hidden by a piece of sacking the same light brown colour as the sand and stones. They had moved towards Kandahar and then, inexplicably, tacked away, eastwards. Now they were waiting. Brodick was waiting. The donkeys had been led away. He was brought tea and bread. No one could tell him what they were waiting for, or why. He smoked the last of his Lucky Strikes. Gazing out of his lair, Brodick saw there was no vegetation other than the odd weed. Certainly there was not a single tree. It was a desert-within-a-desert and if Brodick's guess—based on his possession of declassified U.S. satellite maps of Afghanistan—was correct, they were resting up in a guerrilla staging area known as Arghastan, about halfway between the Pakistani border and his destination. The hours went by and Brodick played his one cassette over and over: a Kate Bush album. After a few hours, he couldn't make up his mind if he loved the artist or hated her. Relief finally came in the late afternoon with the arrival of a tractor and trailer, the latter containing a dozen local men with a variety of weapons. There was also a mortar, broken down into base plate and tube, and a 12.7mm DShK machinegun with a tripod. Brodick joined the men in the trailer.

At the base of a small hill they disembarked and clambered up to the ridgeline, where the machinegun was set up. The mortar was established on the reverse slope but no attempt was made to dig a proper firing pit.

Forefingers showed him where he should look. 'See? You see? There? Yes? Communists. There. There.'

About three thousand metres to the west was another low hill. Below the peak stood what appeared to be a fort, or a clutch of buildings, reinforced with a sand wall and wire. At least that was what it seemed to be, but the light was beginning to fade. In the valley between the two hills was an orchard and what seemed to be a small farm.

Brodick almost felt sorry for the scrofulous bunch of ill-paid, badly-led, poorly-equipped militiamen or soldiers, left like bait out there on the hillside. How many would there be? Fifteen? Twenty? According to Mirwais and Mungoo, those lads hated their officers, the officers despised the rank-and-file, the Khalqi junior officers hated and feared their Parchami commanders, the Parchami senior officers distrusted their subordinates, and everyone loathed and despised the Soviets. To say it was not a recipe for good morale and a healthy fighting spirit would be an understatement. Most Afghan soldiers were pressganged until the Afghan Army stood at around 80,000 at the start of the fighting season, only to decline to less than half that number through desertions, disease and casualties by the onset of winter—right about now—when the cycle would begin all over again. Officers pocketed much of the pay of the rank-and-file, especially that of absent and dead soldiers.

Afghans crowded around the machinegun, watching the ammunition belt being fed into the breech, apparently arguing about who would have the honour of firing it first. Someone cocked the weapon, someone else fired, the weapon seemed to leap, flame rushed from the muzzle, and tracer fire sped in a long, red, festive stream towards the enemy. Everyone had a go, firing a deafening burst of three or four rounds each. Some wouldn't stop, firing continuously until pushed away by their companions eager to have a go as if this was a funfair and you paid your pennies to shoot at a wooden duck—and miss.

It wasn't clear if they hit anything animate. Probably not. No one was getting a teddy bear prize tonight.

But the enemy could not have failed to notice the muzzle flashes and hear the firing even if the tracers had missed their hill completely. Eventually the enemy fired a mortar in response. The first round soared over their heads with a flutter and fell well behind Brodick and his companions, some three or four hundred yards away, detonating harmlessly, the thud shaking the ground under Brodick, oily grey smoke rising and slowly dispersing. A few minutes later the mortar was fired again, with similar results.

Had both sides planned and coordinated this pathetic exhibition of firepower? Maybe they were all local Pashtuns, related to one another by blood or marriage, and while Mohamed would no doubt want to demonstrate to the foreigner what his brave men could do, those involved had no wish to spill the blood of their neighbours and cousins. Among Pashtuns, blood could only be avenged with blood.

Brodick sat with his back against a large rock, ensuring it was between him and the PDPA post just in case the other side inadvertently succeeded in lobbing a 60mm mortar bomb close enough to pose a real threat, though he knew full well there was no hiding from a mortar bomb. Unlike artillery rounds, which throw forward in an arc, mortar bombs fall vertically, their killing grounds being circular. It occurred to him that he could turn this pointless action into a lucrative business, luring wealthy Americans to Afghanistan at the rate of maybe five hundred dollars a day to have a turn at firing a heavy machine gun at communists. All those rich, retired dentists and their bottle-blonde and surgically modified wives from Florida—the husbands being the kind who enjoyed the fantasy worlds conjured up by *Soldier of Fortune Magazine* and *Playboy*—would just love it. Of course, he would have to hire both *mujahideen* and the Afghan army or militia post to perform in just this manner, avoiding casualties. The clients could be driven over the border and back in groups of perhaps three or four every couple of days, those on the return trip clutching colour photographs of themselves posing as freedom fighters in turbans, waving AK-47s. War tourism. Why not? Where was the harm? At least these Florida dentists wouldn't be shooting elephants or giraffes in Africa. Wasn't he a war tourist, after all?

His journey so far had taken two nights and a day and Brodick still seemed a long way from Kandahar; in peacetime his destination could have been reached in a straightforward drive of three or four hours at the most from the border at Chaman. Not that he was complaining, he told himself: not at all. He had every reason to be grateful. He was alive, in one piece, in good health—thanks to the Afghans and thanks to Mohamed in particular. Never mind the fucking crab lice.

Now it was night again and he was on foot with an escort of five men armed with an assortment of weapons: a shotgun, a bolt-action rifle held together with strips of wire and bands of metal, two Kalashnikovs with the blue worn down so much that they glinted silver, and a Soviet semi-automatic pistol. They were led by another mullah, this time a younger man with very thick, pebble glasses and enormous white turban. He was the one with the 7.62mm Tokarev in his belt, and he walked in zigzags, but quite why this was necessary wasn't clear to Brodick. He kept this up for two hours, but his followers didn't argue or question this weird tactic. They had too much respect for the fellow. Perhaps he was avoiding minefields. Something clever at any rate. But what was certainly unusual was the weather: it started to rain.

It rained very little in Kandahar Province, and some years it didn't rain at all. When it did so it was in the winter months. In any event, the rain was a fine mist, making the desert sticky underfoot and Brodick's clothing and face clammy. The mist descended from low cloud and reduced visibility to perhaps twenty or thirty paces, but it was constantly shifting, moving, a dance of the wet veils. Brodick sensed that his companions didn't enjoy it one bit; they seemed frightened, unnerved by the ghostly shapes moving all around them. Then, out of nowhere, there was a light ahead—diffused, without a source, such as a lamp might shine through curtains. It strengthened as they approached, narrowing and becoming two, then four, burning a gully through the dark and the fizz of drizzle, spreading from right to left in front of them. The mullah kept walking towards whatever it was.

The strengthening light was accompanied by noise: a mechanical sound, like an engine. It was an engine. Engines plural. Powerful engines, a chorus of them. The sound became a roar and, without any warning, an immense shape rose up right before them, hovered right over their heads, and Brodick thought of an alien spacecraft. Lights pulsated through the mist, burning through the haze. It turned away and another monster rose and took its place. The noise was now so loud it seemed to reverberate up through his feet, his legs. Brodick instinctively put his hands over his ears while he looked up and resisted the temptation to throw himself flat, but not before seeing that his fellow travellers were doing the same thing: staring, mouths agape.

They'd wandered into the perimeter of Kandahar airport, now a Soviet airbase.

They stood facing a twelve-foot chain link fence. Brodick realised he had witnessed a Soviet helicopter patrol of two aircraft taking off. Two others had just landed.

Didn't they have infra-red sensors? They must have.

They were going to die. Right there. Now. Either the choppers would get them or the airport protection force would send out a patrol and catch them up against the wire fence. Brodick took another step, put out one hand and touched the cold, dripping wire with his fingers to make sure he wasn't imagining it. At least it wasn't electrified. Yes, they would die here, cut down with a few bursts of automatic fire. And all because of a silly sod of a preacher blundering around in the desert, unable to find his way to the fucking city.

Why didn't the gunships open fire?

Apparently the Afghans began to have similar thoughts. Three turned and stumbled away, their sandals now clogged with heavy mud, weighing them down and slowing them to a stagger, forcing them to raise their knees high, at the same time clutching their baggy trousers, trying to hold them up so they wouldn't get mired in the mud. They blundered off singly into the mist. One man slipped, fell on his arse, dropping his rife. Brodick laughed out loud at the sight as he too backed slowly away from the fence. The preacher was on his own; he called out to them but they took no notice.

What a lovely war.

When headlights cut through the drifting rain, Brodick was ready to put his hands up, drop to his knees and surrender.

It was another motorcycle. 'Mister Richard? We thought we'd lost you.'

*

It was nearly midnight. Brodick had his boots off and lay on his side, a Kazakh rug under him, a pillow supporting his elbow. He was comfortable on the floor: warm, exhausted, but happy to be alive. He'd eaten part of a scrawny chicken. He scratched fondly at the vermin infesting his crotch. He was safe, relatively speaking, having ridden pillion on another motorcycle, one of three machines, the trio roaring around central Kandahar, red and green tracers flying around them, streams of red in, streams of green out. Terrifying, certainly. Exciting, definitely. His hosts had given Brodick a city tour, sweeping through the city's central market, which Brodick realised was intact and showed little or no war damage despite a recent U.S. State department briefing pegged to a single, unnamed "carpet merchant" who'd reported the market totally destroyed by a Soviet airstrike.

The fireworks above their heads—and disconcertingly close around them and between them—was simply the nightly firefight between PDPA militia and military centres dotted throughout the city, and those positions held by the resistance. It was a street-by-street, house-to-house thing. The ritual took the place of television, of pub brawls, of neighbours meeting to chat on corners and over fences. It was entertainment, the Afghan wartime version of the *passegiata*—without females, naturally enough—and it wasn't clear to Brodick if anyone got hurt in those pyrotechnic displays.

A lot of ammunition got wasted, though.

He was in someone's house and they were putting out the candles and kerosene lamps. The firing had died down in the streets. The fun was over; both sides were going to bed. Some of the fighters stretched out on either side of Brodick were already asleep and snoring.

At Brodick's feet was the object of his mission: a large green canister with a screw top chained to the canister itself by a metal chain, much as Mungoo had described. It was curved and resembled a very large hip flask. It would have to be a giant's hip. Poison gas? Biological agents? A vacuum flask for hot coffee? It seemed empty, but then if it was gas how would anyone know? All he could think was that it didn't look dangerous. Brodick's companions had no idea what it was or what it contained, and neither did he.

12

'*Assalaam Aleikum.*'
          '*Waleikum Salaam.*'
     'How are you today?'
     'Well, thanks be to God.'
     'And your family?'
     'They are well, also.'
     'And the sheep? The goats?'

The Special Branch man blushed under his tan and giggled, showing his perfectly white teeth, finding this almost daily ritual both amusing and also somewhat embarrassing. Brodick pretended not to notice.

     'They are well, *insh'Allah.*'
     '*Nashkur Allah.*'
     '*Al-hamdu lil-lāh.*'

The first time Brodick had stopped and talked to his new watcher—the day he'd moved into his new home back in September—the man had told him he was a farmer and, questioned further by Brodick, informed him that he had sheep and goats on his farm. Ever since—and that meant every day except Fridays, the day of prayer—Brodick greeted the man outside his front gate, using the occasion to improve his Pashto and the conventional Arabic greetings common among all Afghans, which was actually coming along well thanks to the time he spent among Pashtuns. Even Mirwais had got into the habit of testing Brodick, teaching him new phrases and correcting his pronunciation. Brodick sent out the occasional glass of tea to his watcher, and sometimes food. Now and then he took refreshments out himself. The secret policeman was portly, with a round head, round eyes and he wore a round white cap. His beard was but a tentative fuzz. He might have been in his twenties. He didn't look in the least threatening. They were unfailingly courteous to each other, and both were scrupulous in maintaining the agricultural fiction. All Brodick did in response to the watcher's presence was to direct visitors whose identity or business was of a sensitive nature to his new home before 9am or after 5pm. For the Special Branch kept pretty regular business hours. Maybe his presence was also a form of security, even if unintentionally so.

Brodick liked his home. It was new, modern, spacious and had big windows that let in plenty of light. It didn't matter to him that it was ugly; he wasn't the owner, he hadn't wasted his own money on it. Someone from General Service Branch, brought in from the SIS Station in Islamabad, presumably, had had blue carpet tiles laid down in the enormous living area, and two air conditioning units fitted to the main bedroom where Brodick slept and worked as well as the living room. Cheap curtains—plain blue—had been provided for both living room and all bedrooms, and someone had had them fitted. Brodick had himself bought two leather and wood folding armchairs and a coffee table from a German-owned furniture factory in Peshawar for the living room; he reckoned on needing something decent to welcome visitors. The walls were painted uniformly white, the floors tiled in what looked like white marble but most likely weren't. For the rest, he'd bought the cheapest stuff he could find as long as it was functional: half a dozen single wooden beds for the four bedrooms along with bedding and foam rubber mattresses, half a dozen upright wooden chairs, a dining table, also wood. There was nothing on the walls except Brodick's maps, and they were everywhere, attached to the walls with masking tape. It was not, then, a home that would find its way easily into *Country Life*.

The property had a garden out back, comprising a big rectangular lawn and a paved area for a table and chairs. When he moved in, the place had had a faded, neglected air. The grass had withered, the plants had long since died for lack of water, but Brodick had resolved to bring it all back to life and it was indeed much better, though now it was winter again the early frost had killed most of it. The front yard was gravel—in itself an early warning alarm if anyone got over the wall and approached the house—and big enough to park three or four cars. The house faced the street, a single lane road that ran along the western perimeter of University Town. On the far side was a scene like the backdrop to a theatrical play: deep blue sky at the top, then hazy, soft azure veils representing the mountains, below that a big, wide band of farmland and, at the very bottom of this expressionist portrait, a dirty brown stripe representing a canal.

There were fields of what looked to Brodick like grain of some kind—wheat, barley, corn, whatever—in which buffalo and other livestock could occasionally be seen browsing, along with storks and sometimes the odd farmer. Sitting out there at the side of the road and facing the big double metal gates of Brodick's rented home, the Special Branch man had the farmland and the Hindu Kush as his backdrop. As for Brodick's place, it could be approached from either end of the street, and it was located on a corner. It was a textbook safe house, pretty much. He reckoned it would take eight watchers working shifts to monitor all comings and goings 24/7; plainly, Brodick did not rate such intensive scrutiny.

But he was being watched quite openly, especially when on the move, and it wasn't because of his by-lines and his magazine articles questioning Pakistan's foreign and security policy. There was much more to it than that. He was watched because of the people he knew, his contacts, his sources. That's what they must be after, and Brodick was having to work harder in an effort to protect them, not just himself.

Brodick had acquired a manservant, a Pashtun named Omar. Of mild disposition, he cooked and cleaned and did odd jobs, and he had enough English to make himself understood. He was from Peshawar, born and bred. He said he was fifty-eight. He had asked for too little money in Brodick's opinion. They argued about it, Omar insisting on the pay he'd asked for, Brodick maintaining it was not enough. Brodick knew because he'd asked around—and he knew he couldn't do everything himself. He also wanted someone who would be loyal and wouldn't tell tales behind his back. Brodick hoped a decent wage would encourage Omar to maintain some degree of discretion, at least in the local community. Of course he had to assume that Omar—his name indicated he was a Sunni Muslim—would share information about his employer with any one of half a dozen Pakistani security and intelligence agencies. That was a given.

*

The following Friday, Hermitage was about to pay only his second visit to the house, ideal timing because the Special Branch man would not be in attendance. Omar had been briefed to keep the double doors unlocked, and to drag them open as soon as the white Land Rover appeared, and then close them again. Brodick certainly didn't want to advertise the fact that his guest was an SIS officer. Hermitage duly turned up in a swirl of dust, precisely at 3pm, and he ran up the front steps two at a time, briefcase in hand.

'Well, this has come along. You must be pleased.' Hermitage strode around with a proprietorial air, inspecting rooms, opening doors, switching on taps, leaping up stairs and dropping down again, Brodick on his heels.

That night guests were expected; all four French and/or Belgian doctors, young, newly-graduated volunteers on their way into Afghanistan, hopefully changing over with four who would, or should, be coming out after a two-month stint. They worked for a Paris-based charity that functioned on a small budget. It couldn't afford hotels for its people. As for Brodick, it was a chance to spruce up his schoolboy French and perhaps learn something about the places where the medics had worked. It was self-interest on Brodick's part, not generosity. He saw it as another potential source of intelligence or at the very least useful background.

Hermitage studied the maps on Brodick's walls, amused by them, smiling broadly as he walked from one to the next.

What did he expect? Tiepolo?

Omar—who'd relinquished his Friday off at Brodick's request so as to be on hand to help out during the Hermitage visit—brought tea and digestive biscuits.

The object neither man had mentioned so far stood on the coffee table, next to the tea tray.

Brodick closed the living room door so they wouldn't be overheard by Omar in the kitchen. He announced that he would play mother. He poured the tea and invited his guest to help himself to biscuits, then excused himself, returning from his study-cum-bedroom—a room secured with a sturdy padlock—carrying a file containing his latest week's CX reports: twenty-seven of them. He no longer expected Hermitage to pay them more than a cursory glance and Hermitage didn't, of course: merely stuffing them into the briefcase and handing back the empty file.

'How is Professor Mungoo?'

'Working hard on the next issue.'

'Good. Glad to hear it. And the fellow who calls himself Mirwais? Have you a name for him yet—other than his nom de guerre?'

'No, I don't. He doesn't feel secure here and I can't say I blame him. There are rumours circulating about the two of them, the usual stuff we've come to expect from ISI.'

'What was his last job in government? Has he said?'

Brodick said he didn't know and Hermitage, by his silence, let him know he was disappointed.

In fact, Brodick hadn't seen Mirwais for months, and Mungoo had muttered something about him having taken refuge somewhere outside Peshawar, but refusing to be drawn further on his friend's whereabouts and activities.

'And this?' Hermitage could no longer ignore the military canister, though Brodick felt sure Hermitage knew perfectly well what it was. 'You brought this back from Kandahar?'

'I did, yes. I should have got it to you earlier, but I was busy and decided to wait for your visit.' Brodick sat down, holding his mug of tea in his lap. He desperately wanted a Lucky Strike but knew Hermitage disliked cigarettes. Hell, this was his own home, for Chrissakes. If he wanted to smoke, he would—with or without the approval of his case officer. When Hermitage patted his own pockets, searching for pipe and tobacco, Brodick immediately put his mug on the coffee table and lit up. 'I'm pretty sure it's not what we thought it might be, but I wonder if you would be good enough to take it back with you and have someone look at it and let me know. If possible.'

The Hermitage foot started its circling, signalling its owner's suppressed annoyance, and it wasn't the cigarette.

'May I speak frankly?'

'Please.'

'I'm not entirely sure, Richard, that you'd really be suited to a career in the Service.'

The moment of silence that followed seemed to last an eternity. Brodick felt he'd been slapped. It hurt, but it was anger not pain that he felt stirring.

Brodick did his best to stay calm and not overreact. 'Why do you say that?'

'Frankly, I think you'd chafe against the bureaucratic restrictions of a peacetime Service. Not that I would wish to detract from the extraordinary contribution you've already made in terms of the quantity and quality of intelligence you're producing.'

Smug bastard. 'Really. Why would I?'

The foot moved faster. 'You have a tendency to go off and do what you think whatever you think needs doing without asking our advice or informing us. That's not how we work. As you should well know by now.'

'I don't want to waste time or bother you whenever there's a new development or opportunity. Not over the telephone. How would I call you and explain this canister over an open landline?'

'Time isn't the point, Richard.' Hermitage pointed at the canister. 'You were in no hurry to hand that over when you got back.'

'Not when I realised it wasn't what we were looking for.'

'But you don't know that yet.'

'In any case, this isn't peacetime. There's a war going on over there.'

The foot carved circles like a propellor. 'But *we* are not at war, Richard. Do you understand? *We* are not at war.' The twin caterpillars locked together.

Brodick could not restrain himself.

'So what are you saying, Colonel? You people want to terminate the contract now, is that right? I take it this has been discussed already with Dryden and London and you've been charged with the job of telling me. Fine. That's why you're here. We're only what, a few months into it, but hey, if that's the way you feel, better end it now than drag it on for two years. I get it. Why not? Pity Cal went to so much trouble over the house, but it's better to clear it all up, I agree. I see that now. I'm glad you've decided to be so open about it.' Hermitage tried to interrupt, but Brodick was in full, furious flood and nothing was going to stop him. 'I'll happily stay on as a journalist. In fact, it might be better for us both. I could take over the contract for the house. I may not have told you but I've a retainer of eight thousand a year from *The Orient*. I've split it down the middle with their Pakistani economics correspondent in Karachi as it seems only fair, but even so, my half will pay for all the basics. Rent. Transport. Food. Clothing. Everything else on top of that will be profit.'

Brodick sounded as if he was talking to himself, an outburst as soliloquy, thinking aloud as if Hermitage wasn't there. 'There's a couple of thousand already from the Inquirer and about the same amount from the *Telegraph*. I haven't calculated earnings from *Voice of America* at sixty dollars a news item, inclusive of expenses, fifteen to twenty-five quid an item from the *BBC Eastern Service*, but I could probably live on radio alone. Yeah, sure, let's do it if that's the way you feel. I don't mind at all.' He obviously did, though, very much. Now Brodick seemed to wake up again to the presence of an audience. He jumped to his feet, strode to the window and looked out, his back to his visitor. His hands were shaking, so he pushed them into his pockets. 'No hard feelings, Colonel. Really. Might be the best thing for everyone. I'm sure you'll find someone else just as able if not more so and certainly more—what's the word—more pliant.'

He didn't believe that last bit about finding a replacement. As for no hard feelings, that was untrue. He didn't believe Hermitage had sought London's clearance. Hermitage was chancing his arm, and Brodick was prepared to call his bluff, though he knew it was a gamble. What an arse.

His sour little speech done, Brodick turned around to face Hermitage. The last few seconds were a blank. He couldn't even remember what he'd said. He marched forward, picked up the canister and gave it to Hermitage with both hands, pushed it at him, in effect, forcing him to take it. It started to come back to him now—where had that come from? Did he really say all that? Was that what he really thought? Jesus. He saw himself standing there, dropping what was left of the Lucky Strike in his half-empty mug, hearing it fizzle, then hitching up his pants, standing back, turning away towards the door to the kitchen, throwing it open and calling Omar to take away the tea things—a signal that as far as Brodick was concerned, the exchange was over.

'My guest is leaving, Omar. Please open the gates, will you.'

What he really wanted to do was beat Hermitage over the head with the bloody canister.

Whatever Hermitage was saying to him now, Brodick didn't hear it. Couldn't. Wouldn't. His ears thrummed with his own blood, deafening him. Rage could be a pure thing, a cauterising fire, but it numbed him. He felt he wasn't in charge of himself. Was this what he really wanted? Was he giving it all up and so soon, without a fight? Things had been going so well. He was a one-man intelligence factory. He was producing more Afghan product than an entire SIS station and probably the whole of the fucking CIA, NSA, DIA and the rest of those rubbish acronyms put together with their billion-dollar budgets and their spies-in-the-sky. And it was no longer chickenshit. He was only writing up the class stuff nowadays. The dross he turned into brief news stories for the ANB, then recycled the ANB material as a source for his own outlets. Yes, of course he'd make out as a freelance journalist. He'd proved he could. He had the by-lines, didn't he? He had his freelance income; he didn't touch his SIS salary. But was it really what he wanted to do? He was dismissing his own case officer, sending him away. Throwing him out, actually. Agents didn't do that. Absolutely not, but he just had. It was insubordination. But there it was—Brodick went over to the living room windows again, hearing the crunch of gravel outside. He saw the white Land Rover reverse out of the drive, Hermitage at the wheel and Omar standing to one side, waiting, ready to close the gates. As Brodick watched, the vehicle straightened out on the street and moved off in a cloud of dust. The gates closed. Omar shot the bolts home, top and bottom, wiped his hands together.

There would be consequences. There had to be.

13

The French medics didn't turn up that evening: neither the fresh quartet of replacements from Paris, nor the exhausted foursome from deep inside Afghan territory. There was supposed to be a handover in two or three days, but something had gone wrong. Or maybe Brodick hadn't been told of a change in plans. To them he was wasn't anyone important, he knew that. He was a housekeeper, the provider of free beds-and-breakfasts. Perhaps the Air France flight to Islamabad had been cancelled. Perhaps it was something to do with whatever was happening in Afghanistan itself. The charity's young doctors were working with Jamiat-i-Islami and given the time of year and the onset of summer and the fighting season, it was possible that Soviet and PDPA military operations had disrupted the medics' withdrawal as well as their replacements' deployment.

There was general talk in Peshawar of an imminent Soviet assault on the Panjshir Valley, and it was in the valley that the medical teams concentrated their work.

Omar had the visitors' rooms prepared. Whenever it was that the two teams did finally meet up, they'd have to share rooms and one bathroom. It would be the second *roulement* that Brodick had hosted and, based on the first, he wasn't looking forward to the second at all. The French—the males in particular—seemed as arrogant as they were ignorant. They seemed to think they were an elite, superior to other mortals, having recently qualified as doctors. They were also phenomenally messy, dropping food on the table and floor, leaving cigarette ends everywhere, never emptying the ashtrays. It never seemed to occur to them to remove their boots at the front door, to help out by carrying food from the kitchen to the table or remove their plates and to wash up. All that domestic stuff was beneath their dignity. Or maybe they hadn't been house trained. They didn't smile, say 'thank you', and they pointedly refused to speak English. They were rude, contemptuous. Some of the females weren't any better. They didn't tip Omar for all his extra work cleaning up after them, laundering their clothes and scrubbing the bathroom which they left in a disgusting state. So much for the beating heart of European civilisation.

Brodick decided that if this next lot—when they eventually did turn up, if they did so—proved to be no better than their predecessors, then he'd scrap the project and tell the charity he couldn't cope and they'd have to look elsewhere. He sent Omar home. There was no point in keeping him at the house, making him wait around all night.

*

He slept badly. He was drinking his second black coffee when Omar rapped lightly on the gate just after 6:30am, and Brodick walked gingerly on bare feet across the gravel to let him in. No, he didn't want breakfast, thanks very much. He turned back to the house as Omar picked up a broom to start the morning ritual of sweeping the floors. Brodick made faces at himself as he brushed his teeth, shaved, took a lukewarm shower, dressed. He had given up on the French; he would put the crisis in his relations with Hermitage and the SIS to one side too if he could, and try to focus on journalism.

Mirwais had promised to introduce him to a military defector, a brigadier-general named Faisal from the Afghan defence ministry who, until a few weeks previously, had been working on integrating supplies of Soviet equipment into Afghan army units. Until his defection or desertion—it wasn't clear which—he had been one of the very few Khalqis left in a senior position and not in jail. Possibly the last of the radicals.

And there was Faisal himself, already waiting quietly in Mungoo's office along with Mirwais. Dapper in ironed shirt and tie, a slight figure in glasses and civvies, he didn't cut an impressive figure, but it quickly became apparent that he was intelligent and self-possessed, a graduate of Moscow's Patrice Lumumba University and various staff officer courses in the DDR. He was still an unrepentant Marxist-Leninist. To Brodick he looked like an accountant or lawyer rather than a combatant. There was none of the usual Afghan swagger. Mirwais acted as translator, sometimes with Mungoo's help, though the officer clearly knew more English than he let on. His home tongue was Pashto, but he was fluent in Dari and Russian.

'You say the Soviets don't occupy Afghanistan. What do you mean?'

'They can't occupy the entire country, even if they wanted to, not with one hundred thousand troops. One hundred and eight thousand, to be exact. They couldn't do so with twice that number. Or half a million like the Americans in Vietnam. So they hold key positions, control major locations and routes. They hold the ring, that's all. They leave the rest to us Afghans, or they try to do so. Though they have a talent for telling us what to do and what not to do!' He gave a loud snort in response to his own sarcasm.

'I don't understand.'

'They see this fight as an Afghan one. They offer their support to us as allies, but they insist they will not shoulder the entire burden of the war; they constantly emphasise that the responsibility for military policy and action lies with the Afghan government, though they have an increasing influence on both.'

'That must lead to all sorts of arguments and difficulties.'

'Yes. Of course it does. They don't have a high opinion of their

Afghan allies, it's true. In any case, they don't want to be dragged deeper into the war.'

'Are they racist in their attitudes and behaviour towards your people?'

Faisal shrugged.

That meant yes.

'So what is the Soviet military role? Can you explain?'

'The Soviets hold the major airbases from which they provide air support. For example, Bagram near Kabul. Ghazni, an important link in the chain between the capital and Kandahar in the far south. Then Kandahar itself. Mazar-i-Sharif and Kunduz in the north. Herat in the west near the Iran border. They fly constant patrols to keep the main ring road—the highway connecting the cities—open. Second, they have major fire support bases—'

'By fire support you mean what exactly?'

'Artillery, armour. Fire support that can bring down indirect fire to support their troops and ours on operations. Direct fire support, too, on occasion. But they don't try to occupy the countryside, villages and towns. They leave that to us, to our army and militia. You don't see much evidence of Soviet forces unless you're in Kabul in the security ministries or near the Makroyan complex where their families live—or unless you fly into somewhere like Kandahar and see their aircraft taking off and landing. They don't use their infantry to try to "take" territory only to have to leave it again and then return months later and do it all over again. It's wasteful. Too many lives lost. They're not like the Americans in Vietnam. They don't use their infantry as expendable bait.'

Brodick shook his head in disbelief. 'Are you suggesting they're sensitive about public opinion back home? There isn't any public opinion in the Soviet Union. Everything is censored. It's one thing they don't have to worry about. The war isn't on Soviet television and there's no opposition to kick up a fuss. Surely the body count isn't much of an issue.'

'How would you know? Have you lived in the Soviet Union? Or do you base your opinion on what you've been told to think by your capitalist media?'

'Be that as it may, General, it's still an occupation.'

'Did the United States occupy Vietnam?'

Faisal was combative, braced for a scrap with Brodick. He wasn't behaving like someone afraid of exposure, of arrest. He seemed remarkably self-assured.

'That depends on your point of view. Many Vietnamese no doubt thought so, but the South Vietnamese government often went its own way despite opposition from its American ally, or simply ignored Washington's advice. I don't think that happens in Kabul, does it?'

'You're not the usual kind of Western journalist, Mr Richard, if you really are a journalist. But even so, your opinions are still second-hand and driven by your imperialist masters.'

'If I may, I'd like to turn to the issue of chemical warfare.'

'There's no such thing in Afghanistan. It's propaganda.' Faisal was annoyed and showed it by looking away.

'Nevertheless, I'm told there is something called the chemical field battalion under the Qal-e-Jangi HQ and based at Hussein Khot near Bagram airbase to the north of Kabul and that it falls under the 234th Gas and Chemical Department in Kabul. Is this true?'

'No, not at all. It's rubbish. Who told you this?' Here the English term "rubbish" was debated by Mirwais and Mungoo. 'Crap', 'shit' and 'balls' were among other possible translations but there was consensus on 'rubbish' so 'rubbish' it would be. Faisal continued: 'The 234th is the designation of a battalion that is used to guard state property in the capital. Ministries, telecommunications. Places like that. It's composed of the sons and nephews of party bosses— in other words, it's what you would call protected employment, and much sought-after. They are conveniently close to home for weekends and will never be called upon to do any fighting.'

'Bottle washers and jam stealers.'

'Something like that, I think. They are Parchamis, of course. Privileged people. Lucky people. Their mummies and daddies are in the Party. As for Hussein Khot, there's nothing there. There's no base. Nothing. It's a ruin, I assure you.'

'It's been reported that the 18th Division of Mazar-i-Sharif and the 20th at Nahrin are responsible for chemical warfare operations in the north and that all chemical warfare units are kept at full strength.'

'It's fiction. A lie. I know the divisions you mention. Someone has been paid well in dollars to make up this story.'

So much for the CIA allegations. But was General Faisal any more credible?

'Tell me about Soviet military supplies to the Afghan authorities. Does Afghanistan have to pay for this aid?'

'Most, yes, though payment is really just a matter of accounting, and like the interest on your capitalist debt, the numbers just keep growing. It's bookkeeping. But not all. Sometimes it's supplied as grant aid. I mean that it's free.'

'And what does the Afghan military want and need more than anything else from its Soviet ally?'

'It's obvious. Helicopters—and more helicopters. Especially the'—another four-way discussion of terminology interrupted the narrative—'helicopter gunships. Yes? You know? The army needs battlefield mobility.'

'Why did you defect?'

'It was only a matter of time before I was arrested. Or worse. I planned it for months, and I had to get my family out first. Once they were out, I could worry about getting myself out.'

The interview continued until lunch, prepared by unseen women in the kitchen and served by Mungoo and his son Fawzi. It was a cheerful occasion, and Faisal joined in. Everyone—every male, that is—sat cross-legged on the floor and ate with their hands. For at least a couple of hours, Brodick forgot all about his meeting with Hermitage and the ill-mannered French medics. He laughed along with everyone else, even though he didn't understand the jokes. The Afghan food was delicious.

And yet. Something about Faisal wasn't right. Brodick couldn't put his finger on it. It was as if he'd delivered a message: namely, that the Soviet occupation was, in reality, a partial and lawful intervention by invitation and that the affair of chemical and biological weapons a fiction dreamed up in Washington. Was he a plant? If so, what did it say about Mirwais, who'd produced him like a rabbit out of a magician's hat? Or Mungoo, for that matter? Was he being played by his two friends?

On the way home there were the usual two motorcycles, but instead of a Peugeot there was a van—a green Ford Transit, very dented and muddy—that brought up the rear. The van didn't disappear this time along with the bikes, but parked at the side of the street as if prepared to spend the night there. It gave Brodick the shivers. It was the sort of vehicle that could be used to snatch someone off the street.

14

Brodick couldn't see who it was at first. He heard something move behind him and turned, startled to see the outline of someone standing in the open doorway, the declining sun behind the stranger. Brodick put up one hand to shield his eyes, but he still couldn't identify whoever it was. He had just returned to the house and was on his way to his room, and had been surprised, even a little frightened, to discover another being in his home. He took two steps back, turning towards the figure, unsure how to react.

'Bonjour.'

He was close now, and he could make out the stranger's features.

She was petite. She was barefoot. She wore what seemed at first to be a nightdress or shift, but which turned out on further inspection to be an Afghan shirt, several sizes too big. It came down to her calves. Her light brown hair was short; it looked as if she'd slashed at it herself with shears for some reason. It looked very dry. Brodick was reminded of a 1928 silent French movie, *The Passion of Joan of Arc*, the heroine's hair savagely cut short in preparation for her execution by burning. A warrior, then: a martyr.

'Richard?'

'Yes, that's me'.

'Mélusine.'

She went up to him and put out a hand. Brodick took it. It was small and warm, and he noticed at once that the skin of her palm was hard and the fingers were particularly strong.

Mélusine held herself erect, head up. She wore no makeup. Her mouth was wide, full. The eyes— well, Brodick couldn't make up his mind about the eyes—were light. They were green or grey, or both, depending on the ambient light. He realised they were each studying the other with great curiosity, openly and without any sense of embarrassment.

'You must be hungry…'

'Not at all. Your man…'

'Omar.'

'Omar made tea and gave me some lunch. It was good.'

'He showed you your room?'

'Yes.' She nodded. 'I took a shower. It's so great to have really hot water and a clean towel. and a bed with sheets, my God! Real, five-star luxury.' She laughed at herself for her outburst. 'I must thank you for this.'

'No need. And your companion.' Brodick looked around. 'There must be someone else, another doctor, with you.'

'No.' Her face darkened. 'He should be here, but Marcel had some difficulty getting out. Unfortunately. He will come later. I hope. A few days, perhaps.'

'What happened?'

'We were separated for a time during a Soviet assault, we were working in different places, and a few days later after the fighting I left.'

'This was in the Panjshir Valley?'

'Yes. Do you have a cigarette?'

'Of course.'

'I never smoke back in France. Only here. Let's sit outside, in your garden. Do you mind?'

'No, not at all. Would you like something to drink? Whisky?'

What wouldn't he do for this woman; any woman come to that.

'Of course!' She smiled at him.

As he went off to get his sacrificial bottle of single malt, Brodick realised that they'd been speaking French, both of them, from the outset. He had even forgotten his own atrocious accent.

Already he was hoping that this Marcel would not appear—not for a while, at least.

*

Early the next morning Brodick found Mélusine sitting on the front doorstep, head between her knees, doodling with a stick in the gravel, totally absorbed in her miniature world of blue, grey and white stone chips. Brodick sat down next to her, but he was careful to do so at arm's length, leaving plenty of space yet not so much as to seem unfriendly. They were in shadow and it was still pleasantly cool. Neither spoke. He watched the stick as she stabbed and poked, dragged and pushed it through the stones. It created hills and valleys, spirals and diagonals, then flattened them. She was building and destroying, making chaos in this world-within-a-world.

Finally, she spoke. 'I need some clean clothes.'

'You can borrow anything of mine. T-shirts, shirts. Whatever you think useful.'

The stick scraped away.

'Okay,' she said after a long pause. Then, 'Are you really a journalist?'

'Yes. Or we can go to the market and you can buy whatever you need.'

'Who is it that you work for?'

He told her.

'But you don't ask questions, Richard. A journalist always asks questions. You haven't asked me any questions. Not one. Maybe you are too polite to be a journalist. Too nice or too shy. You know what people say about you?' She didn't wait for his response; Brodick was sure what was coming next. 'They say you are a spy. A British spy. Or maybe a spy for the Americans. Are you a spy,

Richard?'

'That's impossible to answer.'

The stick stopped its prodding and digging, no doubt to the relief of terrorised ants. 'Why?'

This time they both spoke English.

How many times would he have to go through this?

'Let's assume I am a spy as you suggest, and you ask me that question. I answer by saying, yes, I am indeed a spy. Now what kind of spy would that make me? Absurd. Irresponsible. A fool. If, on the other hand, I deny it: would you accept my denial? Would a denial be sufficient? Would you accept it at face value? I don't think you would. No one would. And if I am in reality not a spy, and I say I am a spy, what would that make me? A fantasist, or something worse, certainly someone mentally or emotionally unhinged. And if I am not a spy and I deny being one, would that convince you? Whether I am a spy or not in reality, you would always get a denial, and it would be up to you to believe it or to disbelieve it. Your question can only ever have one answer.'

She cut through his talk. 'But I would know if you were lying. I always know.'

'Really? You do? But maybe I'm a very good liar with much practice. Aren't spies always good liars?'

Mélusine turned to him and laughed.

'I would still know, my dear. It's called intuition. It's interesting to me that you assess the alternative responses not by whether they are true or not, but that you judge them by the effect they might have on me. Should I be flattered? Or frightened by someone who lies so easily?'

'We'll have to see, won't we?'

Brodick had made a point of not staring at her. Not at her face or her body or any part of it. He forced himself not to, to drag his eyes away. But he did glance at her, did make eye contact in quick flashes, rapid, surreptitious glimpses the way a camera constructs a narrative from a series of stills. And he did begin to see her as a whole, and what he saw intrigued him. She was so small. Were Mélusine to stand in front of him, the top of her head would probably just reach his chin, or maybe not. So, five feet, or a whisker over five feet. Maybe five-one. She was slim, but far from skinny. Again, perhaps fifty kilos, if that. Her hands were as small as a child's but much longer, the fingers tapering and, curiously, he saw that the tips of each finger pointed up like the tips of Turkish slippers. They were beautiful, he decided. But the most striking aspect of her wasn't the wonderful smile, the fullness of her mouth, the eyes, no, it was quite simply the feet. They were small yet cherubic, plump, and Brodick tried and failed to imagine those feet walking across the Hindu Kush, the peaks of Kunar Province, the arid hills of the Panjshir Valley. It seemed physically impossible. He wanted to feel those feet, take them in his hands, feel their plumpness, their shape.

She'll think me a foot fetishist.

'But you haven't answered my question.'

'I'm not going to.'

'You're afraid I'll know you're lying. You're afraid of being caught out.'

'Not at all. I thought I'd just explained that there is no satisfactory answer to your question.'

'You're evasive. I didn't expect that, Richard. It's up to me to decide if your answers are satisfactory or not. So—why haven't you asked me any questions? By now I thought you'd be thirsting for details of the latest fighting.'

'I'm sure you will tell me what it is you want to say when you're ready. I'm not going to badger you with questions. Not now. You're my guest. I think you need sleep and food and rest—and a clean shirt—not an interrogation. That will come later, maybe.'

'You're far too polite to be a journalist. It follows that you must therefore be a spy.'

'Perhaps I'm both.'

'Both? Both? No. Impossible, I think. You would end up schizophrenic, caught between being forced to keep secrets and being compelled to tell everyone everything you know. The stress of the contradiction would be too much, even for such a polite Englishman.'

Brodick heard the sound of bare feet shuffling towards them from the front door. It was Omar, announcing breakfast. Brodick wondered if the van was still parked out there on the street.

*

'You still haven't asked me anything.'

'I'm sure you'll tell me when you're ready.'

'So courteous, you English.'

'I try. But I'm not English.'

'What are you?'

'I'm a Scot.'

The conversation was sporadic, interrupted by mouthfuls.

'You don't sound Scottish.'

'Is that a prerequisite?'

She shrugged. 'Do you live there? In Scotland?'

'When I'm in the UK I do.'

'Were you born there?'

'No. In Lebanon.'

'Your mother was Scottish?'

'No. French. With some Irish blood thrown in.'

'Your father?'

'Yes and no.'

'Sounds complicated.'

'My ancestors have been Scottish since the 12th century. They were Normans.'

'Colonisers. Settlers. Invaders.'

'Yes, I suppose that's right. It's called history.'

'But that was a very long time ago, and they became Scots, but you aren't. Maybe you want to think you are, and like many people you want to wrap yourself in this flag or that one, because it gives you a better sense of who you are, but it's not real, Richard. It's no more real than a pretty fairy story. We are more than our passports and our genes and our flags. I hope so, anyway.'

They tucked into soft white cheese with cucumbers, mint, basil and loaves of hot, round, thin bread, washed down with milky tea, very sweet and flavoured with cardamom. Perhaps Mélusine expected Brodick to say more, but he didn't. Omar placed a bowl of small apples and pomegranates on the table.

They ate with their fingers, occasionally using knives to spread cheese on the bread.

'Well, as it so happens you're in luck, Richard, because I do want to tell you a little story.'

'I love stories, especially true ones.'

'I don't think you will love this one. It's about my colleague, Marcel, and his boots.'

'His boots?'

'Yes, particularly his boots. Marcel is very attached to his boots. Or he was. I'm afraid I was unkind about them and hurt his feelings and now I feel quite guilty. You see, if I hadn't been so horrid, we would not have separated. It's all because of the fucking boots. He will blame me, I'm sure, but I blame the boots.'

15

'I don't know how much you know about us. I mean, the charity. We work in teams of two, usually male and female. A newbie is always accompanied by someone with at least some experience of working in Afghanistan. There's no attempt to match people in terms of personality or background. We're not that well-funded. Everything is done in a hurry. Hand-to-mouth you call it in English. It was Marcel's first time, and my second; you might say it was a case of the nearly blind leading the totally blind, and the totally blind in this instance was most unwilling to be led by the partially-sighted. He had the usual problems some males have with females. Fear. Fear of me proving to be better than he was. And like so many pairs, we hadn't met before. In fact, the first time we saw each other was on the flight out, and even so we didn't sit next to each other. Then a day in Islamabad and, in our case, four days at Green's Hotel in Peshawar. I would say it was just enough time to develop a strong mutual dislike.

'And Marcel? Well, he's a certain type, let us say. A Protestant boy originally from Nancy, you know it? It's in the north. His parents are solid bourgeois, comfortably off, whatever that means. Don't the rich always say with a shrug of embarrassment and guilt that they're just comfortably off? The father a doctor, a specialist of some kind—Marcel did say, but I wasn't paying attention—his mother a lawyer. Marcel an only child, badly spoiled. Nice family car, a little one for wifey, big classical apartment in Le Marais, right on the Place des Vosges—in fact, next door to what was once Victor Hugo's home—and a place in the country inherited from his grandparents or great-grandparents. Whoever. What was Marcel like? Well, he was very sure of himself professionally. I think arrogant would not be too strong a term for it. He thought the world of his own skills as a doctor—though just like the rest of us, he'd only just qualified. Out to save the world from its own worst instincts. I'm sure it's partly a matter of his upbringing, his schooling, and partly the effect of his medical training. The arrogance.

'Physically, I didn't think much. He was—to me, anyway—unprepossessing. Not that I think looks matter one way or the other, though I do like good legs on a man. Anyway, he was tall, which is nice, but thin, narrow shoulders, bony, bad skin, long hair, dark. Very French, you might say. Awkward around women, awkward around me. We didn't talk much, and when it became apparent that he wasn't interested in anything I had to say on any subject, including our work in Afghanistan, I basically stopped trying to be nice or helpful. Perhaps too quickly I came to the conclusion that the guy was a prick. My fault, okay? He spent all his time smoking and drinking and eating with the males in the other teams: the pair going in, like us, and the two pairs that had just emerged. He ignored me and the other female team members. I ignored him. He disgusted me, to tell the truth. It was not a good start, and I accept that perhaps I could have handled the situation better, but he just pissed me off, and that was that. I hate a misogynist with a fucking huge ego and that's what I decided he was, and I was so disappointed to be facing months with this guy in the wilderness. Unusually, he didn't even try to make a pass at me. Though that was something of a relief, I have to say.

'Off we went with our friends from Jamiat-i-Islami. He made it clear on the very first morning that he was very proud of his boots. They were the best, of course. They were combat boots, American, and I think the kind used by paratroopers. They had thick soles with steel plates in them, so he said, and the uppers were made of very soft leather. But I saw they were lace-ups and that was a big mistake, but hey, I wasn't going to say anything. Like, haven't you heard of Velcro, asshole? Why should I? I thought, well, Marcel doesn't want advice from me, a mere woman. God's little gift of genius to the medical world can find that out for himself.

'Our first stop he took around ten minutes to remove his boots, and when we moved on, maybe longer to put them on again. He laced them the German way, criss-crossed, and I think there were at least twenty pairs of eyelets.' With a finger she drew the crosses in the air. 'Can you imagine? Maybe U.S. paratroopers never take their boots off. The laces were as long as I am tall. No, I'm exaggerating: but only a little, I assure you. So we had to wait for him to take them off, and wait again for him to get them on. At our third halt I suggested he dispense with some of the eyelets, you know, just do up a few of them to speed things along, but he just cursed me, called me a stupid bitch. That was just the first day. It was not a good start! Every evening he cleaned them, using some special cream on them, then buffed them to a high shine. They were like mirrors. Ridiculous man. He went to bed with them— when we were lucky enough to go to bed, of course, bed being a very relative term in this part of the world—and then he would hug them in his arms as if they were a couple of little puppies or babies. He was afraid, it turned out, that someone might steal his precious fucking boots. I only wished they would.

'As time went on, this fear became a morbid conviction, an obsession. Everyone—the Russians, me, other French doctors and of course every Afghan on the planet—coveted the boots and we were all conspiring to steal them. On the second day an Afghan, half-jokingly, offered to swap a pair of used Afghan sandals made out of tractor tyres for Marcel's U.S. paratrooper boots. He was taking the piss or maybe trying to offer some sensible advice. Both, perhaps. I don't know. Marcel went crazy. He lost it totally, something you and I know one should never, ever do in front of an Afghan, let alone an entire group of Afghan males of fighting age. The loss of face is truly terrible. It cannot be repaired except by leaving or dying and I would have gladly accepted either action on his part. Little did I know then that my wish would come true. He was an embarrassment. Marcel didn't see this at all. He wasn't aware of it. Of course, this kind of sandal is common because they are actually very hardwearing, cheap, and perfect for the terrain. I think the Afghan was joking because he could see how silly those boots really were, and he preferred his peasant sandals anyway.

'Naturally I told myself that Marcel wasn't all bad. There had to be some part of him that was decent, morally upright. After all, he was giving up months of his time and knowingly putting his tender young life at risk just to help save the lives of wounded Afghans. Just like the rest of us. I told myself *that* was what mattered, not his little eccentricity. We're all of us odd in some way, no? Of course we are. You too. Me certainly. Nobody's perfect. I'm sure I have habits I'm not even aware of that would irritate the hell out of anyone who had the misfortune to live with me in close proximity. That's the thing. These trips—these excursions into the unknown, into danger—allow us—force us, actually—to study closeup another human being, like peering through a microscope into someone's else's mind and heart. It's all laid bare, yes?

'Enough philosophy. By the third day the Afghans with us were laughing at Marcel behind his back. When we were resting up they'd throw glances at him and laugh out loud, or just snigger. When they offered to carry his pack, he accepted. Another bad mistake. And he kept falling back, saying he wanted to rest. You can imagine, Richard. It went from bad to worse. He was always hungry, and yet always complaining of the food. When they could they fed us okra—you know it, yes? Ladies' fingers. It's a delicacy here, or at least if not here then in Afghanistan, and the prices are high for ordinary people because the Soviets are buying up the food, draining the swamp of water so the fish can't survive: a deliberate policy. But they kept giving us okra and goat meat because we were their guests, because they have immense respect for doctors, like we are witchdoctors or something, powerful people with supernatural powers. I wish! Marcel said he was sick of okra, that they were trying to poison us. He once threw his plate at the cook. Can you imagine? The precious okra rolling in the dirt, and stamped off in his ridiculous boots to sulk among the boulders. I tell you I blushed. I wanted to hide away, to shrink, to become invisible, to beat him, to bash his teeth out. I swear he made me so ashamed to have anything to do with him, to speak the same language, even to be French.

'God, how I hated him at those times.'

She looked up at Omar and smiled at him. 'That was a lovely breakfast, thank you.' Brodick translated her words into an approximation of Pashto. He was jealous of that smile, he realised. Omar bowed slightly, pleased.

Mélusine continued: 'Nothing much happened at first. People came to us every day with their complaints. You can imagine, no? The usual. The headaches, the stomach pains, the sore throats, the snotty-nosed children with fever. There was always a long queue, and it got longer as news spread of our presence in a particular village. We didn't stay long in any one place, of course, because our hosts were afraid the Soviets and PDPA would be able to pinpoint us. And it allowed different villages the honour of looking after us. That's how they saw it. Not as a burden to be suffered, but an honour to be enjoyed. One thing you must already know. The Afghans in one village very often don't even know the name of the next village. The most remote villages—the ones untouched by government in any shape or form—are not only the most traditional but also the most innocent when it comes to communism or Islamic militancy. It's those with a government school or state-financed irrigation that are tainted with either or both ideologies. Anyway. What was I saying? Ah, yes. Of course it wasn't our role to hand out aspirin or bandage a sprained ankle. We were waiting for the fighting, and the wounded. I had an enormous bottle of red vitamin pills. The pills were big, like miniature flying saucers. I handed them out for everything. A placebo. You have toothache? Take one of these.

An abscess? Take two. You have menstrual pains? Ah, take three of these at four-hourly intervals. Are you shocked? Am I the first cynical doctor you've met?

'We could see the Soviet preparations. You know. First, much aerial activity, not so? Small reconnaissance aircraft were always flying back and forth. Then the armour was massed below the valley, mostly tanks and self-propelled artillery. Like a huge parade, all in rows. Neat. Textbook stuff, by the book you say. Our side was getting ready, too. Special arms and ammunition caches were being prepared and camouflaged. Weapon pits and trenches were dug. We could feel the tension. Fighters were coming in, mostly at night, and were directed to defensive positions. Then came the bombing. The strafing. They seemed to be working off a list, applying so many tons of explosive to villages A, B and C. Then D, E and F. Fixed-wing aircraft. Then helicopter gunships. They were bombing in batches. So many tons of explosive per metre. According once again to some military textbook.

'Now I know what you would like to hear, Richard. You would like me to say the Soviets deliberately targeted civilians. It's an easy thing to say, to believe, to report. But is it true? What they wanted, certainly, was to clear the villages of human habitation, to reduce them as potential centres of resistance. If civilians got in the way, that was just tough. That's my opinion for what it's worth. So civilians did die under the bombardment. Of course they did. Of course. Women, children, the aged. And they achieved their purpose, in effect, because civilians did evacuate, and the villages did become uninhabitable for the most part. All this took about a week. Then the artillery started, and that was terrifying. The sound of the artillery shells whooshing over our heads and crashing with such terrible blows, raising smoke and dust. Horrible.

'Our Afghan friends pushed us into caves or underground irrigation channels. It was scary. Yes. Of course. I was very frightened. Sometimes all I could do was lie flat on my face and pretend to be a stone. The artillery bombardments would last an hour, two hours, and they would roll like a curtain of flying steel and dust up and down the sides of the valley. By this point—I think it was the ninth or tenth day—the wounded started to appear in significant numbers. Walking wounded and others carried by their comrades. Quite a few dead. They seemed to think we could revive them. Maybe they thought we owed them that. The price of all that okra.

'Wounds caused by shell splinters aren't pretty. Many died of shock—blood loss—before we could do anything to help them. Our situation was not good. We operated on the floor of a cave or a ditch. Or a field. We had to operate triage—those most likely to survive took priority. The rest…' She shrugged, leaving it unsaid.

'Hygienic? Of course it wasn't. You know, those Norwegians and Swedes at the Afghan Surgical Hospital here in Peshawar sneer at us. They call us amateurs, and worse. But you know what?' Her voice rose, words bursting out. 'They've never had to amputate in field conditions with so little equipment. They say they get our former patients and when they open up the sutures all they find is sepsis. Maybe so. But they are alive, for God's sake, alive after ten days, even two weeks, of being carried over the mountains on the backs of men and strapped onto mules. But they don't think about that. All they do is criticise. Let them go there and do what we do.

'Let them fucking try!'

She paused as if short of breath.

'Marcel cracked, you see. It was the artillery fire. He was working fine until then. The shooting and bombing—he was okay with all that, as well as anyone is. But he couldn't stand the artillery attacks; the shellfire was too much. Those detonations. He threw himself to the ground and started shaking.' She mimicked the tremors by clenching her fists and shaking them. 'He couldn't work under artillery fire. I don't blame him, not at all. It could happen to anyone. His nerves couldn't take it. It wasn't a matter of choice or willpower. He wasn't a coward, not at all. He would drop, and crawl under any cover he could find. He couldn't help himself, really he couldn't. Everyone has a breaking point, Richard. We cannot judge. We shouldn't judge. Then, one day, our village was attacked for the third time, but this time by ground troops. Marcel panicked. He ran for it—he ran out into the open, his wonderful boots on, shining beautifully in the sun like a couple of sun-kissed children, but unlaced. He didn't get maybe six or seven metres before he tripped. He fell on his face. They saw him, or they saw movement. They were shooting at him, or where they thought he was, with their automatic weapons. Little fountains of dirt where the bullets hit. The Jamiat-i-Islami commander in our village went out and grabbed him by the collar and dragged him to safety, risking his own life for Marcel.

'Those stupid boots.

'I felt pity for him. I didn't know how to comfort him or what to say. I was embarrassed. I felt useless. For once my medical training was no help to either of us. I still feel bad about it, don't you see?

'From that time on, we worked separately, in different places.'

'You're saying Marcel was taken out of artillery range.'

'Yes.'

'But not you.'

'Me? No. It was okay. Well, kind of okay.'

'And then?'

'Well, the Tajiks had a plan. They used a screen—small groups—to fall back, to lure the Soviets up the valley. They resisted the Soviets, but only a little. It was a kind of flirtation. Come and get us, seemed to be their message. The Soviets pushed in. The Tajiks then sent teams to attack the rear elements: the supply trucks, the bridge-laying equipment. They did enough to block the valley, trapping the attacking force inside so they couldn't replenish their fuel or water. Then, finally, the main Tajik force attacked from the flanks, cutting the invaders in two. They launched the main assault before first light to avoid Soviet air power. The Soviets didn't withdraw: they couldn't. They fled. I counted dozens of tanks and other armoured vehicles burnt out, wrecked, littering the tracks and roads. Jamiat-i-Islami said there had been a series of small, running battles, skirmishes really. It was a traffic jam of broken armour. You could smell death all the way down the valley: the stink of Soviet corpses. But Tajik dead as well.'

'So then they brought you back?'

'Yes.'

'And Marcel?'

'They said they would bring him out later, once he'd rested. He was in a bad state. I saw him before I left. He was trembling all over. He was curled up under a blanket and didn't speak, didn't say anything. He was—how do you say—catatonic. In very deep depression. He wasn't eating and couldn't sleep. He didn't respond to anything. It seemed to me to be a complete breakdown.'

'That's awful.'

'It is, yes. Very much so. I stayed with him for three days until he seemed to improve. I didn't want to stay but I felt I had to. I couldn't just leave him. So I remained with him until he was eating again, sleeping a little and moving about, but he wouldn't talk to me, not a single word. So having done what I could—and it wasn't much—I left. And you know what?'

Brodick waited.

'He'd lost his boots, you see.'

*

'Is there anywhere in Peshawar to swim?'

'I think so—at the Khyber Inter-Continental Hotel.'

'You haven't been?'

'I went there for something else, for the *Sunday Times*, to check on some British mercenaries hired by the Pentagon, but I saw the pool. It looked okay, it looked clean and it didn't seem crowded. In fact, I didn't see anyone.'

'You've never been there to swim?'

'I've been too busy.'

'That's crazy, Richard. We all need to take a break, isn't it so?'

'You're right.'

'Will you come with me to the pool?'

'Sure.'

'Today?'

He would, but Brodick didn't get a chance to reply. Someone out on the road was banging on the metal gates. The suddenness was vicious, some sort of assault, and it had made him jump. Omar hurried out as more metallic crashing rang out like cracked church bells rung by demented monks. Both Brodick and Mélusine had run from the table to the window, watching as Omar came back, escorting a visitor Brodick recognised as Fawzi Mungoo.

'Mr Richard.' Fawzi was gasping for air. His chest heaved and his face glistened with sweat. It dripped off his beard onto his shirt. He'd apparently run all the way from his father's house, about half a mile away, and now he stood in the hall, leaning against the wall.

'What is it, Fawzi? What's happened? Omar, fetch him some water, please.'

'Come quickly, Mr Richard. My father's house has been attacked. He's asking for you.'

16

The gate was open, but Brodick could see over the top of it anyway. The front yard was carpeted not in last year's leaves but paper, an ocean of it, sheets of white A4 paper: some of it torn, some stapled together, mostly typed, printed, copied. There were handwritten notes, too, apparently translations. As they walked in he saw that there were pieces of metal and of plastic scattered about. The papers looked as if they were pages from the ANB— Brodick bent down to look more closely and they were in Dari, Pashto and some were in English. Fawzi led the way to the door of the guest room and sometime office. The door leaned drunkenly on one hinge and it was badly cracked. Someone had lifted it off two or three of its hinges to smash a way in.

The Xerox had gone, the smaller photocopier had been shattered and its bits and pieces were on the floor. That was what the plastic and metal outside had belonged to.

Mungoo's table had been broken up as if with an axe, so too the legs of the wooden chairs. All it was good for now was firewood. At least the furniture had been cheap. There was more paper; the place was awash with it, almost ankle deep.

There was no one there.

Brodick had a terrible thought that chilled him.

'Where's the professor?'

Fawzi saw the look on his face. 'He's okay, Richard. He's not hurt. He's at home. My mother is very scared and my dad's looking after her, trying to reassure her.'

Brodick hadn't realised it before now, but he saw that the work room and the house weren't directly connected. The entrance to the house—the family living quarters—was around the side, and usually reached by another gate in an alley. That could have saved their lives.

'They heard nothing?'

Fawzi opened his hands, shrugging. 'My dad heard something, but he didn't know what. It was probably the door giving way. He certainly wasn't going to go outside unarmed, to investigate. My father doesn't even have a gun.'

'Very wise. What time was it?'

'He said a few minutes after 3am. Will you come to see him now?'

'Yes. Did they get the names and addresses of your father's contacts?'

'No, he never wrote them down in there. He says he didn't keep records for that very reason. They're mostly in his head, which is the best place for them.'

Neither Mungoo nor his son knew that Brodick had been assiduously collecting names and addresses of ANB sources and Mungoo's contacts and salting them away in his metal trunk.

'So no one's been compromised: their identities, addresses, telephone numbers?'

'No. My father said he doesn't think so.'

'I hope he's right. Who does he think did this?'

Fawzi sighed. 'It could be Burhanuddin's people. It could be ISI. It could be both.'

'Is that what your dad said?'

Fawzi didn't reply.

They walked from the annexe to the house. In the half minute or so it took to get there, Brodick had already made up his mind what had to be done. He knew it had to be done right away. They had to send a strong, defiant message to the attackers, whoever they were.

Burhanuddin and his ISI patrons were certainly at the top of Brodick's list of suspects.

There would be no time to seek Hermitage's approval, or even to inform him.

First, there would have to be a news release embargoed for 16:00 local time. He would write it, include a quote from Mungoo, obtain Mungoo's approval for the text, and issue it to all the agencies represented in Islamabad: Reuters, the American Associated Press, Agence France Press, United Press International, and Novosti. Maybe the Iranians and Chinese as well. And the local English-language newspaper, the *Khyber Mail*. Also *Dawn in Karachi*. To hell with translations.

Second, he would write his own news story for print and radio.

That done, he and Mungoo would prepare a special edition of the ANB, concentrating on the attack, but bringing in other acts of violence perpetrated in Peshawar and the FATA by persons known and unknown since the Soviet invasion. It should be finished within a few days. There was no such thing as bad publicity—well, there was, of course there was, but in this instance, the event should boost subscriptions. The violence would be tantamount to a stamp of media respectability. The ANB would have to be taken seriously.

Brodick made up his mind to beg, borrow or steal another Xerox machine.

He would try to convince Mungoo to allow him to move ANB production to his own house. The copying, the stapling and the distribution could be done in one of the spare rooms, even if editorial work stayed with Mungoo. Hopefully, it would lower Mungoo's profile, and spread the risk.

And it would give Brodick greater control.

Brodick would encourage Fawzi and his father to put their heads together to try to find a few trustworthy men—hopefully family members or at least close clansmen—who could take turns guarding Mungoo's place, especially after dark. They'd have to be armed and paid, of course, and Brodick resolved to cover the cost one way or another.

He had to persuade Mungoo it was the right thing to do.

Sorry, Mélusine, but there's going to be no swimming today.

While Fawzi started tidying up the mess of paper and splintered wood, Mungoo entered and found somewhere to sit, leaning forward, staring into space. He looked dishevelled, confused, exhausted. Scared, too. Brodick started laying out his plan of action, but it was some time before Mungoo looked at him and appeared to pay him any attention. Brodick went through it again.

17

Brodick dreamed he was talking to Hermitage, who looked irritable. Brodick told him there were two kinds of people: Limpets and Loners. Limpets' lives were measured, determined, judged by their attachment to others and, when one attachment moved away, rejected the Limpet's grasp or died, another attachment immediately took his or her place. Had he, Hermitage, read a short story, *The Darling*, by Anton Chekhov? No? The Limpet's wellbeing depended entirely on the person to whom the Limpet was so firmly attached. Loners, on the other hand, conducted a lifelong conversation with themselves, a perpetual monologue, and Loners were so wrapped up in this internalised selfhood that no one could understand them and they couldn't understand others. They had no real, lasting attachments: or at least, none without incessant conflict. They were no good at marriage or parenthood. Sometimes a Limpet could become a Loner and vice versa. Brodick said he was one of these. He was a Limpet-become-Loner.

Hermitage, definitely a Loner in Brodick's opinion, wasn't listening, but was waving his pipe in the air, waggling both feet— bare for some reason—in time to his writhing eyebrows and telling Brodick off for multiple sins: he shouldn't have written the press release about the attack on the ANB without first consulting Hermitage himself; he shouldn't have borrowed another Xerox machine—from a pleasant USAID couple who'd just settled in Peshawar—nor should he have run off a new edition of the ANB so quickly without seeking approval and, finally, he shouldn't have set up the borrowed Xerox and the production of further editions of the ANB in his own home in University Town; it was bad security. All of it was bad security. Mungoo was responsible for himself and his family; he might be Brodick's sub-agent, but that didn't mean Brodick had to take care of him. On this point they disagreed. Wasn't Brodick Hermitage's head agent? Wouldn't Hermitage take responsibility if he, Brodick, was in imminent danger of being murdered? An exasperated Hermitage took his pipe out of his mouth and said it wasn't the same thing at all. His eyebrows leapt off his face in fury and scurried across the floor.

Then, abruptly, Brodick wasn't dreaming. The dream was over. He was awake. He was thinking that, in a patriarchy, men were encouraged to be Loners, and women instructed, even compelled, into the role of Limpets. He thought of the much-abused Mary, Queen of Scots. Someone had come in very quietly and was standing over him and even though it was very dark in his room he saw at once who it was: not Queen Mary but Mélusine.

At first he thought he was imagining her, another dream extrapolated from the first.

'Are you awake?' She was whispering, though she didn't need to. They were alone in the house. Omar had long since gone home.

He took her hand and she let him hold it, not limply or passively, but encouraging him by pressing it slightly with those strong fingers of hers. This was no dream; she was real after all.

He pulled her closer, put her fingers to his lips. She didn't resist. On the contrary, she bent over him, after a moment's hesitation climbing carefully onto the single bed, her weight on her knees and arms. She slowly pressed down on him.

'You have a good body.'

So did she, but Brodick said nothing.

She raised herself and removed the shirt she'd borrowed, then lay back down on him. He wore nothing under the sheet, which was now on the floor.

He smelled the soap he'd given her: an astringent whiff of Wright's Coal Tar.

They moved, slowly, gently, and it went on for quite a while as they explored each other, breathing in each other's breath, tasting each other, becoming one by degrees. There was a final rush or sprint of pleasure, and Brodick thought the bed was shaking and jumping so much that it would collapse. Mélusine wasn't quiet any longer. She seemed to be talking, then shouting, at herself, in French, and Brodick realised to his surprise that the hoarse breathing—gasping—was himself. Near the end she was growling and grunting—actually growling, he wasn't imagining it—then screaming, rearing up and plunging down. In pain and ecstasy they rode each other.

When Brodick woke in the morning, he was alone. The bed hadn't broken, after all. He had had no more dreams that he could recall, but he realised that for the first time, really the first time, he felt something more than lust or gratitude towards a female human being and the sum of her body parts. What it was he felt he didn't rightly know, not yet.

There were ninety-six words in Sanskrit for love. Only one in English.

Maybe he'd turned back into a Limpet.

✳

They went swimming at Peshawar's Khyber Inter-Continental Hotel, with its broken road sign and its empty guest rooms. The place was still up and running, international tourism's ghost ship, a last and lost port of call on what had once been the hippy highway to the ultimate hashish high. There were still staff around but few, if any, guests. The restaurants and coffee shops carried "Closed" signs on their doors. They paid a youth in a hotel uniform for entry to the pool area and went off to change. When Mélusine re-emerged, she wore a black, one-piece swimsuit and Brodick found it hard not to stare, though the suit could only mean one thing: to Brodick's disappointment this was to be no casual dip, a little flirtation thrown in with a soupçon of romance, but rather a serious business of physical exertion. Mélusine strode immediately over to the deep end, her expression one of serious intent, tested the temperature with one foot, stepped back, jumped, somehow jack-knifed in the air, and dived. There was little splash to be seen or heard. She slipped into the water like some sleek creature that lives its entire life in water and proceeded to cruise up and down in what Brodick knew as the crawl. Her feet scissored, her hips turned, her arms rose and fell, each time a hand poised for an instant in perfect timing before slicing into the water and pulling, her head only turning every three revolutions of the arms for air. Everything worked in unison, yet seemed so effortless. Disturbance of the water was minimal. She turned at the far end underwater, a silent torpedo. Her timing was perfect, a magnificent choreography of movement.

Brodick counted twelve laps before she swam to the side where he sat, pulled herself up on her arms, looked at him and smiled.

'Oh, how I love this. How I looked forward to swimming when I was in Afghanistan. It's superb. Are you just going to sit there or are you coming in?'

His reward, when he did so, was a very wet and probing kiss, a huge hug, her arms around his neck. She pressed herself against him. He couldn't help himself, making her laugh as she reached down.

'Your push-button manhood is impressive, Richard, my dear. Men are so obvious! And by the way, don't let anyone tell you that size doesn't matter because it's a lie, and it's not one you will ever have to worry about, at least not until old age. Maybe we have time before our flight, don't you think?'

They found a spot on the grass out of sight of the hotel windows and balconies, and they agreed that even someone strolling into the pool area from the hotel wouldn't see them, at least not at first. So they spread their hotel towels side by side, and made love in the open, the risk of discovery and the sense of being under an open sky only adding to their excitement.

'I'm going to swim again.'

'I'll join you, but we've only got five minutes.'

'Yes, chief. Sure chief.' She gave him a mock salute and was off again, cutting through the water.

Brodick was nothing less than captivated. His friends at school and the university locker room had had another apt though vulgar term for it. He was, he had to admit, totally cunt-struck. He was pretty sure there was no Sanskrit term for it.

*

Thermals rising from the beige, baking plains of south Asia lifted and dropped the little white Fokker F27 turboprop like a toy so that it bucked and bounced its way across Pakistan. Mélusine remained unconcerned, betraying no sign of nervousness as the passengers were advised to keep their seatbelts securely fastened. Some passengers, Brodick noted, were praying fervently.

'Your father.'

'What about him?'

'He's still alive?'

'No, unfortunately not.' Brodick was looking anxiously out of the porthole or whatever it was called.

'Where did he live?'

'In retirement? Outside the village of Clonakilty, near the town of Cork in the Irish Republic.'

It was too much detail.

'So he retired to Ireland?'

'Many years ago.'

'What was his job?'

Brodick didn't like the direction this was taking. 'A diplomat.'

'And he was born in what year?'

'In 1921, I believe. Why the interrogation?'

'I'm so sorry. Do you object? Do my questions embarrass you,

Richard?'

'No, no. Not at all.' It was easier to lie.

'But you're uncomfortable. I can tell from your body language. You're tense.'

'I'm a lousy flier. I hate flying as a matter of fact. I find it scary.'

'You protest too much and you're not the nervous type, Richard. Truth is, you don't like me to pry. Don't worry. I won't tell anyone your secrets. I just want to know you better. You're not just a casual fuck in the grass. You should be flattered when a woman says something like that to you, no? So, we were saying: yes, in 1939, when Great Britain reluctantly declared war on Nazi Germany over Poland, he would have been eighteen. Right?'

'Yes.'

'But he didn't join the armed forces. Why?'

'He joined the diplomatic service. He was good at languages. He went to school in France, and he was fluent in Russian a while later.'

'So, I think you mean to say he was a spy.'

'I didn't say that—' The plane gave a sudden lurch, dropping like a stone for what seemed like several hundred feet, throwing Brodick's gut into his throat, then rolling over onto its right wing which quivered and twisted outside the porthole next to Brodick, who thought for a horrible moment the entire wing might be wrenched off the fuselage, throwing them to their deaths.

'Richard, it's okay. I'm sure he did important work in the war. I don't question his achievements.'

It seemed so improbable that a newly qualified doctor, a Frenchwoman in her twenties from Bordeaux, would know anything at all about William Brodick. Why would she? True, his dad had written an amusing memoir of his early years as an SIS officer immediately following his retirement, but few people outside the UK were likely to be familiar with it or with its author. It hadn't been translated into French as far as he knew. His father had indeed done important war work, as had so many people, but Mélusine couldn't possibly know anything about that.

His most spectacular wartime achievement had taken place in Lisbon. It was sometime in mid-1943 when William Brodick, just turned twenty-two, succeeded in turning an officer in the Abwehr, or German military intelligence, a young man not much older than Brodick himself. William Brodick had seen at once that the German, the number two in the Abwehr's Lisbon station with the rank of major, was uncomfortable in his role, indeed, he had been uncomfortable in his own skin. He was vulnerable and lonely. He had a dark secret, and—given prevailing attitudes and legality of his situation—a guilty one. He was homosexual, and William Brodick had exploited his vulnerability to great effect in winning the German intelligence officer over to the Allied cause by persuading him that Hitler had already lost, and that his secret would be safe with the British. Extraordinary, in that the previous year had been such a grim period in the fortunes of the Allies, both at sea and in Asia. All it had taken, apparently, was a patient ear and gentle reassurance. Kindness of the weaponised variety. Having an agent in place inside the Abwehr had turned out to be of inestimable value in reassuring London that the breaking of Nazi codes at Bletchley had not been detected by the enemy. Important war work—yes, indeed.

'You'll come to Paris.' It was said as a statement, not as a question.

Brodick turned to her, taken by surprise.

'If you come for a weekend or a few days, and let me know in good time, I'll join you. I'll come up from Bordeaux. We can be together. I'll give you my address and telephone number.' Mélusine put a hand on his leg.

'That would be great. I'd love that.'

'Don't wait too long. Otherwise I might forget you.'

'Why did you ask about my father?'

'I'm guessing, Richard, okay, but I think you admired him very much. You looked up to him. He was a god-like figure. I imagine I can see him; he always wore a three-piece suit, black—or maybe, how do you say, pinstripe—double-breasted, wide lapels, and he carried one of those tightly furled umbrellas—am I right? Yes? The English gentleman, or Scottish gentleman. Did he wear a bowler hat, too? I imagine also that he was away much of the time, for weeks, for months, but the distance only reinforced how you felt. You wanted his approval and you wanted his love. You wanted him to hug you. You wanted him to play with you. They were feelings you as a child would not have understood. But that did not make them any less strong. Perhaps you knew the legend but not the man himself—and perhaps he didn't really know his own son. How am I doing so far?'

'Pretty good. But it would apply to most children, surely.'

They had begun their descent to Islamabad airport, Brodick clutching at the armrests.

'You modelled yourself on him. Forgive me for saying this, but you wanted to be like him. Reserved. The stiff upper lip, born to rule. Boys all want to be like their dads. In your case: persuasive, urbane, sophisticated, suave, manly, a warrior in a tailor-made suit and old school tie. The British Empire personified, no? But you never could quite get him in focus, could you, because he was never there, hmm? He was like a mirage, a little out of focus, always floating away out of reach into a sepia-tinted past. You loved his smell. What was it? Whisky? Cigars? Some kind of cologne? How do you say—aftershave?'

'Gin, pipe tobacco, sweat.'

'Ah, yes. How English. Sorry, Scottish. Though I'm slightly surprised it was gin and not whisky. And of course you were packed off to boarding school in England, which didn't make things any easier. Such an inhumane British thing, tossing children away into institutions like that. Torturing the hearts of young children, killing them silently on the playing fields of Eton! The price of patriarchy. And where were you born, Richard, if you don't mind me asking?'

'I did say. Beirut.'

With a bump they were down and rolling along the runway, to Brodick's immense relief.

'And your point is?'

'My point? My point, my dear Richard, is that you are not going to change the world. Sorry to be the bearer of bad news. You will not end the Soviet occupation of Afghanistan. You are not Lawrence of Arabia or that racist hero adored by the English, Winston Churchill. You will not maintain British colonial power in this area. No. That's all finished with. You have only the power to be the artist of yourself, you understand, to become the man you want to be. You are not your father and never will be. The Soviets aren't your father's Nazi enemies. The so-called freedom fighters aren't the French Resistance. Wanting them to be won't make it so. So sorry. Right now you are trying to be your father and you want to fight his war. Don't. That's in the past. Find yourself, Richard. Be yourself. Live in the future. Don't stunt your own life. Find your own drama and be your own hero. Maybe as a newspaperman. I believe in you, Richard, not in your trying and failing to become someone or something else in the pages of an old history book. Look in the mirror. See what's there. Truly. I mean this. Every word. Talk to what you see. Have a conversation. Listen to yourself. Then become that person. Live within yourself. Trying to live outside what you are is the way to madness. If you want, I will help you by being there for you.' She leaned over and took his chin with her hand, turning it and kissing him on the mouth just as the doors were opening, not caring who saw them.

18

He was a small man with narrow shoulders. Physically, he seemed vulnerable. Had he been a woman, journalists would have called him petite. Instead they described him as slightly-built, being little more than five-three. He dressed in white, the colour of death. Pristine, well-starched white cotton, with a long black beard he constantly fingered, pulling at it nervously with delicate fingers. The white, lightweight and fringed *potu* was folded over one shoulder. His skullcap was white, also. The message seemed to be one of religious purity, of an innocence in direct conflict with the man's considerable reputation as a sociopath and killer. The eyes were large, calf-like, yet his look was penetrating, even intimidating. The nose was an immense beak, a pirate's hook. The voice was deep, strong. On either side stood his bodyguards, a dozen bearded men in shades and black turbans, for the most part clutching the fashionable and sought-after AKSU-74 submachine guns. It was quite a theatrical display, intended no doubt to impress and dominate.

Brodick understood that Burhanuddin was entitled to be addressed as *'Qari'*: that is, a title indicating that he was an outstanding reciter by heart of the Qoran. Burhanuddin was also widely believed to speak fluent English and to understand it well—but he insisted on having everything he said translated into

Pashto—as well as every question put to him. He was not going to speak in the arch-tongue of Western imperialism.

He had chosen for this rare press conference—only the second Brodick had attended—one of the newly-built mosques funded by Saudi Arabia: a massive, brutalist structure in concrete and coloured glass in downtown Islamabad. It was certainly big enough. It could have hosted thousands, and no doubt often did. Burhanuddin's media audience of perhaps fifty journalists, local and foreign—along with a sprinkling of diplomats and Pakistani officials—had no chairs on which to rest their backsides, but a well-polished marble floor and scattered carpets. Brodick didn't intend to plant his arse on a carpet: they were all too likely infested with vermin, especially bed bugs and crab lice. So he squatted on his heels until he became weary and retreated to the edge of the proceedings, partly behind the usual phalanx of television cameras and crews, where he could sit on the cold marble.

Burhanuddin had media appeal: he was always controversial, always fiery and his hostility towards the Western media seemed—not without irony—to attract ever more attention. The first hour of the monologue proceeded with painful slowness, with every paragraph being translated into American-accented English. It was all about the humbling of empires, the inevitable destruction of imperialism, communist and capitalist, being but two sides of the same debased and corrupt coin; this was an inevitable historical process as prophesied by the Prophet (PBUH). Only Islam would be victorious. The Russians had already failed. Communism was the enemy of mankind. The Soviets simply hadn't accepted their defeat, but they would, and soon.

Transcripts of his speech were distributed in English, Pashto and Dari.

None of it, in Brodick's view, was remotely newsworthy. Only the event itself.

The prepared speech was over.

Burhanuddin stepped forward and peered out at his audience.

He raised an arm and swept it around the room as if embracing those present. His voice rose in volume and pitch.

'Among us today there are enemies, even here, even now. In this very mosque. In this holy place. The infidels lurk in the background, hiding themselves under cover of being journalists.'

The atmosphere changed at once. The audience was no longer slumped, bored out their wits. Some—especially the foreigners—were visibly alarmed. Others reached for pens and notebooks. This was what they'd been waiting for. Burhanuddin would not disappoint them.

The translator's words brought Brodick back from his daydreaming, He scribbled the words down, using T-line shorthand and looked up, only to see Burhanuddin turned towards him. The Afghan leader seemed to be looking right at him. Other members of the audience turned, too, and tried to see whoever it was that Burhanuddin seemed to be accusing of being a traitor, though Brodick was partly obscured by the television cameras and their operators.

The translator, again. 'It's no surprise that we have spies in our midst, spies planted by foreign intelligence services in an effort to sabotage the liberation of our country from atheism. What does surprise me, and disturbs all Muslims everywhere, is that Pakistan permits this, that it allows such unbelievers to move among us freely, without hindrance. Some of these spies and saboteurs even live in Peshawar, in defiance of government regulations. We know who they are. We know their names. We know where to find them.' Again, Burhanuddin turned and seemed to stare at Brodick.

Brodick scribbled away.

Burhanuddin was pointing, not using a forefinger—which would have been discourteous—but all five fingers and palm of his right hand, in Brodick's general direction.

'We say this to the traitors and spies. The enemies of Islam will be found out. They will be uncovered. We will destroy our enemies wherever they are to be found and regardless of their identity. Their press cards will not save them. Their passports will not save them. This is not a threat, brothers, but a fact. I say to you traitors and spies: leave. Leave now, while you have the chance to do so. Stay, and you will face the holy warriors of Islam.'

So that was the news story Brodick would write for his several outlets: that the leading Afghan Islamist leader backed by Pakistan and Saudi Arabia denounces Western journalists as spies and threatens to "destroy" them.

Cowley, the Reuters man, grinned at Brodick as they trooped out into the sunshine, and slapped him on the back. They'd occasionally shared a beer or two during Brodick's brief visits to the capital.

'Hey, well done, mate. You seem to have got under his skin and no mistake. I'm quite jealous but, if I were you, I'd take a break for a while. Fame is all very well, but it might be wise to lie low for a few weeks. The south of France should be good at this time of year. In the meantime, are you up for a pint this evening?'

In the street outside the mosque Brodick thought he saw the Transit van, still caked in mud and dust, parked across the street. Was it really the same one? Had it followed him all the way to Islamabad? It seemed unlikely. If the surveillance team were ISI, they'd have no need to bring the same vehicle down the Grand Trunk Road. That in turn indicated that it wasn't ISI—so who did the van belong to? Who else besides was keeping tabs on him?

*

'My dear chap, wonderful to meet you! Really. Thank you so much for coming in to see us.' Brodick's hand was pumped hard, shaken up and down and tugged—Brodick's host held onto it as if it might escape Her Britannic Majesty's vice-like grasp. 'You've been doing great things on the Frontier. You have had the good fortune to make a real difference, and how many of us could say that in all honesty, eh? Damn few, I dare say.'

His name was Jasper-Cole, Sir Stephen Jasper-Cole, High Commissioner. He was short, round, bald, in a starched white shirt, collar undone, the knot of his tie—Club? Regiment? University?—

halfway down his chest, his French cuffs rolled halfway up hairy forearms, his black pants held up by black braces. He was on the toes of his black brogues, bouncing with enthusiasm, faked or real, and still he gripped Brodick's hand, pulling it towards him while simultaneously moving backwards in little hops in the general direction of his desk which seemed as long and as wide as the flight deck or a football field. Jasper-Cole was a human cannonball of diplomacy. 'Now I want to hear all about it, everything. I want to hear about Professor Mungoo. I'm very sorry to hear what happened, but equally I'm very relieved he and his family were unharmed. I don't suppose we'll ever really know who was behind the attack, but I do feel we ought to do something for the good professor, don't you? One can't help but feel sympathy, and I think his *Bulletin* is a splendid effort.'

Brodick's mind was grinding backwards, reversing, trying to get a purchase somewhere in this hosing down of friendly if not overwhelming verbiage. He'd taken a taxi, leaving Mélusine to make her own way to the medical charity's office in Islamabad, and from there to the hotel where they'd agreed to meet up eventually. For some reason he'd been brought in to see the high commissioner straight after the Burhanuddin press conference, and clearly Sir Stephen welcomed him not as a journalist—he'd have had to have been one of the BBC's celebrity presenters to be afforded such an effusive welcome—but as a spy. Jasper-Cole had been fully briefed, that much was clear, and presumably it was Hermitage who had done the briefing. If the high commissioner knew, how many others in the high commission would be in on his little secret? Now he was plunged back into the high commissioner's torrent by the relinquishing of his hand, which he took back gratefully, flexing his fingers to get the blood flowing again. He'd been released, and was being urged to take a seat, and did so, only to realise they were alone, that the high commissioner's secretary had left along with the man in the suit who'd delivered him to Jasper-Cole's lair.

Doing something for Mungoo was at the top of Brodick's own agenda, and the fact that Jasper-Cole seemed to be thinking along the same lines made him feel exuberant with fellow-feeling, almost lightheaded. At last he really was going to do something practical for Mungoo, something that would please the old man and make a positive difference. He'd made use of Mungoo ever since arriving at the start of his assignment—yes, Brodick had exploited him—and now this was his chance to help Mungoo and his wife in return, perhaps by getting them out of the country for a decent break, away from the violence.

Maybe the British weren't really so awful, after all.

But Jasper-Cole's tone changed during Brodick's self-congratulatory thoughts, breaking into the warm glow. 'He's not really on our side, though, is he? Your professor? The chap seems to entertain what we might call leftist views; something of a dangerous luxury, wouldn't you say, in Peshawar?'

Brodick was so taken aback he wasn't at all sure how to respond.

'Is he a practising Muslim? I did wonder. You see, I had the impression that he's rather more secular than your average Afghan.'

'I suppose so. Yes.' Was there such a creature as an "average" Afghan?

'He has leftist friends, too, I gather. Related to the late President Daoud, isn't he?'

'Only by marriage, not by blood. If he does have leftist friends, it doesn't necessarily follow that he's sympathetic to the Soviets. He isn't at all.'

'Well, that's a relief. I did wonder where his loyalties lay. Thank you for setting me straight. In fact I was wondering whether a visit to London at our expense, you know, as a guest of the Foreign Office, might help him work out his priorities, help correct any erroneous views he might hold about us, about the Soviet occupation. What do you think?'

Everything was back on track, after all.

'I think a visit would be wonderful. It would be a great tribute for his work with the ANB. He could do with a break, a rest, especially after the latest incident, and he certainly can't afford to travel abroad on his existing means. It would impress him, I'm sure, though I don't know about sorting out his views.'

'We'll give it some further thought, Richard. Thanks so much for coming to see me. My door is always open. You're doing wonderful work on the Frontier and I really wanted to meet you after hearing about all the great work you've been doing. We're all very impressed. You really are a chip off the old block, eh?'

Jasper-Cole bounced to his feet.

Was that it? What, two minutes? Three? So much for wanting to know "everything".

It seemed a good moment to exploit the situation. 'I was in fact wondering—it's only a suggestion—whether we might award Professor Mungoo a modest monthly stipend of some kind for his work with the *Bulletin*. Or perhaps a British Council scholarship if such a thing exists.'

'Those are useful suggestions, Richard. I'll talk to Tim about it. It's rather in Tim's bailiwick, don't you think?'

Brodick knew that when a British official said something was "useful" it meant it would be consigned quickly, quietly, to one of Her Majesty's standard-issue waste bins, never to be resurrected.

Obviously Mungoo was already taking covert monthly handouts of cash from the SIS, but that wasn't what Brodick had meant. He wanted to help engineer a measure of official recognition for Mungoo's championing of free speech, something overt that would provide a degree of public respectability, placing a seal of approval on his role. An award, of some kind, even an absurd gong presented by a princeling at Buckingham Palace.

The human ball bounced on its shiny brogues towards him and Brodick found his right hand mangled again before being herded away in some haste by the high commissioner's secretary— appropriately clad in black and white very much like the livery of a border collie—to the door, down the stairs and out into the open air. At least she hadn't nipped his ankles.

*

170

Brodick's next ordeal was at the lunch table, an expanse of polished oak, in the Hermitage villa. Hermitage himself presided at one end, facing the windows. Brodick sat on his left. Opposite, on Hermitage's right, was a stranger who'd risen a few minutes before from the depths of a leather Parker Knoll armchair and offered Brodick a limp, clammy hand along with a limp smile and introduced himself as Dr Nathan Pardoner. He'd spelled out his own name, letter by letter.

They'd taken their drinks with them to the table, Brodick's being a very stiff gin and tonic served by Hermitage. Had he done it on purpose? Did Hermitage feel he deserved it? Was it to disorientate him, make him more amenable? Perhaps he was being unduly paranoid and this was simply how Hermitage liked his own drinks. Delicious, of course, but after a few sips he could feel it kick in and his head started to feel a little numb: pleasant enough, but it was not the best choice of drinks when trying to stay alert. Brodick simply wasn't used to drinking. The strange and prudent Pardoner sipped dry sherry.

'Richard, Nathan is your new case officer, with immediate effect.' At these words, Pardoner smiled wanly and the fingers of his right hand adjusted the heavy black frames of his spectacles. 'I'm to be head of station, taking over from Jamie Dryden. He's moving on to bigger things.'

'Congratulations, Colonel.'

'Thank you. It's Tim. Please do call me Tim.'

The dining and living area of the Hermitage villa seemed to have been furnished straight out of a John Lewis catalogue: solid, respectable, middling in taste and cost, understated and entirely predictable was Brodick's judgement. The only personal touch Brodick had seen so far was an Omani dagger and belt lying on the mantelpiece over the fake fireplace. The hilt and scabbard of the traditional weapon, and the belt, seemed to have been hand-worked in solid silver and semi-precious stones. A gift from Sultan Qaboos himself, apparently. No doubt for services rendered— against Marxist rebels—in the scorching wadis of southern Dhofar.

Hermitage poured the white wine, a Riesling.

They began on the starter: grilled aubergine, olive oil, red onion, anchovies.

Brodick tried to show polite interest in the newcomer. 'What was the subject of your doctorate, Dr Pardoner?'

'Religious Studies. Are you a religious man, Richard?'

'Not at all. Sorry.'

'Ah, well.' He looked disappointed.

'Your dissertation was published?'

Of course it had been, but Brodick wanted to seem interested. He needed an ally if it was at all possible, though unlikely by the look of him. Dr Pardoner nodded, fiddled with his glasses. It was quite a "tell".

'And the topic? If you don't mind me asking?'

'Dante's Beatrice: Outrageous heresy or Augustinian myth.'

To which neither Hermitage nor Brodick had any response.

'I understand you were born in the Lebanon, Richard.'

So he'd read Brodick's file. Full marks.

'I didn't have much choice in the matter.'

Nobody found it amusing. The atmosphere seemed strained. It would hardly be surprising, given the frosty nature of his last meeting with Hermitage. The relationship between them was not unlike that of an estranged husband and wife putting on a brave public face for the benefit of an outsider, in this instance Nathan Pardoner. Their little tiff wasn't mentioned, naturally, but hung in the air. Brodick wondered if Pardoner had been briefed on their spat. Almost certainly he had. The question was what he would do about it. Would he try to repair the damage—or wrap things up and send Brodick packing?

'Professor Mungoo… He's your primary sub-agent?'

'You could say that, yes. He is.'

'You have how many now? Sub-agents? All told?'

'I haven't really added them up, to be honest, Dr Pardoner. The number fluctuates. I'd say seventeen or eighteen regulars or thereabouts. Unwitting, all of them, aside from any suspicions they may have about my activities. I'm pretty sure Mungoo realises by now that I'm not simply a journalist. Less than, or more than. I think we can assume that he believes I have some link or links with the UK authorities, formal or otherwise.'

Dr Pardoner leaned towards him, keeping his voice low. 'Most of these sub-agents were provided by Mungoo over the past eighteen months or so?'

'I wouldn't say "provided", Dr Pardoner. That's not the word I would use. Many, not all, were introduced by, or recruited through Mungoo and his *Bulletin*, yes. That much is true. He's opened many doors for us even if he isn't aware of having done so. I'm certain Mungoo isn't fully conscious of just how many or who they are because I have made separate, individual arrangements with several and we meet separately.'

'You're certainly very productive, Richard.'

'But…?'

'But nothing. I meant that quite sincerely.' Dr Pardoner glanced at Hermitage, who responded with the slightest of nods.

Brodick waited to hear what would follow. It seemed to him this little drama had been rehearsed. Hermitage watched, listening to them, thinking only heaven knew what, the script running in his head.

Pardoner removed his glasses and examined them close up. Then he polished them with his white napkin. 'I was so sorry to hear about the attack and criminal damage. I read the news release and I'm glad you managed to bring out a new edition so quickly after the event. That was fast footwork.'

All three men waited in silence while the plates were removed by someone who appeared to be a servant, lavishly turned out in baggy pants, puffed sleeves and turban as if he was an extra in a theatrical production of *A Thousand And One Nights*. He appeared to be Sudanese or Egyptian and a member of the high commissioner's catering team, on loan for the lunch. When the room was clear again, Brodick spoke up, looking at Pardoner and Hermitage in turn.

'I told the high commissioner—'

Hermitage raised a hand. 'We know. We heard.'

'What do you think?'

'About what?'

'About my proposal that something be done to reward Mungoo for his work with the ANB.'

There was something akin to distaste on Hermitage's face. 'We'll consider it, Richard. We will. It will take a little time. These things do. You've heard the high commissioner's concerns about Mungoo, of course. The Americans are, as I think I said before, nervous about your professor.' Brodick noticed for the first time that Hermitage wore a large gold signet ring on the pinkie of his left hand. How had he missed that?

'Presumably they are now your concerns too, Colonel. Sorry, Tim. I recall you saying something similar about Mungoo's politics. Maybe they're being fed this poison by ISI. Maybe they're envious of the amount and quality of product we're producing. Maybe it's a combination of both: professional envy and an ISI whispering campaign.'

All Brodick had in response was a fidget on the part of the twin caterpillars.

Another pause as the main course intruded: lemon sole, new potatoes, asparagus, served up by the man in fancy dress, expressionless and unctuous, bowing as he withdrew. Certainly this was a welcome change from the usual biryani. Maybe the expressionless, silent server moonlighted as an assassin was the next thought in Brodick's somewhat befuddled brain.

Hermitage rose, came around the table with a bottle of Rioja. Brodick could feel the effect the drink was having on him; despite the air conditioner rumbling away it was making him sweat, partly because of the effort to try to stay focused.

'I'd like to know your views about something we're planning to publish as a special edition of the *Bulletin*. I think you'd want to see this and I'd appreciate your opinion.' Brodick reached down under his chair for his document case. He felt the blood rush into his face and neck as he bent.

Hermitage's caterpillars danced, then locked. As he straightened up, Brodick saw one of the Hermitage feet wriggling wildly, a worm on a hook. 'Perhaps we could wait until the coffee, if that's all right. *If* you don't mind.' Pardoner smirked, and Brodick felt a little flicker of hatred, freed from his subconscious by the cumulative effect of the gin and wine.

19

Now was his chance. Coffee had been served and drunk in silence. Brodick unzipped his document case, slid the AA-size papers across the table to both men: two each, stapled together. He kept one set for himself. On the first sheet was a map of Afghanistan and northern Pakistan in outline with North West Frontier Province, FATA and the Durand Line. On the Afghan side, the provinces, provincial centres, airports and the circular highway were delineated. Around the edge of the map were boxes and arrows connecting the boxes to locations on the map. Each box contained the details of Pakistan's special forces units.

Originally, the map had obviously been colour-coded but was now black-and-white with some grey shading where the colours used to be.

'As you can see, of the approximately 6,000-strong complement of Pakistan's Special Service Group or SSG, half are according to this Soviet map currently deployed on Afghan territory, comprising four of the eight SSG battalions, each battalion numbering seven hundred men organised into four companies, and broken down further into platoons and ten-man teams. Let's say 2,800 men—or nearly 3,000. That's the equivalent of a brigade in the UK army, I believe. In addition, you'll see there's a fifth battalion deployed in FATA.'

'Where did you get this?'

Brodick wasn't going to relinquish control of the proceedings.

'In one moment, please. Let's turn to the second sheet. There's a simple key to the map, and the terminology is given in English, French, Spanish and Chinese, representing the languages of the five permanent members of the UN Security Council and most of the ten non-permanent members. At the bottom is a brief description of the SSG, its origins in 1956, and its deployments in Pakistan's subsequent wars and counter-insurgency operations. It claims the SSG has received training from Britain's Special Air Service Regiment, that it works with CIA special action groups in the FATA, and that it has worked closely with both the Jordanians and the Chinese. The balance of the remaining special forces units seems to be deployed mostly in Kashmir facing the Indian sector and in the far north on the disputed Siachen glacier.'

Pardoner looked over the top of his glasses at Brodick. 'Do you have one of the originals?'

Brodick ignored the question and pressed on. 'What we're looking at here is a full battalion of about seven hundred troops divided between Nangahar and Paktiya provinces, another company in Kandahar Province, two more companies in Kunar, and more units—and this surprised me—in the areas around Herat in the west, Mazar-i-Sharif and Kunduz in the north as well as close to the Soviet border. Even in Badghis and the Wakhan Corridor. There are two platoons working in the Ghazni area. Obviously the main focus is on those Pashtun areas close to the Durand Line.'

'Richard, where did you get this?'

'Please, Colonel, er Tim, I'll be happy to take questions when I've finished. *If* you don't mind. These troops pose as Afghan *mujahideen*, dressed and equipped as Afghan resistance fighters. The commissioned officers are mostly Punjabi and the rank-and-file largely Baluch or Pashtun. They sometimes wear black, or carry special markings of black-and-white rectangles. They are sometimes attached to Afghan resistance groups, particularly the forces of Burhanuddin and Hezb-i-Islami, Pakistan's favourite Afghan clients and the ones best equipped and funded. As you well know.'

Brodick looked up.

'Finally, I understand these documents were distributed to the heads of delegation of all fifteen members of the Security Council on July 22 this year, when the Soviet Union put forward a resolution condemning what it called foreign aggression in Afghanistan by the Pakistani armed forces and what it called U.S. mercenaries. The resolution was of course quashed by the Americans, British and French. The Chinese abstained despite close relations with Pakistan.'

Brodick was almost done. 'What I would like to know, if I may, is whether this is genuine.'

There was a long pause. Hermitage's foot waggled and his eyebrows writhed. Pardoner fiddled with his glasses, taking them off and putting them back on.

Pardoner broke the silence, 'So you don't have the originals.'

'No, which means this could be a clever fake. Misinformation. Which is why I asked the question.'

Hermitage looked hard at Brodick. 'It's not a fake, Richard. This is authentic in so far as any photocopy can be. Whether the Soviet allegation, and the details they provide here in their memorandum,' he tapped the papers with his pipe stem, 'are accurate is another matter entirely. Where did you get this, Richard?'

'From one of my informants. One of my sub-agents, I should say. He's a former intelligence officer in the Khad. He says he obtained a copy of the document from a contact still in the Afghan intelligence service and working in Kabul.'

'Does he have a name, this agent of yours?'

'Mirwais.'

'You've mentioned him before as a friend of Mungoo's. His real name?'

'I don't have a real name.' The lie came easily. 'Only a *nom de guerre*. He's a former Khalqi. He was arrested immediately following Taraki's assassination. At the time he was deputy chief in the Khad for the Kabul region. His immediate boss was shot. Mirwais managed to escape his captors. Previously he had headed the Khad offices in Ghazni. He was a student Khalqi, one of the founding members of the PDPA faction in 1968. He's lucky to be alive and he's in hiding. He's very much afraid ISI will track him down.'

'He lives in Peshawar?' Hermitage was asking all the questions.

'Yes, or somewhere on the outskirts.'

'A close friend of Mungoo?'

'I suppose you could say that. Mungoo is no communist, and they're very different in their origins and views, but yes, they are friends. They go back a long way.'

'I'm sure Mungoo will know. Get the name from him.'

'Sure.' Brodick had a notion of what would happen if he did supply the name. It would end with Mirwais in an unmarked grave.

'What are you going to do with this, Richard?'

'We're going to publish. Of course. No question. It's of no value as intelligence, as you've just pointed out. As far as I'm aware, this hasn't been made public before. As you see, it's stamped secret across the top and the distribution list is only thirty: presumably two for each Security Council delegate. We'll produce a special edition of the *Bulletin*. Mungoo and I have discussed it at length. We believe it'll demonstrate the *Bulletin's* non-partisan stance. It'll get him a lot more paying subscribers and just maybe we'll break even, perhaps make a small profit. It will get us more intelligence, more defectors and the like. What's important, though, is that it's going to be a huge boost to the ANB's reputation. It's a scoop, and a breakthrough story for the *Bulletin*. It'll put the ANB and Mungoo on the map. It's to our advantage, too.'

Pardoner wrinkled his nose as if he'd detected a bad smell.

'Thanks to your informant: a former intelligence officer and a Communist.'

Hermitage took the unlit pipe from his mouth and started

scraping out the bowl with a metal instrument, the burnt bits discarded into an ashtray.

What Brodick didn't say was that the Dari and Pashto translations had already been completed, and the first copies were being run off the Xerox machine as they spoke.

Hermitage was on his feet, holding up the wine bottle. Pardoner and Brodick shook their heads.

'May I offer some advice, Richard? I really wouldn't publish this. I strongly urge you not to. It isn't in your interest, or ours or that matter. But for your sake, and especially considering the growing doubts about Professor Mungoo's loyalties, don't. Don't do it. You'll only make Moscow very happy and upset a great many closer to home. I'm talking about ISI and their Afghan clients. People like Burhanuddin.'

Brodick didn't really care what Moscow felt or what Burhanuddin thought. This was too good a story to miss and a wonderful opportunity to build the ANB's cover for intelligence gathering.

*

Pardoner drove. He sat upright and slightly bent forward in the driver's seat as if nervous or short-sighted or both, his pale hands gripping the top of the wheel. He glanced frequently up at the rear-view mirror. Brodick noticed that he was imperceptibly speeding up and slowing down again, the standard method employed by SIS personnel—head agents included—to detect any car that might be following. Brodick had noticed that the battered old Renault carried a standard Pakistani registration, not CD plates as he'd expected, so it had to be a vehicle kept in the high commission pool and used at random by members of staff of various ranks and sections, most of them not SIS. Which was in itself useful when an SIS officer wanted to move around without attracting attention.

'I know things haven't always been easy. In Peshawar, I mean.'

Brodick said nothing, waiting to see where this would lead.

'And I understand you've had your difficulties with Tim.'

Brodick made no reply.

'It must be quite stressful being up there alone on the Frontier.' Pardoner threw him a quick glance. 'Now that you're under surveillance by ISI.'

Brodick grunted. So they knew. He would not allow himself to be drawn.

There was a dirty white Datsun pickup behind them that Pardoner seemed to be watching.

'I hope we'll be able to establish a mutually rewarding relationship, Richard, though I have to say that, mm, I won't be up to see you in Peshawar very often because my duties pretty much restrict me to Islamabad, but I hope we can come to an arrangement that suits us both. Maybe you could come and see me once every fortnight or so. Is that something you think you could manage?' Another glance. 'You can put the air tickets and hotel charges on expenses. I know you file features through Reuters from time to time, so it might not be all bad. Come and have dinner with us. With my family. You can relax, and we can talk shop. There are other perks. I mean the odd bottle of wine or scotch from the high commission commissariat, for which there'd be no charge.' Pardoner turned to look at Brodick, his mouth stretching into a half smile, eyes invisible behind the shifting reflections of his glasses.

'Sounds good.' Brodick's tone was non-committal. He kept his eyes on the road ahead as if he, and not Pardoner, was behind the wheel. So they were offering him free weekend breaks. Nice.

The Datsun had turned. It wasn't following them after all.

'Do you want a woman, Richard?'

The question took Brodick utterly by surprise. 'Do I...?'

Had he misheard?

'Do you want a woman? It can be arranged.' Pardoner was driving slowly now, being overtaken on all sides, oblivious of other drivers sounding their horns. For no particular reason Brodick noticed that his new case officer wore a charcoal suit, white shirt and plain maroon tie, his collar and the knot undone in a concession to the heat.

'No, but thanks all the same.'

Clearly they didn't know about Mélusine.

'Sure?'

'Sure.'

So here was the second sweetener. The evangelical Dr Pardoner, student of Dante, in the role of pimp, offering him tricks with a professional sex worker, airfare and personal services billed to HM Government in return for dropping his pretence at upholding journalistic ethics. Pick our side, Richard, follow orders, and we can make life very agreeable indeed. If you insist on trying to live by standards set by others, choose ours. We're a family and we look after our own. Lie back and think not of Mungoo and the ANB but of Empire and Mrs Thatcher, bless her. Hell, what did Mungoo matter, anyway? He was just another fucking Afghan, and an old, bookish one at that: a relic long past his usefulness and near the end of his particular road. What did this friendship of theirs amount to, anyhow? Envelopes of cash, presents, praise. In return, access to Mungoo's contacts, his information and insights. For a time it had been mutual interest. And temporary; he didn't need Mungoo now. Brodick had vacuumed up all of the old man's contacts, his friends, his sources, their phone numbers and addresses. He'd filched everything of value, pillaged Mungoo's memory and ransacked his mind. The loot belonged to Brodick and he was in control of the ANB. All he wanted now from the professor, alive or dead, was the old boy's name on the masthead.

Espionage was a cruel business. It would be so much simpler to be rid of the ambiguity. A high-end call-girl, endless fucks for a fortnight or whatever, and no recriminations, no damage to the bottom line. Free booze and flights to the fleshpots of Islamabad. This, then, was the sweet world offered by Dr Pardoner. Brodick senior had once laughed at his recollection of a Saudi delegation's visit to London and had marvelled at the princely visitor's seemingly inexhaustible sexual appetites. The UK station had run out of women—maybe males as well—for the VIP guests, and had had to signal SIS stations abroad for urgent reinforcements, which suggested to Richard Brodick they must have had a stable of suitable tarts on standby, at least in his father's time. Presumably, in this instance, had Brodick accepted Pardoner's salacious vision of his future, one such asset would have been flown out to Pakistan in business class, with a fee agreed in advance. But how would the cost be calculated? Was there a budget? There had to be a standard operating procedure for this as there was for everything else in the SIS universe: a clever algorithm, perhaps, that measured both duration of the visit and the number of sexual encounters. How could the latter be predicted? And what if he didn't care for the candidate's hair style, choice of perfume, politics, table manners or Geordie accent? The point being that not even the most talented call-girl could please every client equally. If he'd said yes, would Pardoner have inquired if he preferred blondes or brunettes and whether he was a legs or tits man? Would the lady in question be required to fill in a form presented by Pardoner at the end of her assignment, noting her client's sexual habits and predilections? More box ticking for his personal file in SIS archives? Brodick's mind boggled. Luckily for Pardoner, his role as pimp would have to extend no further, and luckily for Brodick he would not be asked any more personal questions about his sexual preferences.

Perhaps he should accept the offer just to test Pardoner's resourcefulness and to see for himself how it was done, to discover just how awkward it would make Pardoner's job.

Brodick pointed. 'You can drop me just over there, on the left.'

'Going to stock up on books?' The strained smile again, the shy, sideways glance.

Brodick had given the name of The Old Bookshop in Jinnah Supermarket to Pardoner because he didn't want his new case officer to know where he was staying in the capital, and he definitely wanted to keep knowledge of the presence of Mélusine to himself. His real destination was a two-star hotel, a tall, thin and shabby building with a striped red awning and greatly favoured by backpackers, squeezed uncomfortably between two shopping arcades not three minutes away by rickshaw.

Brodick climbed out of the Renault and bent down. He glanced back, but there was no sign of the surveillance van or the Datsun. No that it meant much; whoever they were, they'd ring the changes with cars and motorcycles and the watchers would be almost impossible to detect.

'Thanks for the ride.'

'I take it that I can reassure Tim that you won't be publishing that report? We heard about that business at Burhanuddin's press conference, by the way. You're making things unnecessarily difficult for yourself.'

But Brodick had already turned away. He pretended he hadn't heard.

*

There were images going through his head rather than thoughts. He saw himself shaving, showering, changing his shirt, then sitting at a small, candlelit table in a little bohemian restaurant where they could drink their own wine for a modest corkage, holding Mélusine's fingers in his, then in bed in their dingy hotel room, laughing, hugging, making love. These happy images moved back and forth as he shuffled them like cards, lingering over them, adding details, becoming aroused in the process as he passed through the hotel's glass front doors, not hearing the receptionist's greeting, leaving the front desk behind, dodging a couple of longhaired tourists, impatiently summoning the cranky lift, wheezing slowly up to the second floor, and finding their door unlocked.

That was odd.

There was no sign of her.

The images of anticipated pleasure evaporated.

'Mélusine?'

No response.

He started to panic. From outside the filthy window, down

below in the street, came the cacophony of the city: the traffic, the throngs of pedestrians, the stalls selling brightly coloured women's clothing and shops offering street food. It was dusk and lights were going on across the city. Despite the grime, the window gave him enough light to see more clearly in the dimness of their room, and then he saw a bare leg protruding from what he had assumed was a heap of bedclothes.

Brodick was frightened. The hairs on the back of his neck bristled.

Had she been attacked?

He said her name again, not as a question but a statement.

Bending over the bed, he peeled back the tangled layers. Out came an arm, and another, and then she was hugging him, pulling him down, pulling him close, and he realised the wetness was her crying, sobbing.

'What is it? What's happened?'

'Hold me.'

He was holding her, and his anxiety was starting to curdle into annoyance. So much for their date. Mélusine dropped her arms, finally, letting go of him, wiped her eyes with the back of one hand and sniffed loudly. 'It's Marcel.'

Marcel? What the hell did he matter? What could possibly have involved Marcel and his bloody boots that could upset her so much and ruin their—his—evening? Had there been more to the relationship than she'd let on? He watched her anxiously as she got off the bed, a little unsteadily, and stagger over to the wall mirror. She peered into the glass, inspecting her face, her eyes red and puffy with crying. '*Merde.*'

'Mélusine.'

She turned, looked at him.

'What happened?'

'Marcel is dead, Richard. He shot himself.' She took a step forward and leaned against him, her wet cheek against his chest. 'I should have stayed with him. It's all my fault.'

20

The instructions were clear. That didn't mean they made sense, but Pardoner had insisted. At 13:08 precisely Brodick was to appear in a Peshawar city park. He set off on foot from his home in University Town at 12:35, then took a rickshaw on the corner, heading into town and circling the so-called park. It wasn't much of a park; just a patch of dusty ground, barely a third of an acre in extent and, aside from a few trees and bushes along the circular brick path, entirely bereft of cover. He stopped the driver a couple of blocks away because he was two minutes early, walking back despite the heat, stopping twice, careful to arrive on time. Odd behaviour, he knew perfectly well, even for a Westerner. There was no sign of any watcher on his back, but he could never be completely sure.

He saw Pardoner was already in place under a winter sky bleached white by the sun, apparently studying the frost-bitten plants with great interest and fiddling with his glasses. Brodick entered and loitered on the far side like a footpad, he thought, waiting for a victim. His shirt clung to his back and sweat ran down his face, neck and legs. This felt extremely uncomfortable, not because of the burning sun but the exposed nature of what they were doing. They pretended not to see each other, as if that would somehow make it all seem perfectly normal. If it was any consolation, the author of the exercise appeared to be even more uncomfortable than Brodick.

The third party arrived by rickshaw.

Three male westerners then, trying not to see one another, visible from any of the surrounding streets, and the only people in the so-called park. They could have been members of a rare species in a zoo: peculiar objects of curiosity. And this was the Pardoner notion of fieldcraft? Century House rules?

'Bloody ludicrous,' Brodick muttered under his breath.

Finally they acknowledged one another with furtive glances, Pardoner nodding and leading the way out, together this time, and all three squeezing into a single rickshaw destined for Green's Hotel. Why meet up in a park if they were going to gather anyway in the same hotel?

'This is Clive.' Clive and Brodick nodded at each other and all three sat down at a table in the Green's dining room. Brodick had already met 'Clive' in London, but neither of them acknowledged the fact. Clive was a workname. The former major of Royal Marines and sometime member of the Special Boat Service had had another handle when they'd first met. Not that it mattered.

Why hadn't they met here and cut out the nonsense in the park? It made no sense.

Pardoner removed his glasses and mopped his face with a large handkerchief. 'You'll introduce us: Clive and, for the purpose of this exercise, I'm Mark.'

'Fine.'

'We'll take it from there, all right?'

'Whatever you say.'

'We can't pay the seven thousand, Richard. It's five-eight or nothing.'

Brodick was taken aback. 'But Colonel Hermitage said—'

'I know what we said. London has set a new limit.'

'I negotiated seven and gave my word.'

'Never give your word to anyone in this line of work, Richard. The market value of items like this fluctuates.'

A waiter appeared and Pardoner ordered tea.

Market value? Of a minigun from a downed Soviet helicopter gunship?

'Still—'

'When you've introduced us, you can go, get on with your day. No point in your staying. Clive will organise the extraction with your contact. We'll have a chat over tea and sort it all out. Don't worry. We'll work it out.'

Ruhollah was striding towards them, hand outstretched, grinning at Brodick, who jumped up and clasped the proffered hand.

They exchanged the customary greetings.

'So. These are your friends, Mr Richard.'

'Yes. This is Mark, and this is Clive. Everyone, this is Commander Ruholla aka Mullah Shariati.'

They shook hands and Brodick heard Pardoner say something about it being a great honour to meet the man who could shoot down helicopter gunships. All except Brodick sat down. 'Ruholla, I hope to see you later. Mark and Clive will settle the details and discuss the arrangements to be made. I have to be somewhere else.' He saw the doubt in Ruholla's eyes, the question as to why Brodick was leaving him with two strange Westerners. 'It's okay. Don't worry. Everything will be fine.'

Which it wasn't, of course. Ruholla was about to discover that he wasn't going to get the money he'd been promised, money he needed for his Hazara fighters and their families. And Brodick, by leaving, showed himself not only to have lost face, but to be a coward to boot, unwilling to look Ruholla in the eye and tell him that his word of honour was worthless. Thanks a lot, Dr bloody Pardoner.

Humiliated, Brodick fled the hotel. This had been his project, and now he was being cut out of it. Clive would collect and take the kudos in Century House.

Outside, the motorcycles and van were waiting for him.

*

Pardoner was waiting for him on his return home at dusk, sipping tea in the sitting room. He had apparently inherited the white Land Rover Defender from Hermitage and had parked it in Brodick's driveway. Brodick told himself he would have to have a word with Omar later about opening gates to strangers and letting them into the house. It might be the way of the Pashtun's sense of hospitality, but being so accommodating wasn't Brodick's way and it wasn't secure.

'I apologise for dropping in on you unannounced, Richard, but I have something rather important to ask of you. Won't you join me and have some of your own tea? There's enough in the pot.'

Brodick poured himself a cup and sat down without speaking. The men watching his house could not fail to have seen Pardoner arrive.

'We want you to drop whatever it is you're doing and concentrate all your energies on this. It goes without saying that it's sensitive, and I'd rather you didn't say very much more than you have to in asking questions. It's particularly important these matters are not mentioned to either Professor Mungoo or his friend, the former Khad officer who calls himself Mirwais.'

'Might I ask why not?'

'We can get into that later, Richard. All I'm asking now is for you to exercise discretion and to exclude them from your inquiries.'

'If you say so. What's this about?'

'I can tell you this. There's unusual activity in Kabul. It's ongoing. There are checkpoints going up in the streets and especially the main routes in and out of the capital. Soviet troops are manning the major checkpoints and that's highly unusual. Security is particularly tight around Soviet and Afghan government buildings. The Soviet residential compound has been shut down. There are armoured vehicles parked outside Soviet apartments. Moscow has flown in reinforcements over the past week and they are certainly not part of any normal *roulement*. We know these include additional *Spetznaz* troops, though we're not certain how many. Maybe a battalion of seven hundred men brought in over a three-day period. There's also increased Soviet air activity, both fixed-wing and helicopters beyond the capital. Air patrols have been stepped up considerably. We want to know why. Has there been another coup? Or an attempted coup? President Babrak Karmal hasn't been seen or heard of for a week or more. Is he still in power? Is he in Moscow? Anything is possible.'

'Fine, I'll ask.'

'You have the contacts, I know. But please be careful who you do ask, and how you ask.'

There was only one man Brodick knew personally who would know what was going on in Kabul on a daily basis, and that was Abdul. Whether he would tell Brodick anything of value was another matter. First, he had to find him.

Pardoner put down his empty cup, using both hands to place it carefully in the saucer.

'If you find out anything remotely of interest, Richard, do get in touch. Don't hesitate. Call. Any time. Call me at the high commission or at home—or Angus in the press office and say you're heading to Islamabad for a couple of days and would love a beer: "beer" being our code for having something of possible value to tell us. Any questions?'

'I don't think so.'

'And leave Mungoo and Mirwais out of it.'

'They might actually have something on this, or could acquire something if I ask. They have couriers they could despatch to contacts in the capital.'

'I'm sorry, but I must insist. It's a matter of security. I'll tell you all about that when we have more time. In any case it's not urgent.' Pardoner got to his feet. 'I've got a long drive back, so if you don't mind I'd better get on the road before dark. And thanks for the tea.'

No mention then of the special edition of the *Bulletin*, issued in defiance of the fervent wishes of Hermitage and Pardoner that

Brodick suppress the Soviet report of Pakistani special forces operating on Afghan territory, masquerading as so-called freedom fighters. The *Bulletin* even had a colour front page and dramatic headlines for the first time. No doubt that would be discussed later, too.

'Surely the Americans with all their fancy gear will be able to help?'

'Gear?'

'Signal intelligence and photoreconnaissance. Satellites and spy planes.'

'They might have the *what*, Richard, but we want the *why*. Capabilities are one thing, intentions something else entirely.'

Brodick accompanied his visitor to the front door, relieved that Pardoner was leaving. He couldn't help it; he didn't like his case officer, and he sensed the feeling was mutual. Outside the sky was a fiery red as the sun died in the west and the temperature was falling fast. 'I didn't expect you in Peshawar so soon, Dr Pardoner. I thought you weren't going to be in a position to visit us that often.'

They stood on the doorstep and watched Omar open the gates as the glow turned from red to orange and pink. The sunsets on the Frontier were vivid and short-lived.

'I didn't expect to be here either, Richard. Today was an exception. Which reminds me: I should thank you for setting up that Hazara contact. Well done. Great job.' Pardoner wrinkled his nose, pushed up his glasses: a gesture of embarrassment, of being ill-at-ease. 'Clive should be over the border by now.'

The praise had its desired effect, though; despite himself, Brodick felt less aggrieved.

'Our friend accepted the reduced offer?'

'Ruholla? Oh, yes. Of course. He didn't have much alternative, now did he?'

'I rather think he did, Dr Pardoner. There are always the Americans. Or the Iranians.'

*

The fact that Pardoner hadn't mentioned the subject of Brodick's disappearance even obliquely suggested he hadn't noticed. No one had, thankfully, not even the *Orient* and his other regular outlets. Brodick had slipped the leash for four whole, wonderful days and nights—and what nights!—falling in the cracks between his two worlds of espionage and journalism; and no one had known, or cared if they did know. Presumably no one had seen them together, either: at the Holiday Inn pool in Islamabad, at their backpacker hostel, or when dining out.

It wasn't love. Love was feeling, and feelings came and went. Brodick understood that much. This went deeper. Or maybe it was love, but if so it was of a kind Brodick had never before experienced and might never do so again. He was left stranded by her absence, riven by a craving for her for which only memory—and a shifting, unreliable memory at that—could act as any kind of palliative, but the affection was still there, still present.

That memory was already both pain and pleasure.

They didn't talk much. They didn't need to.

'What do you want to do?'

'Do you have to ask?'

'No, not really.'

'Okay, then.'

'We've four days before my flight.'

'Let's make the most of it.'

'Sure.'

That was the longest exchange, aside from one discussion about Marcel on their first day together. Sleep, food, rest and sex all made a difference. Mélusine didn't blame herself any longer for Marcel's death or if she did, she stopped talking about it. She seemed to accept she wasn't personally responsible. She didn't question Brodick any further about his family, his origins, his outlook on life, nor did she offer more sage advice on how he should live. There wasn't time and they both knew it. She was content to enjoy the present moment, and so was he. Brodick decided he could afford a little luxury, so they checked out of their vermin-infested hostel and into the Holiday Inn, the place where the wealthy Pakistani elite of Islamabad liked to see and be seen, and where members of the diplomatic community went for a change of scenery. Of course there was a risk that either of them, or both, would be recognised. But what the hell. It didn't matter. Mélusine didn't care about her reputation in any conventional sense. As for Brodick, it was like playing truant from school. They both gorged themselves on what, in any other circumstances, would have seemed the unlikeliest choice of culinary delight, the club sandwich. That, and the unhealthiest of drinks, Coca-Cola. It was the best kind of fun—guilty fun.

They sunbathed and swam. They made love, and often. They prowled around second-hand bookshops and read by the pool and in bed. They drank oceans of coffee although they agreed it really wasn't much good but went on to drink oceans more in the vain hope it might change for the better. They ate and drank in little "boutique" restaurants and clubs favoured by Pakistan's self-consciously gilded youth. He smoked her Gitanes. They kissed on the dance floor and groped each other with abandon. They laughed more than Brodick thought he had in all his twenty-nine years. Time surrounded them like the white barriers at a race meeting. They were hurtling on, hours flying like the sods kicked up by the horses' hooves. Brodick could feel and almost see the course stretching ahead of them. The railings on either side, the flags at the far end. Their *affaire d'amour* was like life itself; it had boundaries, a finite limit on movement from start till finish, no turning around or breaking out left or right, no slowing down or stopping, just straight on.

'Come with me.'

'What do you mean?'

'Join me in France. Stop all this. Finish it. Come with me. Stay with me.'

'And what will I do in France?'

'Improve your French for a start. Then find work.'

Brodick was tempted for all of thirty minutes.

What was he going to do: wash dishes?

'You know the West—and I include my own country in the word—doesn't really give a shit about the Afghans, Richard. This is all about bleeding the Soviets, outspending them on weaponry and bleeding them from a thousand cuts in Afghanistan. No matter that it means encouraging Afghan peasants to do the dying so we can play the game of nations. It's dishonest, it's dirty, it's cruel, it's murderous and it's so unnecessary. Give it up, Richard. Do something decent instead, make yourself a real life in the real world.'

She seemed to know he wasn't going to take her advice.

But in his heart of hearts, Brodick had come full circle: the high ideals, the naivety, the exciting start of his adventure, the successful and exhilarating gathering of intelligence over many months—then the mounting paranoia and now, finally, realisation of the awful reality. She was right, of course. How she'd managed it, he could only guess. Perhaps it was female intuition, emotional intelligence—something of the sort. Mélusine had sensed the truth of it from the outset, apparently, and at last he did, too—but he wasn't going to admit it.

So it did end, all too abruptly, all at once. They crossed the finish line, both of them numb while hauling her belongings down to reception, Brodick speechless with fright, his very nerve endings feeling deadened, standing back to watch the ritual of signing out, the taxi waiting, the road journey, the driver talking endless shite, holding hands slippery with sweat, Brodick watching her float away on those tiny feet through the departure gate, holding his breath, restraining unmanly tears and fearing he would shatter into fragments, and she—she refusing to turn, to look back. Then it no longer existed for either of them. All they had left was flimsy, mercurial memory and like everything else, he knew, it would fade. It was a little death. How would he survive his affection for her?

21

Brodick used the trees at the side of the road like stepping stones, moving from one to the next as white discs of headlights swept past in the city's smog of dust and woodsmoke, turning his face away from the street so he would not be identified as a Westerner. He stopped often, turning to see if he was followed. He used his *potu*, draping it around his shoulders and raising it over his head whenever he saw people approach on foot. He rounded the corner and looked over the gate. The guard was there, squatting down by the door, his rifle beside him.

The light in Mungoo's office was on.

'Well, well, what a pleasant surprise—the return of the prodigal son, or, in this case, Englishman. Come in, my dear Richard. Where have you been? We're glad to see you're safe and intact. You are intact, are you not?'

Mirwais was there, too, smiling at him. Neither he nor Mungoo rose from the seats; after all, Brodick was a friend and no stranger. The third man present—and he was a stranger, at least to Brodick—did climb to his feet and placed his right hand over his heart in traditional greeting.

'Am I interrupting something? I can always come back tomorrow.'

'Not at all. Please.'

Mungoo made the introductions. 'This is our good friend Hamid, just arrived from Kabul, with many stories and even more mysteries. But first the good news, Richard. Our subscribers have increased in number by one third. And a lot of extra copies were sold. We're making a profit, my friend. We can afford to pay our contributors regularly. Isn't that wonderful?'

Mungoo now rose to his feet and the two of them shook hands, congratulating each other. Mirwais clapped his chubby hands.

It was wonderful, of course.

Brodick and Hamid eyed each other warily.

Hamid wore a brown *shalwar kameez* and, despite the heat, a dark grey Western-style jacket. He was swarthy and short, with a neat beard and a pot belly, and Richard placed him in his forties; though he could never be certain about the age of an Afghan because he'd been proven wrong so often.

'Hamid buys and sells carpets, Richard, and he's very successful at it, which is why he manages to cross the border every month or so. It's a luxury only important traders enjoy these days.' Mungoo gestured for them both to sit. 'He sells to foreigners, and of course nowadays the Russians are among his customers in Kabul. Along with the few tourists staying in Peshawar hotels. But mostly Western aid and medical workers.'

'What are these interesting stories?'

'You cannot use my name.' Hamid spoke good English. 'Okay?'

'Okay. If you say so.'

'I have travelled to Istanbul, mister. To Paris. To Rome. I specialise in Baluch and Kazakh rugs, also silk rugs from Herat. Persian carpets, too. You like fine carpets and rugs, mister?'

'Richard. Call me Richard.'

'So we agree first, Mister Richard, that you haven't met anyone, or talked to anyone, who is a carpet dealer from Kabul named Hamid.'

'Of course not. I understand. We never met.'

'Good. Then it's okay. I trust you because you are a friend of my friends here and they trust you. Of course.'

'I do like carpets and rugs very much.'

'That's good, that's very good. I will give you very special price. You come to my shop here in Peshawar tomorrow and I will show you many. With special price. Big discount.' He pulled a card from his pocket and reached over and handed it to Richard. 'I have lovely blue and red Kazakh. Big. You will like. I know.'

'Excellent.'

'Come at ten o'clock.'

'Very good.'

Brodick was doing his best to be patient and agreeable.

Hamid turned to Mungoo. 'Shall I tell him what I told you?'

Mungo nodded. 'Go ahead.'

'One week ago, Mister Richard, in the afternoon, something happened, but no one is sure what it was.'

'Last Wednesday, you say?'

'Yes, yes.'

'What time exactly?'

'I don't know the exact time, but I saw from my shop Russian troops on the streets, jumping out of trucks, running. Many. On foot, and in vehicles. Armoured vehicles. At the corner they set up a checkpoint. Very quickly my shop was empty of customers, the pavements were cleared. The big market where I have my shop went very quiet. It happened so quickly. Within minutes. It was a shock. This is so unusual for us.'

Brodick waited. He wouldn't have to ask Mungoo and Mirwais anything—he wasn't breaking Pardoner's order not to raise the issue. The issue had been presented to him without prompting.

'Ever since then, Mister Richard, the Soviet forces have been moving around the city. Patrolling. Many arrests. They grab people and take them away. They stopped cars, opened the doors, pulled people out. Nobody knows where they are taken, or why. For questioning, certainly. But questioning about what? I don't know. I don't think anyone does know. And at night, aircraft flying all the time, coming and going. Helicopters and also the big planes. Transport planes, I think you call them.'

'Last Wednesday—you heard no explosions, no shooting?'

'No.' Hamid shook his head. 'Nothing like that. No fighting. But I heard that sirens were sounded in government buildings, that the airport was closed, and the Soviet residential compound was guarded with Russian civilians told to stay home. There were tanks everywhere. State workers were sent home.'

'What were the Soviets trying to do?'

'They tried to stop people leaving the capital, and they wanted to stop people coming into the city. They meant to isolate Kabul, shut it down. You understand?'

'How did you get out?'

'I have a *laissez-passer* for my business. I said I was going to Khost. Once there, it was easy. In Khost many people travel across the border legally and illegally. You know there are many crossings impossible to close. But even in Khost now there are more Russians.'

'Why did you come?'

'There was no business in Kabul. No customers. There was no point in staying. I do have good business here, Mr Richard, even now.'

'And your family?'

'They are here. They are safe, thanks be to God.'

'So what happened?'

Hamid shrugged.

'You can tell me. I won't give away your name, your identity.'

'There are many rumours.'

'Of course. But you do know. I know you do.'

'Mister Richard—'

'You've already told my friends. I can see it in their faces. And yours.'

Hamid sighed. He got up, took one of Mungoo's cigarettes, lit it with trembling fingers and sat down again, puffing hard.

'Okay. I have very good Russian customer. Nice man, I think. Not soldier, a civilian, some kind of engineer, and adviser. Irrigation. I believe so. That's what he said. There are many Soviet advisers.

He told me a very senior Soviet official had been kidnapped in Kabul. In the street, in daylight.'

'By whom? Who did it?'

'He said it was the *basmachi*. The bandits. What the Americans call freedom fighters.'

'Who was the official who was kidnapped?'

'I don't know. My Soviet friend said he was very senior and from Moscow. Someone of high rank. Top Communist Party member, I think, maybe Politburo. Someone with important connections. My friend said he had met him once in Kabul. He was an old man, he said. I did not ask for a name. I was afraid to ask too many questions, you see. It's dangerous to ask questions of these people. I just let him talk. He's a good customer, too. He said the man who was taken had gone to Khwaja Rawash airport in Kabul to meet his wife. His personal driver, a Tajik, stopped at a place on the road—my Soviet friend said that was planned in advance, you know—and they were attacked by *mujahideen* dressed as soldiers. The driver disappeared.'

'You believe your Soviet friend?'

Hamid shrugged, raised his hands. 'Why not? I don't know what to believe, Mister Richard. Why would my Russian customer lie to me? What for?' He looked at Mungoo and Mirwais in turn as if seeking their approval. 'I'm not an important person. I do no harm to anyone. I have no politics. My friend—his name is Viktor—comes to my shop maybe every week or two and we drank tea and yes, he talks—he tells me about his family and what his life is like in Russia, I think he likes to relax in my shop because he spends an hour or two there sometimes—and we look at rugs and occasionally he buys something. He knows I have no politics, that I am no danger to him. He pays cash. German marks. This time he told me this story. That's all I can tell you. Truly.'

'I believe you.' It didn't matter, Brodick told himself, if he believed this Hamid or not. He would have to call Islamabad and use Pardoner's code. At least Brodick wouldn't have to defy instructions not to involve Mungoo and Mirwais in his enquiries.

They were, as usual, one step ahead.

*

Mirwais seemed in a hurry to leave. He and Hamid stood up together. They said their formal farewells and Mirwais led the way out, protesting that they could find their own way and there was no need for Mungoo to accompany them to the street. Brodick heard the voice of the guard, the metallic squeal of the gate opening and closing.

Mungoo sat down heavily. He seemed out of sorts, bothered.

'What is it?'

He looked up as if surprised to discover Brodick was still there.

'Mirwais won't be around for a while. He thinks it unsafe, especially after the Kabul kidnapping, if that's what it was. He's going to take his family somewhere safer.'

'I don't follow.' Brodick thought he did, but he wanted Mungoo's explanation.

'Pakistan's under pressure, Richard. We've heard the Soviets are flying troops into the border towns. Especially Jalalabad and Khost. They're putting pressure on Pakistan's generals. The last thing Islamabad wants is to have some kidnapped Soviet official hidden in a cave in the tribal areas, prompting cross-border raids by Soviet forces. There'd be a risk of a full-scale military confrontation. So my guess is Pakistan will want to be seen making an effort to ensure the missing Soviet isn't being held on this side of the Durand Line. They'll make a show of being helpful. That means searches, raids, mass arrests. ISI will use the opportunity to pick up politicals. It will be a settling of scores. You understand what I'm saying? As for the Russian, they'll try to do a deal through the Red Cross.'

Brodick did, of course. Mungoo was feeling the stress. It was in his voice, his impatience, his constant fidgeting, getting up and siting down and getting up again. The professor was restless and seemed not to know what to do with himself.

'There's certainly a lot of military stuff moving around tonight, and the police aren't letting anyone in or out of resistance offices.'

'There, you see? Mirwais thinks people like us are vulnerable. They could come for us at any time.'

'People like us?'

'Oh, come on, Richard. Educated Afghans. Anyone in exile here who sticks his neck out. Anyone critical of our beloved Pakistani leader, General Zia ul-Haq and his Islamic hordes. Anyone who doesn't toe the line. ISI has been putting out stories about Mirwais and myself. You must have heard them, no? Of course you have. We're leftists, socialists, communists, Soviet fellow-travellers. Whatever label sticks. You see? Word gets around. ISI makes sure of that. Murderous thugs like Burhanuddin loathe us. We're heretics, devils, unbelievers. The feeling is entirely mutual, of course! And we've been sticking our necks out with the *Bulletin*. Particularly after we published that secret Soviet document about Pakistani troops operating inside Afghanistan. The Soviets will have been delighted, the Pakistanis enraged. Not least because it's true, or I believe it to be true. They'll have seen that in Islamabad. All those extra copies we sold were probably bought by ISI to distribute to the chiefs of staff. It's just a matter of time before we're picked up. '

'Maybe we shouldn't have published it.'

'It was a risk, Richard. You said so yourself. We should be proud we did it.'

Or was Mungoo following Moscow's orders? Had Brodick been too blind to see it?

He saw his opportunity. This was the time to say what he'd been planning to say all along. In a sense, Mungoo had said it for him. He pulled his chair—one of the replacements after the place had been ransacked—closer to Mungoo and sat down facing him so their knees were almost touching, but Mungoo suddenly pushed himself up. 'Wait!'

'What now?'

'I have a little secret I want to share with you, Richard. My wife knows. Maybe Fawzi, also. But no one else. Now you are part of my magic circle.' He had opened a cupboard and was reaching in to find something at the back. 'You do drink on occasion, don't you? Wine? Whisky? Gin?'

Mungoo didn't wait for a reply. He held two shot glasses in one hand, a bottle of Stolichnaya vodka in the other. 'I think Stoli is the best. It's the only one I can drink straight, without mixing it with something else. Such a waste to do that. And it never gives me a hangover.' He bent down, carefully filling the glasses to the brim.

Mungoo held up his glass. '*Za zdarovje!*'

'Cheers.'

They emptied their glasses and Mungoo refilled them.

'You're a very subversive fellow, Professor.'

'Oh, don't I know it, Richard. But it's fun, isn't it?'

'Enough. We need to talk.'

'If you insist. There are times when I like to drink, and tonight is very much one of them.'

'I'm sorry. Maybe another evening.'

Mungoo put bottle and glasses away and they returned to their chairs. 'So. Richard. Speak.'

'I came here tonight with something urgent and important to say, although you have already started talking about it. It's not just the Pakistanis and the likes of Burhanuddin and other Islamists who are a threat.'

'What do you mean?' Brodick had Mungoo's attention. The latter frowned at Brodick, puzzled and alarmed.

'The Americans.' He paused. 'And the British. Even the ambassador expressed doubts about you.'

'I don't understand. What are you saying?'

'They believe, or strongly suspect, that you are working for the Soviets.'

'The Russians? Me, working for Moscow? Do they think I'm a spy? That's ridiculous. It's beyond ridiculous. It's insane!'

'They think you're some kind of agent of influence.'

Brodick watched Mungoo sit back, scratch his scalp, look up at the ceiling.

'How? Why do they think this?'

Brodick remembered what his father had told him: that a case officer was often the last person in the world to believe one of his own agents had been turned by the enemy.

'Your guess is as good as mine, Professor. You said it yourself: ISI spreads lies, tells its friends in the resistance and the CIA, the CIA tells the British and other allied governments. The lies circulate, are repeated, grow in strength. If you tell the same lies often enough, they become the perceived truth. Even Abdul told me you were a Communist working with the Soviets.'

'Pah! He's ignorant. A fighter, and a very good one, but uneducated. Naive.'

'Of course, certainly, but it shows just how widespread this is. How dangerous it is.'

'And you? What do you believe, Richard?'

The truth of it was that Brodick didn't know what to believe, not any longer, but that there was very real danger—of that there could be no doubt.

'It doesn't matter what I believe or don't believe. We're friends. But that isn't the issue. The issue is what we do about it. What I want you and your wife to do is to pack an overnight bag. One each. Enough to keep you going for two or three days, small enough in size to carry onto a plane. Only the bare essentials. Make sure you have some cash in hard currency. Dollars, German marks, it doesn't matter. As much as you can safely carry. Be ready. Have your passports in your pocket at all times. Make sure everything is to hand so you can just walk out of here day or night with no more than ten minutes' notice. Can you do that?'

'You're really serious about this.'

'Damn right. By all means tell Fawzi but no one else. No one.'

'And then, Richard? What do we do then?'

'I have a plan.'

22

As soon as he reached home, Brodick called the high commission, which of course was shut. It was nearly 9pm, after all. Not that he considered the carpet dealer's tale really worth the urgency; but still, they'd asked him to call if he found out anything at all. He rang Pardoner's home number, but there was no answer. He did not leave a message. No doubt Pardoner was out to dinner or at some diplomatic reception. Finally, Brodick left a message on the high commission press officer's phone, saying he would like to take up the offer of a beer. He tried to sound friendly, as if they were best mates.

'Don't know about you, Angus, but I could do with a bevvy and a chat. As soon as possible, okay, pal?'

The landline had to be monitored, he reasoned, at least some of the time. Occasionally there were strange clicks, or an echo that suggested the Pakistanis were listening to his calls and recording them.

He went out again, leaving the lights on in the house, locking the gates behind him and got into the back of Ahmad's taxi.

Abdul was nowhere to be found. Which was not surprising, given that even after dark the headquarters of the Hezb-i-Islami Yunis Khalis faction was ringed by police, both uniform and plainclothes. It was normally shut by lunchtime and deserted—and now the windows blazed with light. The uniforms weren't allowing anyone in, and refused entry to Brodick despite his press card. One cop stood in front of the taxi and shouted at Ahmad to get the foreigner the hell out of there or they'd both be arrested. He struck the bonnet of the Toyota twice with his truncheon to make the point. Undeterred, Brodick went on to Abdul's house, but there appeared to be no one in residence. No cars were parked in the drive or in the street outside. The metal shutters in the windows and over the front door were down. The gate was padlocked. A solitary uniformed policeman stood outside, waving his hand at Ahmad to keep moving.

Peshawar airport was lit up: both the two runways and the terminal building. Aircraft were landing and taking off, a Hercules 130 lumbering around in a half-circle over their heads as it lined itself up for a landing. There seemed to be more of the old Pakistani Mig-17s and Mig-21s than usual parked on the apron and, for the first time, the Vietnam-era Huey helicopters the Americans called "skids". On the road itself, they passed a convoy of Pakistani military vehicles going the other way, heading away from the Peshawar cantonment in a northerly direction—Chinese-built jeeps in army green mounted with U.S. TOW anti-tank missile launchers. Brodick counted thirteen of them.

'What's happening tonight, Ahmad? What's going on?'

'I don't know, Mr Richard.'

It was not something worth pursuing. He'd get nothing from Ahmad.

'Take me back to my house in University Town, please.'

Five minutes later Brodick paid off Ahmad, adding a tip for the late hour, and had just unlocked the gates when he heard the wail of a motorcycle. Ahmad's Toyota was already moving away, only the taillights showing. Brodick turned his head towards the noise. He saw the motorcycle coming on fast—directly towards him, headlight blinding him and the speeding bike trailing a cloud of orange dust as if on fire. He put up a hand to shade his eyes and stood back, facing the road. At first he thought it must be one of his watchers. Brodick considered trying to run inside, but it was too late. His back was against his front wall and he told himself this was where he would make his stand.

As it drew level, the motorcycle skidded to a halt. The pillion rider jumped off and jogged over, head and face hidden in his turban. Brodick fully expected he was going to be shot.

Something was pushed at him at chest height. It wasn't a gun. It wasn't a knife. Something white. Instinctively, without thinking, Brodick took it. No words were exchanged. The pillion rider ran back into the road, jumped back on the bike, the driver revved the engine and it screamed off into the night.

Brodick held a crumpled envelope in his hands.

*

Brodick pushed the note across the table. Hermitage picked it up and peered at it.

'Who the hell is Yuri Polivanov?'

Hermitage looked at Brodick, then at Pardoner. 'Anyone? No?'

Brodick felt he was back at school, facing his scary Latin master. Maybe he should put his hand up and start his reply with 'Please, sir...'

'I do know Polivanov is officially listed as counsellor at the Soviet embassy in Kabul. His official title is chief of the Soviet meteorological survey in Afghanistan. Unofficial sources say he is KGB, but they would, wouldn't they?'

Hermitage glared at Brodick. 'And you know this—how?'

Pardoner leaned across and snatched up the note. 'May I?' He left the high commission interview room, closing the door behind him.

'I was sent a note with the name, which I then looked up in the Kabul diplomatic directory. I have a copy and I presume you do, too.'

'Don't get fucking fresh with me, Brodick. Who gave you the name?'

'I told you. I was sent the note last night. Around 2100 hours.'

'By whom?'

'How do I know? By messenger. He didn't show his face and he didn't wait to exchange pleasantries.'

'You don't know? People just turn up at your door at night with anonymous notes? That sounds more than risky. It's asking for trouble. I heard about the Burhanuddin press conference— you're supposed to tell us when this sort of thing happens.' The caterpillars were working overtime and Hermitage seemed to be working himself up into a storm of disbelief. Brodick felt curiously unaffected by the sudden change of climate in the room.

'They do sometimes turn up, yes.'

Pardoner was back. He nodded at Hermitage and resumed his place between them at the table, placing Brodick's note in front of him.

Hermitage scowled. 'Well?'

Brodick remembered the first day on the lawn in Islamabad; how much he had wanted to impress Hermitage, how much he'd cared what Hermitage thought of him. How quickly that respect— even admiration—had evaporated.

Pardoner adjusted his glasses with thumb and forefinger. 'If it's the same man, then he's believed to be sixty-six years old, a senior Party veteran and a personal friend of Prime Minister Nikolai Tikhonov. And yes, he is accredited as a diplomat in Kabul. Been there for years, on and off. Knows the country well and speaks the lingo. An old hand. More of which later.'

Pardoner muttered something *sotto voce* and it sounded as if he'd said: 'No wonder the Paks are getting antsy.'

'Tell us what you do know, Richard, not what you don't know.'

'A motorcyclist and pillion rider sped up to my front door. The pillion rider handed me the note and they rode away. Their faces were covered and they didn't say a word. There was just this name on the note, written in pencil and in capital letters.'

'Jesus Christ.' Hermitage leant back, hands behind his head and gazed at the ceiling. 'That's all? Nothing else on the note, you say?'

'No.'

'Where's the original?'

'I didn't keep it. I put a match to it.'

'Why?'

'I didn't think it important, but I didn't want to leave it lying around.'

Did they believe him? He was lying. There had indeed been the name, but there had been three more words, also in pencil and capital letters. *"READY THREE DAYS."* It had all the hallmarks of a message from Abdul, and as far as Brodick knew, only Abdul had the men and means to organise a kidnapping in central Kabul in daylight and get the captive out of the city safely without being detected.

'So no demands?'

'Not that I know of, no. Not yet.'

Pardoner took off his glasses. 'Early days.'

Hermitage sat up, put his elbows on the melanin tabletop, steepled his fingers and looked at Brodick. 'We'll break for coffee. You do drink coffee, don't you?' He didn't wait for Brodick's response. 'We have other matters to discuss after the break. Dr Pardoner, could I trouble you to ask David to bring us the coffee now? And those chocolate biscuits, too, if there are any left.'

*

Nibbling a chocolate Hobnob, Pardoner squeezed his eyes shut, stopped chewing, swallowed and turned to Brodick. 'Tell me, if the kidnappers sent you another message, asked you to meet them in Afghanistan, interview this Polivanov and bring back the kidnappers' demands, would you agree to do it?'

'Yes.'

'Despite the obvious danger? You are already at risk as recent events suggest.'

'Yes, I would. Why do you ask?'

'I just wondered.' He took another nibble of the biscuit.

'It's a bloody good story. For any journalist.'

Pardoner nodded. 'I suppose it would be, yes. For a journalist. But is it a story worth dying for? Is any story worth dying for?'

It was almost as if he knew what was in Brodick's mind.

*

The young man named David took away the coffee things and returned with an easel and flip chart. He set this up under the gaze of a rather stern Elizabeth II then stood to one side, waiting for Hermitage's instructions. David was in shirtsleeves with some sort of striped, representational tie. Hermitage and Pardoner had both taken their jackets off, hung them on the back of their moulded chairs and loosened their collars.

'First page, please David.'

It was a large photograph, black and white, grainy and much enlarged, giving it a fuzzy, unfocused look. It appeared to have been taken in a garden or park.

'Recognise him? Yes? No?'

It was without doubt Mungoo.

'It's our friend with a full head of hair and his usual impish expression. Here he's young, a junior lecturer at Kabul University, starting out on his academic career. Get a good look. Take note of the ears, the smile, the manner of the man. It's 1968. The year of so-called student revolution in western Europe.'

Hermitage paused, letting the details sink in.

'Let's have the second page, please. Thank you.'

Another blown-up photograph of Mungoo, this time in colour.

The likeness was obvious. 'Does anyone think this is not Mungoo?'

Apparently they did not.

'Two guesses where this was taken. Any takers, gentlemen? Does anyone bet me a fiver? No?'

Mungoo was smiling his lopsided smile, this time wrapped up against the cold with a furry *shapka*, a scarf, thick gloves and boots.

'Leningrad University, three years later. 1971. Mungoo attends a Russian language and culture course, free of charge for selected and talented young people from fraternal socialist countries and paid for by the Communist Party of the Soviet Union. Mungoo was the only Afghan national on this particular six-month course. The young woman in the picture is his official Soviet escort and guide—and maybe much more besides. Tell me, Richard, did Mungoo ever tell you he speaks and writes Russian with remarkable fluency, and that Pushkin is his favourite poet? No?'

Brodick objected. 'That doesn't mean a damn thing—'

But Hermitage shut him up with a wave of his hand. 'Wait, Richard, please. You'll have your say at the end. There's not much more.'

David turned the page.

The final photograph, sharper than its predecessors and also in colour, showed three men, Mungoo in the centre. Much older, thinning hair, a serious expression and the beginnings of a paunch. They sat side by side on a bench in what appeared to be identical grey suits, Mungoo in the centre, looking cold and rather unhappy, his palms together and both hands squeezed between his knees.

'Berlin-Karlshorst, April 1978, so little more than three years ago. The buildings in the background are interesting. They look like a school or barracks, with an annexe. It's part of the massive KGB headquarters in the DDR, employing hundreds of officers. Mungoo and his two comrades—one we believe to be Bulgarian, the other Czech—are receiving specialist training. We believe the main topic to have been clandestine communications. The Czech later defected which is how we obtained the photograph. Incidentally, Mungoo's wife travelled with him to East Germany and later they went on a little holiday together in the Harz mountains.

'Thank you, David.'

They waited while David removed his apparatus.

Brodick's cheeks were burning. He couldn't help taking it personally. This was his best sub-agent they are talking about. His best friend, too, come to that. His only friend in this country, anyway. So maybe he was one of theirs—but he was still a friend, wasn't he?

'You wanted to say something, Richard.'

'This is circumstantial. It may add weight to your theory that Mungoo is a Soviet stooge or fellow traveller, but it's not hard evidence. It's supposition. You've put down a few pieces of a jigsaw and claim to see the entire picture. I don't buy it.'

'Point taken. But let me put this to you. London—London, not the CIA—suggests that Professor Mungoo is your Soviet mirror image, Richard. He's a head agent, just like you—only he's been trained for longer and cultivated far more intensively. The *Afghan Bulletin*—which you helped produce and which we financed—was a masterstroke on Mungoo's part. The Soviets provided much of the material—oh, it was true enough, real intelligence, but well worth the price. Chickenfeed, we call it, and you were the chicken fattened for slaughter. You didn't recruit Mungoo at all; he has recruited you.'

Brodick opened his mouth, but again Hermitage held up his hand.

'Let me finish. Thank you. The natural course of events was to have been the following. The British Council—or the FCO— invite Mungoo and his good wife to London for a well-earned break and as a reward for their courageous work in exile. They achieve a degree of celebrity as champions of freedom, as upholders of a free press, as moderates. On this basis, they also spend a few days in Washington, where they are feted. More funds are pledged to the *Bulletin*. It takes on staff, opens an office in the West. It expands. Mungoo is a salaried editor-in-chief. He wins press awards. He rubs shoulders with influential people. He has access to those in power. Are you getting the picture? The journalists, the contributors, are in effect his unwitting agents of influence and the Soviets are his investors and his beneficiaries. From acorns mighty oak trees grow, etcetera, etcetera. And maybe they hope that they might have a chance of eventually turning you too into a fully-fledged KGB agent once we take you on fulltime. Two penetration agents for the price of one. Do you see where this is going?'

'I do, but this isn't proof. It's supposition.'

'Look, Richard.' Hermitage changed his tone to one of sympathy. 'I am sorry about all this. I know how hard it is to accept that one of our best people—especially someone you count as a friend—is working for the other side; but it does happen, believe me, and it happens all the time in this business. It happens to us and it happens to them. It's not your fault. No one's accusing you. It's no one's fault. Mungoo is a penetration agent, and a pretty good one. He's being groomed by the Centre as a future illegal in the West. But we can't let it pass. You do see that, don't you? What we have to do is limit the damage, and then carry on as normal and build on our undoubted successes. The ANB can continue to flourish. No reason why it shouldn't. No reason at all. The Professor will still be remembered—and honoured—as its founder and first editor.'

'How?'

'How?' Hermitage nodded, smiled—Pardoner nodded and smiled, too—as if to say that they understood the question perfectly, just as they appreciated Brodick's apparent bafflement. They were at their most solicitous. 'Well. We have to root out the canker, Richard. Destroy it root and branch, and we have to do it now.'

'Meaning what exactly?'

As if he didn't know.

'Meaning, Richard, that Mungoo's contract must be terminated. Unfortunate, yes, of course, but essential. We leave the method and timing to you, naturally, but it should be soon. I don't think you need any help from us, any special equipment or skills. You have everything you might need right on your doorstep. In Peshawar, anything can be bought. But do let us know if you do need assistance or advice.'

*

In a way, the decision had already been made, years ago. During a holiday in the Scottish Highlands as an eighteen-year-old, he'd gone stalking for one day with a gillie and a Finnish .308 bolt-action rifle borrowed from his father. They had managed to crawl downwind to within three hundred yards or so of an elderly doe, one that should or would have been culled anyway, or so the gillie said later, no doubt to make Brodick feel better.

From a prone position in the heather and squalls of horizontal rain, Brodick shot the animal just behind the shoulder, a heart shot, precisely where he should have—but even so the creature managed to walk a few paces before going down. She lived just long enough for Brodick to reach the spot, stand over her and see her go, those huge, dark and glittering eyes watching him with what seemed to Brodick to be the terrible knowledge of her own imminent death. The eyes glazed over and she was gone. Brodick was shocked, stricken by the beauty of the deer and at what he'd done. He felt terrible, physically sick. He turned his face away to hide his feelings, but the gillie knew enough about his clients to recognise what Brodick was going through.

'Next time you should bring a camera, laddie, not a rifle,' the gillie said, not without sympathy. Richard was no killer, that was the fact of the matter. He couldn't take a life coldly, deliberately. He might, in a moment of madness and extreme exhaustion, try to shoot an Afghan assistant cook, but there had been mitigating circumstances.

And if he couldn't stalk and kill a red deer with equanimity, he knew he couldn't murder his best friend even if the target was an old man on the KGB payroll who'd betrayed his trust, no matter how much Brodick wanted to be a fully paid-up career intelligence officer. It might be hard to admit, but hadn't Brodick betrayed Mungoo's trust, too, by not confiding in him about his SIS role? It worked both ways, surely.

The decision made, Richard knew he had urgent arrangements to make. He paid his friend Ahlberg a visit and they talked for almost an hour. He bought two one-way domestic airline tickets.

He cashed some of his own money and changed it into U.S. dollars in the money market.

That done, he turned to his journalistic tasks, filing the Kabul kidnap story to his radio and daily print outlets at the local telex office. While it was good to be first with a major story, an exclusive, it wouldn't be at all good to be alone with it for long. Editors would begin to doubt him and his copy. So he went to the Reuters bureau, filed a long piece on the kidnapping to *The Orient*, and, in passing, tipped off the delighted Cowley.

The latter insisted Brodick join him for a celebratory beer once the Reuters story was out, wouldn't take no for an answer and they chatted cheerfully in Cowley's office, but as soon as he left, Brodick realised he couldn't remember a thing they'd talked about. He had too much on his mind.

By the time he flew back to Peshawar on the last flight that evening, Brodick had the satisfaction of knowing he had a by-line on the front page of the next morning's *Washington Post*, another in the *Daily Telegraph*, the *Philadelphia Inquirer* and the *Glasgow Herald*. But once again his thoughts were elsewhere; this was no time for self-congratulation.

Brodick reasoned it might be some time—days, hopefully—before SIS realised what he'd done, or rather not done, moreover that he'd helped the Mungoos escape, that the latter were alive and well and nowhere to be found, at least for a while—until it was too late and they were safe and sound abroad in a neutral country, out of reach of both the Centre and SIS. When that happened, he was sure Century House would wash their hands of him. Hermitage would give Brodick the benefit of his unrestrained wrath. A right bollocking. He'd let them down. He'd disobeyed orders. He'd ignored their advice, their warnings about Mungoo. He'd rescued a fucking KGB agent. It would be the premature end of his contract. He was unsuitable material. Well, he could live with that—he would have to live with it. Indeed, in some circles it might even be regarded as an accolade. In the meantime, though, it would be better if he made himself scarce for a week or two. Let things simmer down.

Omar hadn't gone home.

'What are you still doing here?'

'I'm sorry, sir, I thought I should wait to give you this. I thought I shouldn't just leave it here in case it was important.'

It was another grubby envelope.

'Don't apologise, Omar. Thank you. It is important. You were right. But please go home to your family now.'

'Sir?'

'Yes, what is it?'

'Your phone—many calls. Again and again. Never stop.'

Brodick took the envelope inside, locked the front door, went into his bedroom, snapped on the light, dropped his bag in a corner, closed the door and tore open the envelope. Inside there was another note, again in capitals, again written in pencil.

Just one word this time.

'*TOMORROW.*'

The phone was ringing again. He went into the living room.

'That you, Richard? Angus here—from the embassy. Sorry to call so late, but it's official business, I'm afraid. We in the press office are reliably informed that Burhanuddin has put a thousand dollars on your head. That's rather a lot, considering it's generally fifty bucks a hit in Peshawar these days.'

'Thanks for letting me know. When did this happen?'

'We're not sure. Probably a few weeks ago, but we've only just had confirmation.'

'I see.'

'No need to panic, but I advise you take a few sensible precautions. There are at least four other foreign journalists and a score of local ones on his list. Just keep your head down and by that I mean stay indoors if you can. Perhaps it would be wise to get away at least for a while. Can you do that?'

'We'll see, Angus. Thank you, though, for the warning.'

'I've passed this on to other interested parties at the high commission and we will notify the Pakistani authorities. Please do take this seriously. Take care now.'

Brodick took the phone off the hook.

In just five hours he would send the Mungoos off on the first stage of their journey.

23

He was awake, lying on his back on the bed in his shorts, thinking about his rescue plan for the Mungoos. It was just after 2am by the luminous Roman numerals of his wristwatch. Brodick had got into the habit of waking in the wee hours. It was when he did most of his thinking, chaotic though it was, images pushing their way into his mind at random and disturbing whatever order he might have wished for. Images of those four wonderful days in Islamabad, images of her, snatches of conversation with Hermitage and Pardoner, amusing remarks of Mirwais, intelligence reports he'd written and which he'd failed to write, his forthcoming trip across the frontier into Kunar. No, he decided he wouldn't go with the Mungoos into the terminal when the time came; he would attract too much attention to himself and his friends. Better if he just dropped them off and let the Mungoos check in to the departure desk by themselves.

Had he forgotten anything? He didn't think so. His gear was packed and ready.

He heard something right behind him, through the headboard, the curtains, the glass of the window. Brodick would have sworn it was a footstep, the scrape of a shoe or sandal on gravel or cement— the cement of his porch out back. Someone seemed to be trying the back door, slowly turning the handle. Thieves? Unlikely—this was more personal.

Christ, they're trying to get in. Thanks, Burhanuddin: this is your doing.

Without a sound, he rolled off the bed onto the floor. Brodick pulled on his pants and short-sleeved shirt without getting up.

Nothing worth stealing—he reminded himself his trunk was padlocked and under his bed and in any case there was nothing valuable or particularly sensitive in it; Brodick never left intelligence reports lying around for thieves to find.

There were low voices, male voices, further away but still, Brodick thought, somewhere in his back garden. He could make out Pashto but they were too distant now to make out whatever it was they were saying. They seemed to have circled the house, perhaps checking for an easy point of entry.

Brodick rose to his feet, stood by the edge of the window, used a finger to move one of the curtains a fraction of an inch. He was dripping with sweat. Nothing. Blackness. Some reflected light on the rear wall and the side of the house beyond the back wall, pale reflections from those ineffectual streetlamps.

Something moved. Brodick thought it was the shadow of someone against the rear wall, a fleeting glimpse of a figure heaving himself up and over the back wall.

Was he imagining it? Dreaming it?

His heart thudded, the pounding reaching his throat, making him pant. He'd never been conscious of being watched at home and at night—until now. His adrenal gland had jumped into overdrive. Brodick had no guns in the house, no weapons of any kind other than a kitchen knife. He wasn't about to go out there to investigate, alone and unarmed. He found his sandals, pushed his feet into them.

Maybe he should make a run for it before they came back. On second thought, maybe that was what they wanted him to do.

The bedroom was abruptly lit up, a flash of light from outside so bright there were no shadows.

A loud *whoosh*.

An enormous crash threw Brodick backwards, made the building quiver, the detonation so loud he was temporarily deafened and his head rang with it.

Dust everywhere, in his mouth and eyes.

His head hurt and so did his neck. It felt like a whiplash injury; he touched his head gingerly. He realised he might have lost consciousness when he fell, for his fingers came away sticky with blood and the skin at the back of his head stung. He knew it was blood because he put his fingers in his mouth and tasted the distinctive flavour of rust and salt.

Brodick had no idea how long he'd been lying there. Seconds, minutes, an hour.

He got to his knees, crawled to the window, wincing at the pain in his head and neck. He peeked out. There was nothing to see or hear.

The white dots on the floor turned out to be flakes of paint fallen from the ceiling.

Brodick struggled to his feet, clawing his way up the wall with his hands, worked his way along the wall, out of the bedroom, into the kitchen and to the back door, picking up a flashlight on the way. He stepped carefully; stuff was all over the floor, thrown from cupboards by the impact, steel pots and broken crockery. Were they waiting for him? Was the idea to force him out?

He waited a full two minutes before venturing outside. At first everything seemed perfectly normal. He made two slow, cautious circuits of house and garden. He played the torchlight on the doors and windows before he caught sight of what appeared to be marks left by a giant cat's paw—a strike that had torn away the paintwork above the kitchen—the plaster, too—and cracked the exposed concrete beneath but failed to penetrate into the interior. It was jagged and circular, well above his head, maybe eight feet up, like a splash as if someone had thrown a bucket of mud at the wall, and the fragmentation of the rocket-propelled grenade had left jagged tears in a rough circle around the main area of impact like giant claw marks.

The kitchen window had caved in, or rather had been sucked out by the blast, leaving a sea of broken glass on the patio along with the twisted metal frame. Mixed with the glass were chunks of plaster and concrete and jagged lumps of metal—splinters from the grenade itself.

Whoever they were, they'd missed, the grenade impacting several feet too high and wide of his bedroom. Enthusiastic amateurs. At a range of forty metres or so, from a firing position Brodick assumed had been on the other side of the rear garden wall, it had been a poor shot, even if the launcher itself was an older model and had only iron sights.

Bats flitted and dived in the light of his torch. He put it off and stood still, listening, wrapped in darkness, neck, head and shoulders aching, his mouth open to hear better. There were no police sirens; no voices, no footsteps or gunshots. No one had emerged from neighbouring houses to investigate.

The assailants had tried and failed to collect their thousand dollars. There was nothing to prevent them from trying again.

*

Three days later Brodick was on his knees in Kunar Province, moving uphill inch by inch, foot by foot. Exhausted, he persuaded himself this was the last ridge he could climb. He had lost count. These northern mountains were both massive and seemingly endless. He felt as if the whole world had turned on its side, that there was no longer anything resembling the horizontal. He wanted to stop, roll onto his back, wedge himself against a tree trunk, and sleep. He'd reached the limit of his endurance. At that moment, a tall, elderly man with a long white beard marched past him, striding uphill and he gave Brodick a glance—and what a glance.

It seethed with contempt.

He said something as he left Brodick behind.

That glance and tone were unmistakable. Brodick didn't need to understand the Pashto. The meaning was all too clear. What a pathetic Westerner, an unholy unbeliever, so weak, so childish on all fours, wallowing in his self-pity. Fucking pathetic. How could he possibly consider himself a man, or have the respect of other men?

The look galvanised Brodick. The man was already a dozen paces ahead, still moving up to the crest. Brodick was on his feet, pain and fatigue forgotten; he was angry and ashamed. He hefted his pack onto his back, and hurried to catch up.

No bastard looks at me like that, and certainly no Afghan bastard!

He caught up: well, almost. Brodick was right behind him and, when the ground opened up, was alongside him. They marched on without a word. The Afghan, certainly a Pashtun, was tall, very thin and in the Western world would probably have been thought of as someone at least seventy, though his back was straight, his head erect, his stride long. Maybe he was that ancient. Then again, Afghans, especially rural Afghans, aged quickly. He did not shorten his pace or pause. Stick with me or don't, he seemed to say. It's nothing to me either way. He carried an AK-47 so well used that the blue had rubbed off, leaving a silvery steel.

Even if it killed him, Brodick was determined not to fall behind again.

Brodick managed to stay with him for the rest of the afternoon, striding up, then down, then up again until, as the sun began to set, they finally halted at a mountain hamlet.

Fighters and villagers alike streamed towards the biggest building and the open courtyard in front of it. The structure was built of stone, wood and mud and had a flat roof with mighty logs protruding from the walls. The yard was surrounded on three sides and, as Brodick moved in with the old man after splashing cold mountain water in his face and over his hands, he saw that the centre had been covered in plastic sheets and tablecloths of many colours and designs. Boys were putting out tin plates. Steaming platters of food were being arranged around the periphery, along with cups and glasses.

The old man continued on, skirting around to the back. He was someone of low rank, of no importance. Obviously a peasant, his only possession of any value an old Kalashnikov.

The other guests in the front rank, to Brodick's left and right, were the senior people. They were better dressed, fatter, older, balder. They bent their heads towards one another, speaking quietly. Except for the place immediately to Brodick's right, that is, which was left empty.

When he tried to move, fellow guests shook their heads, held his arm and pointed to his place of honour. 'You sit. No, no. Sit.'

The food was ready, jugs filled with water or cola.

Nobody ate. Nobody helped himself. Nobody drank. Brodick's stomach was rumbling with hunger and his legs ached. Everyone was waiting, expectant, the general hubbub of voices falling away until there was almost complete silence, aside from the odd cough, sneeze or hawking of phlegm into a spittoon. It reminded Brodick of a London audience in the Queen Elizabeth Hall on the Southbank, waiting for the conductor and soloist to appear before a concert could begin.

There was a commotion behind him. Brodick turned. A crowd approached on foot, moving quickly. They were *mujahideen*, perhaps fifteen in all. In front, the leader was someone he recognised: burly, bear-like, mouth like a trap.

It was Abdul.

Everyone stood until he had himself sat down, settling cross-legged next to Brodick. He turned his head and they looked at each other, but Abdul gave no sign of recognition and said nothing. His expression remained blank. He began to load his plate with food. Abdul was renowned as a big eater, a man of considerable appetite in all things. Everyone else followed suit, the higher ranks first. Brodick saw that the old man at the back and those around him hadn't put food on their plates as yet.

Once Brodick had piled a generous quantity of food onto his own plate, far more than he could manage—saffron rice with sultanas, raisins and walnuts, okra, chicken thighs, chunks of mutton, tomato, bread—he got up, took his plate with care and walked with it in both hands around the seated guests to the rear, to the old man, and set the dish down in front of him. He went back, fetched a jug of water, returned, and filled the old man's cup.

Brodick returned to his place, was handed another plate and started helping himself. Only then did Abdul turn and grin at him, waving a chicken drumstick at him.

'Very good, Richard. I see you learn how to be an Afghan now. A Pashtun!'

There wasn't much talking because everyone was too busy eating.

Then there was tea and cigarettes and a washing of hands by moonlight. In the mountains, Brodick thought, the air was fresh and clean, free of dust and car fumes. If only he didn't have to spend days climbing to appreciate it.

The old man stood in front of Brodick. He gestured with his head. Come.

He led Brodick up a ladder against the side of the main building. On the flat rooftop stood a *charpoy*, the traditional wood and string bed. From somewhere the old man had also found a large, thick quilt. The old man put his head on one side, a hand to his cheek, mimicking sleep, and pointed a long bony finger at Brodick, then at the bed.

As for the self-appointed bodyguard, the old man wrapped himself in his *potu*, his Kalashnikov close to hand, and lay down at the foot of Brodick's bed. Brodick stared up the glittering panoply of stars. They seemed so close, so big. He fell asleep almost at once.

For the next ten days—the remainder of Brodick's trip to Kunar Province—the old man never left his side.

*

'We have these hills and villages, they have the valleys and towns, at least in the day.'

Abdul and Brodick sat among boulders with plenty of overhead cover from the trees, with a fine view of a wide valley far below.

'I'll try, Abdul, but he might not cooperate.'

'Okay. Good.' Abdul rose to his feet.

'But I must tell you now, Richard, that the Russians and Pakistanis will never take him back by force. We will shoot him if they get too close and we'll dispose of the body in such a way that they will never know what really happened to him. They can't win this one. They have a simple choice, Richard. They make the exchange, or the Russian dies. Then both sides lose. You can say that, too, quoting his—what do you say—captors. No names, though.'

'Yes, captors.' Brodick got up then on his stiff legs.

'I'll take you to him. Then we're going to move him again—this morning. You don't have long.'

As they walked back to the building, Brodick heard aircraft in the distance.

'The morning patrol,' Abdul said with a wry grin. 'They're ten minutes late today.'

24

'My name is Yuri Polivanov. I am Soviet citizen. I am sixty-seven years old, married with two children. I am from Moscow. I am head of Afghanistan Meteorological Survey and my office is in Kabul. I am diplomat. I have diplomatic passport. See? I have been told to hold up English-language newspaper, *Khyber Mail*, though it is week old. More. Ten days old. You can see? Yes? The date, here, at the top of front page. So you know that on that day and the ten days following that I was still alive. I am prisoner. How do you say? Hostage? Yes? That's what these *basmachi* tell me—that I am hostage.'

Brodick kept his questions simple. 'How are you being treated?'

'No complaints. It's okay.'

'Did they question you?'

'No.'

'Have you been beaten or tortured?'

'No.'

'Never?'

'In the beginning, when I was kidnapped, they were violent. I lost—how do you say—they hit my head and was unconscious and when I woke up I had very bad headache. I couldn't see because of blood in my eyes. They gave me tablet, painkiller, and held gun to my head when we left the city. They were nervous. My wrists were tied for short time and they put gag in my mouth. But only then, first day.'

'How did it happen—your kidnapping?'

'Everything was normal. It was beautiful day in Kabul. I was happy. I was going to airport to meet wife. For some reason my driver, Afghan, stopped jeep. Not American Jeep, of course, but small utility vehicle. We call UAZ-649. I was asking him. What are you doing? Why do you stop? What happened? The doors were pulled open. There were several Afghans, all armed. They were shouting. I thought they were soldiers. I saw they had Afghan military uniforms. They pointed their guns at us. They dragged driver out, beat him, forced him down, and others got in next to me on back seat, on both sides. It was very, very quick. Seconds. I protested. I say I am Soviet citizen and diplomat! I speak to them in Pashto and then Dari. What are you doing? An officer—he was wearing the uniform of army colonel—punched me in the face and I fell sideways, then he hit my head with pistol and I lost consciousness. When I woke up I was on UAZ floor. They had tied me up and gagged me. I was under blanket, and they kept their feet on me. It was very hot. It was difficult to breathe because nose was broken. See? Still swollen. My mouth was bleeding and I lost two teeth. That's all.'

'Are you getting enough to eat?'

'Yes. It's okay. Meat, vegetables, rice. Sometimes goat milk. It's okay.'

'Do your captors let you sleep?'

'Yes. But I am not good sleeper.'

'Do they let you go outside?'

'Depends…on situation. Sometimes outside all day. Sometimes walking all day, all night. Sometimes just an hour. Sometimes not at all.'

'Are you in good health?'

'So-so. I have heart condition. I smoke too much as you see.'

'They give you cigarettes?'

'If I ask, they give. Yes. American cigarettes made in Pakistan, I think. Here is packet.'

'You're on medication?'

'I take pill twice every day. But only six pills left. For three days.'

'If you show me the bottle I will take a picture of it and ask the people holding you to find the equivalent medicine in Kabul or some other city.'

'Here. Good? You can see?'

Brodick changed his position. 'Hold it up. Turn it a little. Okay. Thanks. The label is in Russian but maybe someone can translate it. You can put the bottle away now.'

'Finished?'

'Not yet. What do you hope for, what outcome do you want?'

'Stupid question. I want to go home. Understand? I want to be with wife and children, of course. What do you expect? I am human being. It's wish of every person held by force and against his will. To be free. To be home. Even animals want that.'

'Would you be happy to be exchanged for Afghan prisoners?'

'Happy? I don't understand. It's not up to me. I have no influence. I have no power. You must ask the people holding me. You must ask the Soviet authorities and the Afghan government, of course, because we are in Afghanistan. Maybe you ask the Red Cross or some humanitarian organisation for an opinion. I don't have opinion. I do my duty—as scientist. I obey my government and Party. I work in Afghanistan to help Afghan people. I am civilian, not soldier. I have diplomatic immunity. I committed no crime. I am being held illegally. That's all.'

'If there is no agreement, no exchange, what will happen to you, do you think?'

'What kind of question is that? I will die here.'

'You do know your government, the Afghan authorities and the Pakistan government are all searching for you. There are thousands of soldiers from all three countries looking. It means that your captors will have to stay on the move, and you will have to keep up. Are you strong enough?'

'We will have to see, won't we?'

'Would you like to use this opportunity to ask the military leaders trying to rescue you to stop, to call a halt, so some kind of deal can be organised? Otherwise, given your heart condition, you might not make it. You might fall sick and die before an exchange of prisoners can take place.'

A long pause.

'It's not for me to tell my own government what to do. If they bomb, they bomb. If they shoot, they shoot. I am sure they have all the facts they need to make good decision. It will be right decision. I know. I trust my government. They know better than me what must be done. Now I am tired. This interview finished.'

Brodick asked his last question. 'Maybe you'd like to say something in Russian, something private, to your family?'

Yuri Polivanov faced the video camera and began to speak in Russian.

*

All the way back south from Swat to Peshawar, Brodick felt peculiar. Even the colours, sounds and shapes seemed distorted as if he was hallucinating from having smoked the local hashish. He felt sick, dizzy. It was getting worse. He told himself it was exhaustion, that he would be fine once he'd slept and eaten. He didn't even feel hungry. Most odd. Normally, after a trip across the border, all he could think about was food. Now the very thought of it revolted him.

The trip back itself was gruelling; first on foot over the mountains and into northern Pakistan, then by bus, a perilous route on crumbling mountain tracks, followed by a ride in the back of a Willys jeep, knees up against his chest, sharing the space with a Pakistani family of four, all staring at the foreigner, and every bump and every jolt making him wince in pain. A taxi, and finally a rickshaw, which dropped him outside his gates in University Town.

It was night by the time he arrived, and once inside Brodick locked the gates behind him, stripped off and dropped his verminous clothing in a bucket—to be burned the next day—then managed to open the front door and staggered naked inside. He lurched along the corridor and threw up in the lavatory. Just when he thought that was done with, his stomach seemed to explode. The diarrhoea was violent, followed by retching, followed by diarrhoea, followed by retching. The force of it shocked him. He didn't believe the human body contained so much liquid, but then he had read somewhere the body is eighty percent water. It seemed as if he would soon be down to the remaining twenty—just gristle and bone.

It went on all night. By morning he was very thirsty, but when he took a sip of water it started all over again. The stuff he was throwing up was a bitter, thin gruel, increasingly acidic, bringing tears to his eyes and making his throat sore. The dry retching that followed was even worse. It was like being shaken violently and the convulsions wouldn't let up. The dark brown gush from his backside was now a flood of watery fluid with what appeared to be small pieces of vegetable matter. It looked like dishwater and there seemed no end to that, either. He lay on the bathroom floor, right next to the lavatory because it was quicker, easier, and he felt too weak to walk. At least the tiles were pleasantly cool. He was still naked. What was the point of dressing? He would only have to drop his pants every few minutes and then soil himself anyway when he wasn't fast enough.

He managed to crawl as far as the bathroom door to close it.

When Omar arrived, he sensed something was wrong, knocked and asked in a quiet voice if Brodick needed anything. Perhaps it was the vile smell.

'Burn those clothes in the bucket, please, Omar. Don't touch them. Use a stick.'

'Yes, sir. You want doctor?'

'No. I'll be fine. Just leave.'

'Sure?'

'Just go.'

'Sir, allow me to fetch doctor.'

'No. Leave me.'

Omar must have returned on several occasions, but Brodick wasn't counting. Days and nights passed. He slept fitfully, in between the continuing evacuation of every ounce of liquid left to him, or so it seemed. He knew he was seriously ill, but he didn't think he could make it to the local hospital on his own. He would have to be carried, and that would mean an ambulance. He didn't want that. He had conversations with Omar, or thought he did, but they could have been dreams.

On the fourth day, he finally kept down a sip of water.

On the fifth, he managed to stand, by hauling himself upright and leaning against the bathroom wall. The diarrhoea had come to an end, or so it seemed.

On the sixth, he managed to take a cold shower and over the space of what must have been an hour, succeeded in drying himself and dragging on clean clothes. It was a painfully slow process, and he had to take short rests. Once he had them on they appeared to belong to someone else and seemed far too big. The sight made him laugh out loud.

Brodick simply didn't recognise the unshaven tramp staring back at him in the full-length mirror in his bedroom, and he waved and winked at his own image to make sure it was him.

By day ten, Brodick knew he was going to live after all. He had to report his discovery of the Russian, his interview with the man, and send off the video. His stomach still hurt and he still wasn't eating. The most he could manage was hot tea brought to him by a worried Omar.

It was time to find a doctor.

'Well, old chap, seems you're over the worst. Could have killed you, you know. You should have gone straight to hospital and they'd have put you on a drip.'

He was a small, sprightly Pakistani with a cheerful manner, an enormous, white handlebar moustache and a very British manner—he let on he was ex-army and had trained in Britain. 'Lie down over there and I'll give you a going over.'

Cold hands pressed deep into his abdomen.

'Tell me where it hurts.'

Brodick did so.

'You're not eating?'

'I drink tea—without milk.'

'You've got a bad case of worms, no doubt from the bad meat that set you off in the first place. I'll give you something for it. Take three a day at regular intervals. The liquid solution twice a day. Finish the course. You should be able to see the worms with your stools when they emerge. Try to rest, at least for a few days, and start eating again—I suggest non-fatty food. If the diarrhoea and vomiting start up again, go straight to hospital and send me a note informing me. No ifs or buts. You'll need a drip immediately. Don't delay. You don't have the physical strength left to withstand another bout. All right?'

Brodick nodded.

The doctor took his weight. The patient had lost forty-six pounds.

Brodick tried to pay.

'No, no. There's no charge, old chap, except for the prescription. You've been in Afghanistan, haven't you? I won't ask what you were doing over there, but I'm sure it must have been in a good cause. Oh, almost forgot, wash your hands very thoroughly before and after eating and using the toilet, won't you.'

Back home, he started to eat—slowly and carefully. Dry biscuits. No dairy. A little fruit, then vegetable soup. His appetite returned little by little. According to Omar, no one had called him or visited, other than workmen Omar had brought in to repair the blast damage to the back wall and replace the kitchen window. The only news arrived in the form a grubby postcard from Mélusine, postmarked Bordeaux two weeks ago.

He recognised her urgent scrawl at once.

'*C'est votre dernière chance,*' it said. '*J'attends. Maintenant ou*

John Fullerton

jamais!

Brodick was indeed sorry. It was going to be never.

25

Brodick lay on his back on the gurney, the needle in his arm, the bag only half full of blood, squeezing his fist to make it flow faster, when he heard his name being called.

'Richard! Richard Brodick, is that you? I was told I'd find you here. Your man, Omar, told me. This is very public-spirited of you, old chap. Gosh, you put me to shame. Maybe I should give a pint myself while I wait for you to finish… What do you say? Good idea? I've a horrible feeling, though, that they might find it's a hundred percent proof in my case!'

It was none other than Harwood, hale and hearty, laughing at his own schoolboy joke and making a pretence of friendship for anyone watching and in earshot, a broad grin on his face as he stood over Brodick, arms akimbo, biceps bulging out of the short sleeves of his tennis shirt. He looked disgustingly fit. School chums at Rugby, Wellington or Charterhouse. Whatever. It was all make-believe, an act. Brodick hadn't seen him since that first meeting on the Drydens' front lawn in Islamabad, doing the heavy lifting with plates, bottles and glasses, playing the willing acolyte to Mrs Dryden in the hope, no doubt, of impressing his boss, James Dryden.

It seemed a lifetime ago but in fact it was only what, almost two years?

Brodick struggled to work it out, arriving at a current date of February 1983.

Whatever had happened to Christmas and New Year?

'So this is the famous Afghan Surgical Hospital. Well, well. I've always meant to pay a visit and never got around to it. I should be ashamed of myself. Pretty impressive, isn't it?' Harwood gazed around and Brodick thought he was doing so not out of curiosity but because he wanted to be sure he wouldn't be overheard. If he was searching for pretty nurses he was going to be disappointed; they were all male and mostly Afghan.

'Do this often, do you?'

'No. They send someone round to my place when they need my blood group.'

It was true. Brodick wasn't fully recovered, and still felt disoriented and unsteady on his feet—but he knew they didn't ask for his blood unless it was urgent.

'Ah.'

'AB neg. They never seem to have enough of it when they have a new influx of wounded.'

'Uh-huh.' Harwood couldn't have cared less. 'I was passing by, you might say. I was asked to pass on an invitation, actually. You're wanted, Richard. An invitation to lunch from your old mate Colonel H, no less. Today. We have a VIP visitor from London and he insists on meeting you.' Again, Harwood glanced back, over his shoulder, but everyone was too busy doing what people did at this hospital: trying to save lives. 'Chap by the name of Hazlitt. Denis Hazlitt. Ring any bells? No? Regional director, making a swing through Asian stations. They do that occasionally. Keeps us on our toes, which is, I suppose, why they do it in the first place. He really does want to see you. Can't think why. Asked for you by name. Fame at last, eh.' Harwood pointed at the blood bag. 'Looks to me as if you're just about done. You must have done something to get them excited on the fifth floor.' Harwood glanced at his huge diver's watch, a flashy affair bristling with dials and knobs. 'Shall I whip the needle out? Only joking. Thought I'd offer you a lift. I'll take you back to your place and you can get whatever you need. I imagine you'll want to spend a night or two in Islamabad at least. What do you say? If the traffic isn't too bad, we should be there in good time for your aperitif.'

Saying no wasn't an option, that much was clear. He was to be escorted by Mr Muscleman himself. Delivered in person. Brodick told himself he had no illusions about what this was about, notwithstanding Harwood's fake bonhomie. He was going to be hauled over the coals, keel-hauled SIS style, and given the boot. This Hazlitt was there to provide London's imprimatur.

*

'Need to have a quick word, old chap, before we join the others. If you don't mind.'

To Brodick's surprise, almost alarm, Harwood pulled in to the side of the road, cut the engine. They were on the city outskirts, maybe ten minutes from Hermitage's villa.

'This is between us, Richard, okay?'

'What is?'

'I want you to agree first. I never said this and you never heard it.'

'All right. If it makes you happy. I agree.'

'You know about Mungoo, I take it.'

'Know what?' Brodick was genuinely puzzled.

'They sent me to Peshawar to sort it all out in your absence.'

Brodick waited, watched Harwood and wondered where this was going.

Sort what out?

'Don't tell me you didn't know.'

'For Chrissake, *what*?'

'He's dead, chum. Did you know? The prof and his wife. Both of them.'

Harwood turned in his seat and stared Brodick in the face, trying to read his expression.

'Tell me.'

Brodick was stunned at first, quite numb, then he felt sick.

'You didn't know, did you? You've gone white under your tan. It wasn't you. Am I right?'

'I don't know what you're on about.'

'I think you do. You took the two of them to Peshawar airport. You were sending them to your pal the Swedish ambassador. Ahlberg. Right? The idea was to get them out of Pakistan, to seek asylum in Sweden. They'd stay at the Swedish ambassador's residence until the papers were ready. I guessed as much. Mungoo might have been a KGB asset—I stress might have been—but he was still your friend. I get it, I really do.'

Brodick said nothing. He felt queasy. He would have liked to open his door and get out, walk around, get some air. He put his hand out, feeling for the door handle and braced himself, ready to jump out if he couldn't stop himself being sick.

What was Harwood's game, then? Was it a setup? A test of some kind?

'I found someone at the airport who remembered you. I talked to Mungoo's nephew who was on guard duty at the professor's home overnight.'

Brodick was shivering with sudden cold and he stared straight ahead, seeing nothing.

'So, tell me: what happened?' His voice was flat, toneless.

'The flight was delayed by military troop movements in connection with the kidnapped Soviet. They were flying them into NWFP through the airport. Others were heading up by road. The Mungoos and the other passengers were told to go home and wait. The airport was shut to civilian traffic, so they did as they were told and went home again. Mungoo had just inserted the key in the front door lock when three unexpected visitors arrived and shot them both, right on the doorstep.'

Brodick shut his eyes.

'I know it wasn't you, Richard, okay? You didn't order the killing. Never mind—I don't expect you to admit it. Now I'm going to give you some good advice. I strongly suggest you take it for your sake. Are you listening?'

Brodick nodded. He couldn't speak.

'Keep your mouth shut. You say nothing. You listen, but stay schtum. Got that?'

Brodick took a deep breath. 'Got it.'

'Okay, then.' Harwood pulled out onto the highway and drove on, watching his mirrors for any tag.

'I'm pretty sure it was Burhanuddin's people,' he added.

Brodick was emerging from his daze, looking around, trying to get a fix on where they were.

This wasn't some kind of deception, after all.

'Why are you sticking your neck out for me?'

'You're not a bad fellow, Brodick. You're pretty good at what you do. You managed to surprise us all, I think. Even Hermitage. It isn't quite the basket of roses you thought it was going to be, I know, but it would be a shame to lose you now. Don't overreact when they tell you. Just keep quiet, don't react and it'll be fine. You'll see.'

*

'The man himself!' Hermitage came outside, one hand outstretched, the other shading his eyes from the sun blazing in a sky leeched white by the heat. 'You're just in time, Richard. Five minutes more and the last of the Pinot Grigio would have vanished. Good to see you.' Brodick noted sourly the hail-fellow-well-met change in tone. The Colonel was quite the actor, it seemed. 'Come on in and let me get you a glass, quickly. Everyone, this is the guest we've all been waiting for. Thanks very much, Harwood, no need for you to wait around. You can go.'

Harwood backed out, dismissed.

Brodick stepped in gingerly through the double glass doors and for a moment he couldn't see anything of the open plan living area; it took a few seconds for his eyes to adjust to the sunless interior. Hermitage slid the glass doors shut behind him. There were figures standing at the faux fireplace, and he recognised Dr Pardoner. Next to him stood a stranger, presumably Hazlitt, a full head and shoulders taller than Pardoner, a big man, blond, stout and tanned, wearing a blue shirt and chinos and holding Hermitage's curved dagger, unsheathed, its wicked blade winking in the dim light. Brodick was on his guard, and the sight of the blade wasn't reassuring.

'Denis, may I introduce Richard Brodick. Richard, this is our boss, Denis Hazlitt, who's on a whirlwind tour of Asia and who wanted to meet you before he jets off somewhere or other this afternoon. Lucky man has all the fun.'

Hazlitt put down the dagger and came forward.

His voice was deep, slow, a little husky. He looked like a successful yeoman farmer, outdoorsy and prosperous. 'Delighted to meet you, Richard, a real pleasure. We've been hearing so much of your exploits.' His big fist swallowed Brodick's right hand.

Hermitage tried to move them along, arms wide as if herding recalcitrant livestock. 'Let's go to the table, shall we? Sit wherever you like, gentlemen. We're all friends, so there are no formalities but a friendly gathering and no one minds if we talk shop while we eat. It'll save time and in any case there's no hired help today. It's only salad and cold cuts, I'm afraid. But the ham and potato mayonnaise are rather good if I say so myself. All right everyone? Nathan here will provide us with a refill, and we'll begin.' Hermitage was being as agreeable and hospitable as Brodick had ever seen him. It was almost unnatural. His furry caterpillars seemed content to remain comatose and even his feet were behaving themselves, both of them.

Brodick ground his teeth together and avoided eye contact.

Hermitage turned to him. 'I'd like to say, Richard, how much I admired your interview with the Russian. Polivanov performed rather well, I thought, given his situation. Stoical. Your video was everywhere. BBC, of course, The American networks. Your stories were on the radio and in print. All the wire services struggled to catch up and compete, though I see our Reuters man had the edge. Tip Cowley off, did you? You must be very pleased. So must he. Quite an achievement. Well done. You showed great initiative. We certainly don't have to worry any more about your cover, do we, eh?'

The man was effing unbelievable.

'Thanks.' It was all Brodick could manage. He was confused. This was supposed to be leading up to his dismissal and a ticket home in disgrace. He had convinced himself and was braced for a grilling and a grownup telling off, his nerves on edge, tingling with flee-or-fight adrenalin pumping through his blood vessels. So much so he didn't notice that he'd finished the first glass of wine and was already reaching for the second. He looked down at his plate and realised he'd eaten his starter, though he couldn't for the life of him remember what it was he'd just eaten. Only the garlic taste remained.

What the hell were they playing at?

Surely, if Harwood knew, they too must have found about by now about the Mungoos.

'Any news what's happened to the Russian, Richard?'

'No, Dr Pardoner, I thought you'd tell me.'

There were smiles, but no takers.

'There are rumours.' Brodick looked at them in turn and heard himself speak as if from afar. 'That he died because of exhaustion or exposure, or because his medicine wasn't renewed. In fact, his pills were replaced. Abdul always said that he would execute his prisoner if the Soviets or anyone else got too close, and I do know they've been bombing the suspected hideouts.'

Silence except for the clatter of knives and forks on porcelain.

Hazlitt leaned forward. 'We're very pleased that you managed to resolve the Mungoo issue, Richard. Our American friends are also relieved at the outcome. It was greatly worrying at the time. You handled it with considerable skill, managing to be away when it happened. Pity about the wife, of course, it goes with saying, but then again, it made complete sense. If she hadn't died with her husband, it might have raised questions. As it was, it looked like a couple of callous extremists were responsible. Well done, old chap. You played a blinder. Congratulations are in order.' Hazlitt raised his glass.

Brodick's stomach lurched violently as if he'd been kicked in the gut.

They really did think he'd done it, that he was the bastard who'd hired the killers.

It was what passed for man-management in the Service, presumably.

He opened his mouth to protest, deny everything, but remembered Harwood's advice just in time. Stay schtum.

Very well: he would.

Pardoner cleared his throat and played with his glasses. 'In fact, Richard, it might interest you to know that a contact of ours in the airline business told us the Mungoos had actually gone to Peshawar airport the morning they were killed. They had booked a flight to Islamabad, you see, but all civilian flights had suddenly been suspended without warning because the military was flying troops into Peshawar and stepping up air patrols in the tribal areas in pursuit of your Russian. The Mungoos along with other passengers were told to listen to the news and to return later once domestic, civilian flights had resumed, but the Mungoos never did return. Instead they went back home to wait, and that's when they were shot. On their own doorstep, front door key still in the lock, apparently. According to Harwood, who went up there to sniff around and talk to people. Of course by that time you were already on your way across the border.'

Brodick was on his feet. 'Excuse me.'

He bolted for the bathroom, threw water in his face, sat on the toilet seat and counted up to sixty, slowly, rocking back and forth. He was surprised to find himself in tears.

*

'All right, old chap? You look awful.'

'Thanks. Good to know.'

Laughter greeted Brodick's retort. 'So sorry. My stomach isn't yet back to normal after the trip to Kunar province, but it's nothing to worry about.'

Pardoner frowned with feigned concern. 'Have you seen a doctor, Richard? You do seem to have lost a lot of weight since we last saw you.'

'I have, yes, thanks. He gave me a bottle of truly disgusting pink stuff and a course of what looked like huge horse pills. All done now.'

Had they heard about the attack on his house? So far nothing had been said.

Hazlitt rose from the table. 'I'm sorry to break this up, everyone, but I've a plane to catch. Thanks so much for the lunch, and thank you, Richard, for coming all this way. Once again, I must congratulate you. And I have to tell you,' he looked at Hermitage and Pardoner in turn, 'that we in London would like to make you a formal offer of a full-time position as an intelligence officer with the Service. I know there were doubts a while back, but I think I speak on behalf of everyone here that those doubts, such as they were, have been laid to rest. Starting as soon as you're ready. Give it some thought. No rush, but let us know. You'd probably have to join one of the regular intakes of the intelligence officers' six-month training course, but I think with your experience it would be a mere formality and you'd sail through it without so much as a hiccup. You have the makings of an outstanding officer. Your father would have been proud of you. Well done.'

He'd done it. Despite everything, his wish had been granted; the dream he'd had all these years of being accepted into the Service was a reality. Brodick felt a great calm descend on him. It was a form of elation, he supposed, but he gave no outward sign. He didn't smile or laugh. He felt dazed. This then was the taste of victory.

They shook hands, Brodick surreptitiously wiping his right

palm on the back of his pants and hoping Hazlitt wouldn't notice how sweaty it was.

'You really are one of us now, Richard.'

When Hazlitt had gone, Pardoner trotting alongside having offered to drive him to the airport, Hermitage invited Brodick to take a walk around his garden. Despite the heat, Hermitage said, he wanted to stretch his legs and hoped Richard didn't mind. Provided his stomach was up to it, of course. Brodick assured him it was.

'I've something to tell you. In confidence, now that Denis and Nathan have gone.'

'Of course. Go ahead.' Brodick wasn't really listening.

They walked side by side down a flagstone path at the back of the house, shaded by a vine-covered trellis, shrubs on either side with fat, lolling leaves like the tongues of panting dogs.

'It wasn't your fault, Richard. I want you to know that. None of it was your fault, and it doesn't change anything. We were wrong, though. I was wrong. Not you. You're still in line for Century House and all it involves, if you still want a career with the Firm, of course.'

Wrong? About what? Brodick said nothing, gave no sign one way or the other. He was still trying to digest the news about both the Mungoos and himself, and he almost stumbled, clumsy with guilt and confusion. What was Hermitage talking about? It was all gibberish. Ahead of them was a pond with a fountain dribbling in the centre and, as they approached, Brodick saw the water was coming out of a vase or urn or whatever these things were called and held by what he supposed was a naiad made of plaster or cement.

'We think Mungoo may have been innocent, but I suspect we'll never really know.'

Brodick halted, momentarily off-balance, dizzy as if he'd been clubbed. He put a hand out and grabbed the trellis to steady himself. It wasn't a vine overhead and on either side, he realised, but some type of clematis. The heavy scent made him feel nauseous again.

'The man you called Mirwais. Remember him?'

Brodick's world swam back into focus by sheer willpower.

'Real name Umar Jaji. But of course you knew that. I asked you and you said you didn't know, but of course you did. You were trying to protect your sources. I don't blame you, Richard. In your shoes, I might very well have said the same thing.'

Brodick was in no state to admit or deny anything.

'Mirwais, or Umar Jaji, whichever you prefer, was the real head agent. We suspect Mungoo was his sub-agent. So-called Mirwais was still operating as a fully paid-up senior officer in the Khad, but was working, we suspect, under Khad cover, for the Centre. He ran networks all along the frontier and across it, in the tribal areas. And in Peshawar itself. A busy man. Ostensibly for the Khad; in actuality, for Moscow. Mungoo was probably one of his most important recruits, as he was yours. And no doubt he did want to use Mungoo to ensnare you if he could. Mungoo was the hook to reel you in. But as I say, we'll never really know.'

Brodick wished Hermitage would stop his endless chatter. Hermitage had also turned to face Brodick, caterpillars arching like twin question marks. He seemed unaffected by the heat, unlike Brodick.

'Incidentally, we also heard about the attack on your house, Richard. We were all greatly relieved that you escaped injury or worse. It must have been the night before you left for Kunar Province and the Mungoos were killed—we have to wonder whether there's a connection. Any views?'

Brodick said nothing because he couldn't. Shock in Harwood's embassy car had given way to elation at lunch which now gave way to horror at the whole messy business. He broke away, stumbling off the path, brushing aside the clematis, away from the pond and its ridiculous fountain. He didn't have any idea where he was going. He blundered into a bed of flowering purple agapanthus, right hand clamped over his own mouth to stem the tide of acid, cheeks bulging with vomit as he waded in among the tall stems.

It occurred to him that the place was probably infested with tarantulas or something worse, but he didn't care. He doubled over, hands on his knees to stop himself falling onto his face, and threw up his lunch. He didn't stop retching until his stomach was empty and then some. He'd had plenty of practice of late.

He straightened up and regained the path.

He felt better.

He'd won the prize. He'd got what he wanted. A career as an intelligence officer was all his at last. He'd earned it and the Mungoos had paid for it with their lives. But the man vomiting into the African lilies moments ago was not the same man who'd sat on a rug in this same garden with a beer in his hand two years before, deferential and idealistic, keen to serve, keen to please.

It was as if there were two Brodicks: the naive Brodick-as-he-was and the wiser, cynical Brodick-as-he-now-is, the latter's attention firmly fixed on his own future as a professional spy. Guilt, shame and doubt he shoved aside. They would pass. He could live with the deceit, of course he could. What spy did not make good use of dishonesty? This older, tougher version of Richard Brodick was looking forward to it.

The End

Did You Enjoy This Book?

If so, you can make a HUGE difference

For any author, the single most important way we have of getting our books noticed is a really simple one—and one which you can help with.

Yes, you.

Us indie authors and publishers don't have the financial muscle of the big corporates to take out full-page ads in the newspaper or put posters on the subway.

But we do have something much more powerful and effective than that, and it's something that those big publishers would kill to get their hands on.

A committed and loyal bunch of readers.

Honest reviews of our books help bring them to the attention of other readers.

If you've enjoyed this book we would be really grateful if you could spend just a couple of minutes leaving a review (it can be as short as you like) on this book's page on your favourite store and website.

https://burningchairpublishing.com/product/spy-game/

Acknowledgements

My thanks to Peter Oxley and Simon Finnie of Burning Chair Publishing for their support, encouragement, total commitment and thorough professionalism in preparing and publishing Spy Game.

Coming Soon

The following is the prologue from John Fullerton's next Richard Brodick novel, provisionally entitled Spy Dragon:

A tall Westerner with a lined face and greying hair emerges from an apartment block onto a one-way street still in shadow. He wears a suit and carries a Samsonite briefcase. He marches rather than strolls, shoulders back, to a Renault 5 Turbo in a nearby parking lot, unlocks it, opens the driver's door and drops the briefcase—containing a 9mm semi-automatic pistol and walkie-talkie—on the front passenger seat. He settles behind the wheel, turns the ignition, releases the handbrake and reverses out onto the road. At the intersection, a black Mercedes lurches out in from of him. A second Merc screeches up behind, braking hard and cutting off any retreat.

Masked men jump out brandishing handguns and an AK-47.

One smashes the driver's window, which explodes with a popping sound and a cascade of glass; his comrade lunges forward and punches the foreigner twice in the head and opens the door. They drag him to the first Merc, force him into the back, down on the floor. They leave the briefcase.

The first car races away, the second reverses out of sight, burning rubber.

It's all over in under eleven seconds.

Not yet 7am, the morning has that special west Beirut fragrance, a mingling of sea air and cardamom-flavoured Turkish coffee. A woman pegs her family's washing onto a line across her second-floor balcony, an infant wails, the sublime voice of Fairuz drifts from a doorway, at street level a metal shutter clatters up to reveal a bakery; a queue forms in anticipation of breakfast: mouth-watering *ma'noeshe*, hot flat loaves crusty on the outside, drenched in olive oil and *za'atar*, the latter a mixture of dried oregano, salt, sesame, sumac and basil.

The Renault is stranded on the street, the driver's door open.

William Francis Buckley, United States national, veteran special forces officer and the current CIA station chief in the Lebanese capital, has vanished.

*

You can find out more about this and other books by signing up to the author's website for the occasional newsletter and blog post at http://www.johnfullertonauthor.scot

About the Author

During the Cold War John Fullerton was, for a time, a "contract labourer" for the British Secret Intelligence Service, in the role of head agent on the Afghan-Pakistan frontier. This experience forms the basis of *Spy Game*.

All told, he's lived or worked in 40 countries as a journalist and covered a dozen wars. For 20 years he was employed by Reuters as a correspondent and editor with postings in Hong Kong, Delhi, Beirut, Nicosia, Cairo, and London.

His home is in Scotland.

About Burning Chair

Burning Chair is an independent publishing company based in the UK, but covering readers and authors around the globe. We are passionate about both writing and reading books and, at our core, we just want to get great books out to the world.

Our aim is to offer something exciting; something innovative; something that puts the author and their book first. From first class editing to cutting edge marketing and promotion, we provide the care and attention that makes sure every book fulfils its potential.

We are:
- Different
- Passionate
- Nimble and cutting edge
- Invested in our authors' success

If you're an author and would like to know more about our submissions requirements and receive our free guide to book publishing, visit:

www.burningchairpublishing.com

If you're a reader and are interested in hearing more about our books, being the first to hear about our new releases or great offers, or becoming a beta reader for us, again please visit:

www.burningchairpublishing.com

Other Books by Burning Chair Publishing

The Curse of Becton Manor, by Patricia Ayling

Near Death, by Richard Wall

Blue Bird, by Trish Finnegan

The Tom Novak series, by Neil Lancaster
    Going Dark
    Going Rogue
    Going Back

10:59, by N R Baker

Love Is Dead(ly), by Gene Kendall

A Life Eternal, by Richard Ayre

Haven Wakes, by Fi Phillips

Beyond, by Georgia Springate

Burning, An Anthology of Short Thrillers, edited by Simon Finnie and Peter Oxley